NINA'S FRIENDS

TAJNA CIRCLE BOOK ONE

JAMES IRWIN

VAGUE APPARATUS PRESS

HUMAN
AUTHORED
Aɢ Authors Guild
9846872

For everyone who has drifted away and come back

"Life being what it is, one dreams of revenge." – Paul Gauguin

1

THUMB DRIVE

Mickey was eating a spicy chicken sandwich and waffle fries in the Chick-fil-A at the mall in Willow Grove when the South Philly meathead walked in. Bomber jacket, thin gold chain, weightlifter build, plenty of product in the hair, a theatrical swagger, and not a lot sparking behind the eyes. This would be Rob, or at least he claimed that was his name on the phone. The guy looked the way Mickey expected, which was a disappointment, but it was all he could get at the price he was willing to spend. Mickey nodded at the meathead, who nodded back and sat down.

Mickey pushed a drink across the table. "I got you a Coke."

"Why we meeting here, making me drive all the way out?"

"I'm the one hiring you, so why should I drive down to your shithole neighborhood? You can come up here to see me."

Rob sneered. "This suburban dump? You live here?"

"Not here, but close." Mickey had a disconcertingly high voice, with a hint of a lisp. He offered fries, which Rob refused. "When I was a little kid, before this mall was built, right where we are now used to be the biggest bowling alley in the world. Had this huge, pointed roof over the entrance, like a rocket ship taking off."

"Rocket ship?"

"Yeah. And a little over from that, one of the top amusement parks in the country."

"You kidding me? We're sitting here talking about local history, just because you're old?"

"God forbid you might learn something." Mickey slid an envelope across the table. "Half now, half when it's done. The address is in there. They need to be dead, and it needs to be done in their house. Not on the street, in the car, or the back yard, in their house. That's the way the client wants it."

"How am I supposed to get inside?"

"Part of your job is to figure that out. Watch the place for a while, you'll see an opportunity."

Rob took the money, put it in a pocket inside his jacket. "What's their deal, besides being rich Russians?"

"A big gay guy and his hot wife, I hear. I never met them."

"You mean big like fat?"

"I mean big like a bear."

"Why would a big gay guy have a hot wife?"

"You ever been anywhere?" asked Mickey through a mouth full of spicy chicken. "Never saw a rich gay guy hide behind a pretty wife?"

"It's fucking stupid."

"You might want help, since there's two of them, that's out of your fee. Keep whatever you find in the place, and they're likely to have all sorts of nice stuff. There might be cash around."

"Nobody keeps cash these days."

"These people might. I'm told they're the type. If you find any you can keep it."

"That sounds good."

"Something else – you know what a thumb drive is? For a computer? Sticks in a USB port?"

"Yeah, what do you think, I'm an idiot?"

Yes, actually, Mickey did think he was an idiot. "You find any in the house, if it's one or twenty, you bring them back to me. There's a bonus in it for you."

Rob nodded.

"One last thing." Mickey tapped Rob's jacket where the envelope sat. "In there is a postcard with the Ukraine flag on it."

"Is that a country?"

"You don't see the news? Nothing about the war?"

"You mean them fighting the Russians?"

"Yeah, that's the one. You need to leave it with the bodies, where it will be found. This is important."

"Jesus, why don't you do it, everything has to be so perfect?"

"Do I look like the kind of guy goes to high tea at a mansion in Society Hill? Cops will pick me up just for walking around."

Rob looked the man over. Mickey was at least in his late fifties, maybe on the other side of sixty, balding on top, the hair he had left kept long and pulled back into a frizzy ponytail. Thick drooping mustache, round wire rim glasses, and a battered leather jacket. It seemed like he could use a shower.

"You got a point," said Rob. "You want them to suffer?"

"No. Just make them dead. Don't forget the postcard."

2

<JUDAS

The shriek of the phone emerged out of the staccato pellets of rain on the big window. Black outside, no moon, nearly the devil's hour. Dragan Markov, still a little drunk, only answered the phone once he saw it was Sergei's private line. Sergei Golubev was a mid-level Russian oligarch, not the sort of man to make his own calls unless it was both important and personal. In that case he wouldn't hesitate to bother someone well after midnight with a demand disguised as a favor.

"Someone has stolen pieces from my collection," said Sergei. "I need you to get them back."

"Are they stolen or just missing?" Dragan was annoyed; why couldn't this wait until tomorrow?

"Stolen, I'm sure of it. They're all very good items, small so they are easy to move. They knew what they were doing."

"I'm in embassy operations, not security. What value would I add?"

"We think it was Ivan. You'll put him at ease, while you look out for my interests."

Oh, fuck me, thought Dragan. He said, "You're joking, that can't be right."

"There's a security team going to his house. I want you there on my behalf."

"Dammit Sergei."

"I want all my art returned."

"I can't promise that."

"Yes, you can. As far as I'm concerned you already have."

Dragan blinked from the glare of the lamp when he turned it on. He had to sober up, fast, and jump start his engines. He had some crystal meth stored in the back of his night table drawer, which would help. He put on coffee for the drive. He entered the shower, trying to make himself presentable so he could threaten and interrogate one of the few friends he had.

***

Dragan arrived at Ivan's little post-war cape in a quiet residential neighborhood in Arlington, south of Washington D.C., as the day was getting started. Surfaces glistened from the overnight rain, everything looking damp and forlorn. Down the block someone drove off to work, and at the corner the lights of a school bus flashed.

He entered the house only to find that the drama was very nearly over. Three security officers stood in the living room. At the center of this circle Ivan Bortnik, a slight man in his sixties, sat in a winged armchair, his head down and his hands clasped between his knees. Dragan nodded to the senior security officer, a humorless prima donna named Sacha who didn't much care for Dragan, either.

He was expected. Sacha directed one of the officers, a young woman in tactical pants and a hooded sweatshirt, to provide an update. She walked over to Dragan, and together they stepped out onto the porch. The woman gave Dragan a handwritten list of the missing artworks.

"It didn't take much effort to break him down," she said in Russian. "He seemed relieved to tell us, actually. He admitted he had been taking artworks for years and selling them to a gallery owner in Georgetown."

"Please speak English outside. We don't want a neighbor to hear Russian and become agitated."

"Yes sir, I understand."

"Do you have the info?"

"Yes, sir, I wrote it on the back of the page, there." She showed him. "The dealer's name is Collins. That's the address for the gallery, and that one is his home."

Dragan made a call. He read off the addresses, and asked the person on the other end to go to the art dealer's home and drag him out of bed. "The idiot's been fencing paintings stolen from Sergei Golubev," he explained. "Take him down to his gallery and get what you can out of him, I'll join you later."

He took a deep breath. Across the street was a stone wall, and beyond it were the sprawling sports fields of a private academy. Mist clung to the grass, not yet burned off by the sun. He imagined Ivan waving at neighbors in the evening as he watched the sweaty children of privilege play their matches.

"Are you okay sir?" the woman agent asked. Dragan nodded.

The front door burst open and the other junior officer, a thick, red-faced man, pulled Ivan along by the arm. Struggling to keep up, Ivan fleetingly looked at Dragan before descending the steps into the rear seat of a black sedan squatting at the curb. The thick man leaned against the sedan, lit a cigarette, and waited. The woman joined him.

Sacha stepped out, his suit pressed, his grey hair immaculate, wearing sunglasses even though there was no need for them.

"I asked Leonid to pick up this man Collins," Dragan told him. "I'll talk to him first."

"Trying to track down the artworks?"

"Yes, of course. You can have him when I'm finished."

Sacha tapped the paper in Dragan's hand. "That's what Ivan remembers taking from the collection."

"Do you think this is everything?"

"I think he thinks so. He's nervous. People get nervous, they forget things."

"Work with him through the weekend. Learn what you can then send him back to Moscow, let them figure out what to do with him."

Sacha took a mint out of a tin and placed it gently on his tongue. "The invasion of Ukraine has gone from a quick victory to a giant mess. They turned our troops away from Kyiv and our casualties are humiliating. You think Moscow cares about a few stolen artworks?"

"Probably not. Sergei does and that's who I answer to right now."

They both looked at Ivan. Sacha asked, "Do you want to say anything to him before we go?"

"I probably should."

Dragan walked over to the sedan and asked the two officers for privacy. He opened the rear door and crouched so he was eye-level with Ivan, who looked small and defeated.

"Of course they would send you," said Ivan. "Sergei's favorite errand boy."

"I'm here because I'm familiar with the art."

"Don't you have anything better to do than be his majordomo? You need to get a life."

"Stop it."

"Judas."

"He thought I might put you at ease."

"You mean distract me, let my guard down as you slip the knife in my back?"

"I'm here because we're friends."

"We're not friends, not now." Ivan glanced at the security guards standing off to the side. "Unless you can get these gendarmes to set me free."

3

PRIVATE COLLECTORS

Dragan frowned. "You know I can't do that."

"Last time you were here we drank bourbon on the porch and talked about Franz Hals, of all people," said Ivan, smiling slightly.

"I remember." Dragan gestured with his chin. "You're bleeding."

Ivan touched under his nose and looked at the wet red smear on his fingers. "It happens sometimes, when I become stressed."

Dragan handed him a handkerchief.

"Thank you," said Ivan, handkerchief against his face. "You've always been kind to me."

"You did the right thing, talking with us."

"It's 'us' now? Throwing in with those three?"

"Ivan, please."

Ivan waved him off. "I knew it was coming. Did they tell you how they found out? A request came in from a curator at a small art museum. Kansas, middle of nowhere. Wanted to borrow two pieces from Sergei's collection for an exhibition. Good ones, I have to admit. A small Malevich and a Rodchenko photomontage. Of course, I was supposed to prep them, but I knew they were gone."

"Because you already stole them."

"Years ago. I tried to get them back from Collins; he said they were sold. So, I had to report them missing. They did an audit and found out about the others."

"They blamed you right away?"

"I can't fault them. I managed the collection. All that work couldn't walk away without me knowing it."

Dragan nodded. "Why did you do this?"

Ivan deflated a little and sighed. "I don't know."

"Was it money?"

"No." A shrug. "A little. If it was money I'd be the fool, wouldn't I? I sold them to Collins for nickels and dimes, really."

He giggled, which Dragan found slightly disturbing.

"It was mostly resentment I think." Ivan lowered his voice so only Dragan could hear. "Sergei has so much. Of everything. So much art he doesn't appreciate what he owns. I wanted him to have a little less." He looked down at the bloody handkerchief, as if he was surprised to be holding it. "Are you going to talk to Collins?"

"I had him hauled down to his gallery."

Ivan giggled again. "Oh, I'll bet he liked that!"

"I'll find out soon enough. I need to locate those pieces and put a lid on this."

"I'm sure you'll track them down. And when you do, destroy them. Burn them. Tell Sergei they were lost. Don't give them back."

"That's not going to happen."

"It could. Don't let him have everything he wants."

Dragan sighed in exasperation. "Stop making this harder than it needs to be." He patted Ivan's arm. "Continue to cooperate, it's best for you. Please don't repeat what you said about Sergei, there's nothing good can come from it."

"Okay," said Ivan. He looked up and for the first time directly into Dragan's eyes. He leaned forward and whispered, "Before you leave, check the files in my desk."

"What am I looking for?" Dragan also leaned in.

"You'll recognize it when you see it. I don't want these pigs to get it first. You need to warn Nina."

Dragan stiffened.

Ivan had already moved on. "I'm sorry I put you in this position." He leaned back and closed his eyes.

Dragan stepped away and told Sacha, "Make sure he understands he has to tell us everything if he ever wants to hug his grand-nieces and -nephews again."

Sacha nodded.

"Also," said Dragan, with the slightest touch to Sacha's arm, "I'd like the keys. I want to give the house a final look."

"We already did that."

"One more time wouldn't hurt." He held out his hand.

Sacha dropped the house keys into the open palm. Dragan stood on the sidewalk and watched the sedan drive off.

Ivan had turned the small suburban home into something resembling a city loft space, with a nearly professional kitchen, and walls a pale cream to show off an eclectic art collection. Upstairs, down the hall was the second bedroom that Ivan used as an office. Dragan sat at the large, antique wooden desk and opened the deepest drawer holding a couple dozen hanging files. He rifled through them. Bills, utilities, his car, and other household things. Toward the back he came to a file labeled "Crown Street LLP." That got Dragan's attention, as Benedikt and Nina Petroski lived on Crown Street, in the Society Hill section of Philadelphia.

It was thick with documents. A few related to the formation of the limited liability partnership in Virginia; Ivan was listed as the registered agent, with both Petroskis as partners. Most of the others tracked the sales of paintings, drawings, and prints. The seller of record for all of them was listed as Crown Street LLP. Facilitating the sales was Collins Fine Art, the same gallery that fenced the artworks Ivan stole from Sergei's collection. All purchasers were anonymous, simply "private collectors."

There were several sheets listing the artists and their works from those sales, along with a handwritten column of valuations, most of them substantial. Each artwork had a note of where it was acquired. Three were purchased from Galerie Strid in Malmö, a city in the southern part of Sweden, across the Øresund Bridge from Copenhagen. The sources for all the rest were referred to as anonymous private sellers.

He scanned the list of artists and their work, frowned, then reread it more carefully. He exhaled in a long whistle. His heart raced, and he looked out the window onto the dour grey morning, thinking about how to handle the mess Ivan just handed him. It had already been a terrible day, and it was now becoming so much worse. The paperwork in his hand told him the woman he had been having an affair with, and her husband, were working with Ivan to launder money through bogus art sales, and it was about to blow up in all their faces.

4

BURBERRY COAT

Nickel-gray clouds gathered as Dragan drove across the Francis Scott Key Bridge over the Potomac, and into the Georgetown section of the city. The art gallery was a block off Wisconsin on the corner of an alley, in a wood frame Victorian painted cream and what the gallery owner might describe as Aegean blue. The lettering on the sign above the front window said Collins Fine Art in an elegant serif. A small sign hanging inside the door window announced the gallery was closed. Dragan walked down the alley to the back of the building where there were double doors, large enough to accommodate bulky sculptures. The doors were unlocked.

In the back office were two desks, a table littered with stacks of paper and a few oversized art books, two wide multi-drawer flat file cabinets for storing works on paper, and wooden racks holding paintings. Two men in nearly identical navy suits stood in the room. They were security personnel attached to the embassy. One was a thick man named Leonid, while the other was a thinner and quieter man named Lev. They often worked together, and Dragan thought of them as the "Els." They were his allies in the security team, as balance to the hostile relationship he had with Sacha.

In the middle of the room was an Aeron chair, and in the chair was a lean, tall man with a mustache and wavy auburn hair, still in his slippers and expensive paisley pajamas, topped by an open Burberry chocolate brown wool coat. He looked a little the worse for wear, with bruises on his face and a few spots of blood on his pajama top.

"He must have objected to being taken from his home," said Dragan in English, so the man in the chair would understand what was happening.

"Objected aggressively," said Leonid. He spoke English in a rich baritone with a strong Russian accent.

The two men stepped outside to talk.

"How has he been behaving?" asked Dragan, standing near the back fence.

"Well, he's an annoying prick," said Leonid. "Also, a little odd."

"Define odd."

"He's afraid of us, and worries that he'll never leave this building alive, which is good, we want him frightened. He realizes Ivan is talking and seems defeated. Yet he's stubborn and defiant, and has told us nothing."

"Do you think he's protecting someone?"

"No, I think he's an asshole. How did it go with Ivan?"

"He claims he was paid hardly anything. In fact, he doesn't appear to have gained much from this fiasco."

They returned to the office, and Dragan pulled a chair into the middle of the room so he could sit facing the gallery owner. "Mr. Collins," he said. "A little earlier this morning we removed Ivan from his home after a lengthy conversation. He told us all about stealing artworks from the collection of Sergei Golubev, and that you were his partner, which is why my colleagues visited your home and transported you here where we could talk."

"They assaulted and kidnapped me," complained Collins, sullen.

"Ivan is now in what could be called a remote location at the end of a cul de sac in Falls Church, where we will learn as much as we can about what you and he were up to. You may be going there too, eventually. On Monday he'll be taken to Russia, which may or may not be an act of kindness given the current state of things over there. Your fate, on the other hand, is still undetermined. That will depend on what you can tell us about where the stolen artworks are now, and how helpful you are in getting them back."

Collins stared silently at the floor in front of him. He seemed like he was about to cry. Dragan pulled the list of missing artworks out of his jacket pocket and looked it over.

"This is what Ivan gave us. Approximately two dozen small paintings and works on paper, no sculptures, nothing past 1930 I believe." Dragan read randomly from the sheet. "A Tatlin, two Malevich pieces, Kandinsky, Rodchenko. A couple of early Chagalls, very nice ones I hear. A self-portrait sketch by Pasternak."

Dragan showed the list to Collins, who ignored it.

"I don't have a lot of time," said Dragan. "Which means I don't have a lot of patience." He held the list up in front of the other man's nose. Collins took a minute before lifting a trembling hand to take it and lower it onto his lap without looking at it. Dragan stared at him, then glanced at the other men. Leonid shrugged.

"What is happening here?" asked Dragan. "Are you unclear about your position?"

Collins lifted his eyes. "I don't understand what to do."

"What do you mean?"

"You're going to kill me."

"My purpose here is not to kill you."

"You're going to kill me. If I tell you about these pieces, you'll kill me right away. If I hold out, you'll hurt me, and then you'll kill me later. What should I do so you don't kill me?"

Dragan felt no sympathy for the man, only impatience. He reached out and tapped the sheet of paper. "The list, please."

"They're downstairs."

Dragan looked at Leonid and Lev, both of whom frowned and shook their heads.

"Who or what is downstairs?"

"The artworks. They're downstairs."

"My colleagues checked the entire building. They aren't here."

"Your men didn't realize where to look." Tears ran down his cheeks, with a single drop falling on the chocolate Burberry wool.

"Would you like to show us?"

Collins nodded.

5

PAPER TRAIL

The four of them walked down the wide steps to a basement that ran the length of the building. Wooden racks held paintings wrapped in plastic, shrouded small sculptures sat on and under an oak table, and off to the side was an area for preparing works for shipment. In the rear of the basement, shelving held document storage boxes. The shelving was on wheels, and Collins swung one end outward revealing four large, wrapped paintings.

"Help me please," said Collins, and he and Lev moved the paintings out of the way. A canvas tarp nearly the color of the basement walls hung from a thick wire near the ceiling. Collins pulled the tarp away to expose a door.

"It might have once been a root cellar," he said, opening the door. He reached in and flipped a switch. A bare overhead bulb illuminated a small, low-ceilinged room, roughly finished with plaster on stone walls. An array of artworks, tightly wrapped in plastic, sat on shallow pallets at the perimeter of the room.

"They're all here," said Collins with a sweep of his hand.

"Please explain," said Dragan, as they stepped inside the naturally cool space.

"I never sold any of the pieces. They are all known and documented. I couldn't put them on the market in any way, not the gray market, not even the black market, without people wondering how I acquired them, their history. I was resigned to have a great personal collection no one could ever know about."

"You understood who they belonged to."

"Of course, who do you think you're talking to? He's one of the fucking oligarchs ruining Russia. Word would get back to him, he would look into it and talk to Ivan. Ivan is weak, he would crumble and give us both up in five minutes, just like this morning. And that would be the end of that."

"If you had given them back when he asked you, he could have covered up the thefts. Instead, it's all crashing down on both of you."

"I guess I didn't think it through at the time."

"Damn, you're a stupid ass." He glared at the art dealer.

Collins looked away toward the wall.

"Can you give us a minute?" asked Dragan, closing the door against surprised looks from Leonid and Lev.

The room was already claustrophobic; now it felt too small for both men, too airless, too quiet. Collins took a step back, afraid.

"There's one more topic we need to discuss, quickly, the two of us," said Dragan. "Tell me about Crown Street LLP and the artworks they sold through you."

Collins was surprised. "They didn't sell to me, I only served as a broker."

"I know that. I've seen the invoices."

"It was consignment. They brought me the pieces, I found the buyers. Quite normal."

"Early century Russian avant-garde, right?"

"Mostly, yes. A hot market right now."

"Also a market with very poor documentation. Who knows how many pieces are out there, waiting to be discovered in attics, right? For instance, one name I recognized was Lyubov Stepanova. While I'm no expert on her, I know she made her name based on a few works exhibited in Moscow in the twenties. Caused quite a stir, but then she died in childbirth, shortly after. Correct?"

"Correct," said Collins, confidence draining. He seemed stunned by Dragan's knowledge, and sensed danger.

"I think there's only, what, eight or nine known pieces in existence? And yet, astonishingly, you and Crown Street managed to move no less than seven previously undiscovered Stepanovas. And I'm thinking that is complete bullshit."

Collins physically recoiled. "Who are you?"

"I'm the man standing here in front of you in this tiny soundproof room, with my friends outside the door."

"Are you with the police?"

"Do I look like the police?"

"A little."

"The four of you were laundering money."

Collins hesitated. He was trapped with an angry, unidentified Russian who, he assumed, was probably going to have him killed. He nodded.

"You want to explain how that worked?" asked Dragan.

"Okay, but I would deny this in a courtroom, right?"

"If you think there's going to be a courtroom you haven't been paying attention."

Collins sighed. "They had money – a lot of money – they needed to account for."

"Who?"

"It wasn't Ivan, but his partners. I never actually met them, I only talked on the phone, mostly with the woman, a few times with the man. Ivan was the go-between. We set up paperwork. The invoices said they were bringing me pieces that they picked up in their travels, or bought from private collections, that sort of thing."

"But there weren't any artworks at all."

"No. After a little time passed, I created sales records that said I sold the pieces, normally to anonymous buyers overseas, who supposedly paid me well. Then I created a receipt that said I passed the sales money over to Ivan's partners."

"But they had the money all along. You just created a paper trail."

"Yes. They had their money cleaned, and they paid me a fee that I documented as a commission. I assume Ivan got a little something too. Everyone paid their taxes and it was all good."

"It was a lot of money?"

"Oh yes. All the invoices taken together – well, you've seen them, you said."

"Okay. We're going back out. It will be better for you if you say nothing about this."

Dragan opened the door to a noticeably annoyed, and curious, Leonid and Lev. He ignored them and walked to the opposite end of the basement and made three phone calls.

The first was to Sergei Golubev's office, where he left a message that the artworks had all been recovered, and they would get them back into secure storage as soon as possible.

The second was to the private line of Sergei's wife, Julianna. He told her he needed to speak with her alone, as soon as possible.

"How alone?" she asked.

"Completely."

"Come by the house tomorrow morning. Sergei has an event in the city, you can update him on the stolen items before he leaves. Then you and I can speak."

The third call was to Sacha, explaining the situation and telling him that after the artworks were loaded in a truck to be returned, Leonid would hand Collins over to him.

"Fine," said Sacha. "Now here is something for you. We can't get Ivan to shut up, and one of the things he told us is that Collins is not the man's real name."

6

— · —

SERGEI

Dew sparkled across the meadows as Dragan drove through the Virginia hills. The estate owned by Sergei Golubev was accessed by an iron gate that led to a long, paved drive gently snaking through a grove of oaks and chestnuts before cutting through a field of lush grasses, leading up to the courtyard in front of the main building. It wasn't a huge estate if you compared it to Kensington Palace. It boasted a tennis court, swimming pool with nearby guest cottages, riding stables for Sergei's wife and daughter, and even a small brick Russian Orthodox chapel on the side lawn connected to the main house via an enclosed walkway.

Dragan was shown into an expansive sitting room with a fireplace and gaming table. It smelled of lilacs. It was in this room that he first met Ivan, the manager and archivist of Sergei's art collection. They had been playing euchre, part of a nostalgic gaming phase popular for a few years with the Golubevs and their circle. Ivan had been randomly assigned as Dragan's partner, and the two of them had a grand time together, winning hands and finding common ground chatting about art history. Dragan thought about that evening as he looked out of the tall windows, across the lawn to the line of trees at the border of the property. The leaves were just starting to become green, a little late that year because of so much cool, cloudy weather. A few cherry trees and flowering pears were in bloom, adding splashes of pink and white.

Sergei Golubev walked in from a side door with the energy of a younger man. He was immaculately dressed, the fabric of his carefully cut suit showing the merest hint of a gray chalk stripe. Now hovering somewhere around seventy, Sergei had been in his prime during the post-Soviet economy arriving with Russian reform in the nineties, and thanks to a few powerful friends had been well-positioned to exploit opportunities. He had made the most of it.

"Dragan, thank you for taking care of this," Sergei said, striding across the room to shake hands. "Sit, please. Can I offer you a scotch? I have Macallan Estate single malt, exceptional."

"It's a little early for me," said Dragan.

"Early for anyone," said Sergei. "But I've been up since four-thirty on the phone with partners in Pakistan, working out details of a land leasing deal for a textile plant. It's already been a long, frustrating day, and in a minute I need to leave for a luncheon I don't want to attend. So I'm having a drink."

"If you put it that way, then yes, I'll join you. Thank you."

They took their glasses and sat. Dragan briefly ran through the events of the day before.

"It's a remarkable thing, my collection safe," said Sergei, running his hand through his silver hair. "You handled things well."

"We were fortunate."

"I don't know this person Collins."

"You'd remember him. Dark red hair and mustache, tall, a bit of a dandy. His story is inconsistent. Originally, he blamed it all on Ivan and that he didn't realize the pieces belonged to you. That was ridiculous, of course. Then we found out his name isn't Collins, but Kalashnik, and things became interesting. At first he said it was all innocent, that his mother and her second husband adopted the Collins name when they opened the gallery, thinking it would be better for business. He said he met Ivan by chance at Russia-related art exhibitions and struck up a friendship. He danced around a bit when we pointed out that Kalashnik is a Ukraine surname. Eventually he admitted he stole the artworks as a blow against Russian aggression."

"Why me?"

"He said it was because of your support of what he called 'the modern Russian imperialism myth.'"

"That's a mouthful. And where does he get the idea that I support the war? I think it's a horrible mistake, as you know. The timing was terrible. Trump might have let Putin do as he wished, but not Biden."

"Let's hope it doesn't last long, that they sit down to talk."

"I'm trying to conduct business in multiple countries, so isolation and sanctions are very bad. Why are they going after me?"

"He claims to belong to the left-wing Grusha Party, and says you're on some list. I find it all a bit implausible myself. He risked prison, or worse, to steal something he didn't know what to do with. His story is either a rationalization, or a child's idea of civil disobedience. My advice, however, is tell your staff to be alert in case there's anything to it. Hopefully the war will be over soon. If not, things against you may escalate."

Sergei Golubev's wife Julianna swept into the room in a boldly printed skirt. She was a handsome woman at least a decade younger than her husband.

Dragan stood. "Julianna Titovna, it is good to see you," he said.

"And a pleasure to have you in our home again," she said. She surveyed the table. "We're drinking scotch? At this time of day?"

"A celebratory drink," explained Sergei. "Plus I needed to steel myself for this luncheon."

"You poor man. In a gesture of empathy, I shall join you." She poured herself a finger of Macallan Estate, splashed seltzer into it, and settled onto an overstuffed settee. "So tell us, Dragan, why did our Ivan do this?"

"I wish I knew."

"Were they lovers?" she asked. "Love can cloud minds."

"They claim they were not."

"Utter madness," said Sergei.

Dragan nodded. He said, "Sometimes people do foolish and dangerous things for nearly no reason at all, other than the opportunity presents itself, and no small voice in their heads tells them not to do it."

"Well, I still pity Ivan," said Julianna, "even though he betrayed us."

The driver and bodyguard came to the doorway to signal that the car was ready. Sergei stood. "Okay, I am off to luncheon. I'll be back in a few hours." He walked over to Julianna to kiss her cheek.

"Goodbye, dear," Julianna said. She watched him go. When they were alone Julianna looked at Dragan and sighed. "I think they must have been lovers," she said.

"I don't know," said Dragan, "and to be honest I didn't ask."

It was time to get to the business at hand. Julianna crossed the room, closed the doors against prying ears, and returned to her settee to wait for Dragan to begin.

7

JULIANNA

"Stealing from your husband was not the only bad business Ivan and Kalashnik were up to," Dragan said, leaning forward, his voice lower. "They were in a partnership with Benedikt and Nina Petroski to launder money by creating a paper trail for the sale of non-existent artworks."

Julianna's eyes widened. "Oh dear."

"Yes, indeed."

"Are you sure?"

He told her about the invoices in Ivan's house, and the conversation with Kalashnik in the root cellar. "I don't know if Sacha has heard about this yet, but he will," said Dragan. "Ivan seems eager to unburden himself of all his sins, and Kalashnik will be looking for anything to bargain with, so it is just a matter of time."

Julianna downed the rest of her drink and made herself another. "Money laundering by itself is not necessarily a bad sign," she said, more to herself than to Dragan. "My husband and his friends have parked a lot of cash in American real estate since the financial deregulation of the Bush years." She sat down, and added, "I wonder why Ben and Nina didn't do something like that."

"They may have. The only paper trail I found was about the fake art sales."

"They were likely keeping it from Ben's father, too," added Julianna, thinking it through. Dragan understood the point. Ben Petroski's father was a wealthy Ukrainian businessman, pro-Russian, tight with many of the power brokers in Moscow. There was little the older Petroski wouldn't do to further his business interests, up to and including money laundering, financial fraud, bribery, and – if rumors were true – an assassination or two. He expected the same from his son. If Ben felt compelled to hide income from his father, it must be severely tainted in a way the older Petroski would disapprove of. Or possibly something to do with the Ukraine war, which was a volatile topic throughout the global Russian community.

She took a few quiet minutes to calculate the risks. Ben and Nina Petroski were not just any wealthy Russian ex-pats. They were members of a network of embedded intelligence agents, living seemingly normal lives in Western countries, tasked by Moscow to keep their eyes and ears open, and to convey their findings. If these agents were to become entangled in illegal activities in their host country it would be embarrassing for Russia. It would also be embarrassing for the person tasked with running those agents.

Which was why she was concerned by the news, because in addition to being the wife of a wildly successful Russian businessman, Julianna Titovna Golubev was also a member of Russian intelligence and the person the Petroskis, along with a number of other agents in the northeast United States, reported up to. Any scandal, even if contained within the intelligence and diplomatic community, would reflect badly on her.

Furthermore, given Benedikt Petroski's family connections, when word of the scheme got out, which it almost certainly would, she would be the target of considerable political pressure. Benedikt's father would resent any inquiry that put his son, and by extension himself, in a bad light; he'd expect the situation to be treated confidentially and made to quietly go away. Certainly, Julianna would likewise want it all to remain under wraps, for her own purposes. But Sacha and his security team had no such motivation. They could, intentionally or not, make a mess of things if they handled it with their usual belligerence. The next move in this was crucial.

"How much money?" asked Julianna.

"Quite a bit, and I only saw a handful of invoices. I have to admit it's a smart play. Records around the early Eastern European avant-garde are terrible. It's entirely plausible to find a brilliant work by a major artist hanging in the bathroom at the home of a Romanian grandmother. A lot of pieces change hands without provenance."

"Will the US tax people be all over this?"

"No. Kalashnik says everyone involved in the scam claimed the full amounts and filed their taxes like good citizens, which makes the money that much cleaner."

"Sergei and I ran into them at a theatre fundraiser recently. It happens once in a while, we travel in similar social circles. Benedikt was himself, as always. Charming, funny. Nina was a little withdrawn and looked stressed, as if she weren't sleeping."

"She can be a little high-strung sometimes."

"Some men find that part of the appeal, I understand." She looked straight at Dragan. He ignored her. She continued, "Later I saw her near the ladies, she seemed a bit tipsy. As politely as I could I asked if she was feeling okay. She said she had over-reached on something but was handling things."

"That's an odd answer."

"Yes. I asked her, what things? She turned and walked away."

"You think they're in trouble of some sort?"

"It's likely. I take it they've said nothing to you? They were your people, after all."

She said that as part question, part accusation. This irritated Dragan, in large part because she was essentially correct. Originally, he had been an embedded agent himself, part of her network. But he thoroughly screwed that up years earlier. He had ruined his cover situation, put himself in trouble with the law, and possibly faced prison. Julianna swooped in to rescue him, brought him to Washington, and called in favors to install him as an assistant director of operations at the embassy. This was actually a good fit, given his talents. It gave him a stable role where he could add value. In turn, Julianna acquired someone at the heart of activities downtown, the better for her to keep tabs on prevailing diplomatic winds, while her husband gained a front man for various business and political activities when he preferred to stay in the background. Julianna and Sergei used Dragan to talk to people they couldn't be seen talking to, ask questions they couldn't be heard asking, visit places where they couldn't leave footprints, and clean up troubles they couldn't be associated with.

It was within this arrangement that Julianna eventually asked Dragan to serve as liaison for a number of her embedded agents. She claimed at the time that she had too many and needed to relieve some of the burden. "All they want," she told him at the time, "is someone who will listen to them complain and do them favors." In retrospect, however, he understood it was to buffer her accountability. She used him simultaneously as a lackey and a shield, in other words. He tolerated it, because he had no alternative. Benedikt and Nina Petroski had been among those she handed over to him. This money laundering fiasco had happened under his nose.

Still, he bristled at her eagerness to throw all of this into his lap. He wanted to say, no, Julianna, they aren't my people, I'm just your proxy, they're all your people. Instead, he said, "They've mentioned nothing about this. Of course, I haven't spoken to them in some time."

"I think you need to, as soon as possible."

He anticipated this. "I'm driving up when I leave here. I have an overnight bag in the car."

"You need to be careful," she said, smoothing out her skirt. "Everyone knows you were friends with Ivan. And it's an open secret that you're sleeping with Nina. Or at least were, if the gossip is correct. You don't want to be collateral damage. You need to sort this out."

"I'll try my best."

"That's all anyone could ask of you," she said with a smile. The smile was merely convention. She would cut him loose in a second if he failed her again.

***

Close to four hours of bad traffic and construction delays later, Dragan drifted down Sixth Street past Washington Square in Philadelphia as the bright late afternoon sun cast shadows across his path. He found a parking space on Spruce, flipped his collar up against the breeze, and walked towards Crown Street. It was a charming Society Hill neighborhood, refurbished homes shimmering with colonial history. It was the first time he had been there since Nina had broken things off and said she didn't want to see him again. On the stoop he looked at the forest green door, took a breath to compose his nerves, put his game face on, and rang the bell.

8

FIRE

It began at a party at that same Philadelphia brownstone. Dragan wasn't entirely sure why he was invited. He was familiar with the Petroskis because he had become their liaison at Julianna's direction, but it was not a social relationship. Nina explained later they invited him because he was an art historian by training so he "would have things to talk about with the artsy people" there. By artsy people she apparently meant other wealthy patrons who sat with Ben and Nina on the boards of local non-profits. An introvert by nature and resentful of inherited wealth by choice, Dragan didn't do much mingling. The food and the music were good, however, and he drifted around the edges of the party, watching the people. He noticed Ben was fixated on his current boyfriend, leaving Nina to play hostess. He thought he saw sadness in her eyes and talked to her. They spent most of the rest of the evening together until, quite late, they found themselves in the backyard getting air. The music drifted out of the open kitchen door, and they slow danced on the patio. She was electric where he touched her and smelled of vanilla and subtle musk and he wanted to consume her. She looked into his eyes and held it for an eternity. He felt it down to his toes.

A disgraced agent, without a career, he was treading water with no clear path forward, and here was this astonishingly attractive woman throwing him a buoy. She was looking deeply into what he believed was his twisted, lost soul, and she wasn't frightened by it. He was a Russian with a Serbian name who had spent half his life in the United States, and he belonged to none of those places, not much more than human driftwood at that point, and Nina felt like a warm, inviting beach where he could land. Under the stars, on that patio behind their elegant townhouse, he felt a sexual and emotional attraction beyond anything he had experienced before, and it was nearly terrifying. He was unable to resist it.

He was staying at a hotel by the river, and when he got back to his room he phoned her. She was still up, and they talked for another two hours. He told her they needed to give it a shot together, knowing full well it would be an inappropriate relationship.

"You felt it as much as I did," he said, confident of how real the attraction was, and that it was shared. It was like he was diving from the top of a cliff in the dark, unsure of how long the drop or what was waiting for him at the bottom, but thrilled to do it anyway. "Together we'll light a fire around us so hot no one else could come near." In a soft, breathy voice she complained that he was making her so wet she was going to stain the chair, then she laughed, and said she could buy a new one.

Dragan had never felt so much like an object of lust. They were insatiable. They tried to be discreet. They never flaunted it in front of Ben even though he had his own affairs. People still picked up on it because it was instantly recognizable to nearly anyone who saw them together.

This continued on for over a year. He loved her, and felt certain she loved him back, and eventually it drove him over a line he shouldn't have crossed. He wanted her to leave Ben, to divorce him, and run. Leave the agency, leave the area or even the country, start a new life.

He was serious, and it was madness.

Intra-organizational affairs happened, everyone was adult enough to know that. More than one embedded couple wasn't a couple at all, but an arranged performance, like Ben and Nina, each with their own personal lives. But the one rule was that you didn't break the arrangement. You didn't squander years of investment in an under-cover identity because of one rash, emotional, self-centered action. It was too much to ask of Nina, even too much to ask of himself. They fought over it, more than once, culminating in a painful night in a hotel in Manhattan after a Broadway show, Nina standing across the room shouting that they weren't teenagers in a romance movie. There was no running away and no happy endings, she said, angry and heartbroken that he had pushed them to this moment. She said she was out, she couldn't take the stress, she couldn't live that tragedy. She didn't want to be with him any longer.

And now, here he was, on her doorstep once again.

9

PURPOSE

When Nina answered the bell and opened the door, she was surprised to find him there. He could see that on her face. She was barefoot, dressed in old jeans and an oversized fisherman's sweater the color of marigolds, her long hair pulled back. She was lovely and it hurt Dragan to look at her.

"Oh, hello," she said, recovering her poise. "You still have a key. Why didn't you let yourself in?" It was said more as a dare than an invitation.

"I didn't think it was appropriate, considering the last time we spoke."

She looked him over and invited him in with a jerk of her head.

Brandywine, Nina's beloved Lhasa Apso, had been there to see what was happening and excitedly greeted Dragan. "Hello Brandy," he said, stooping to pet her. "Have you been behaving yourself?"

"As much as the rest of us," said Nina, heading toward the kitchen. "Can I get you something?"

"Coffee would be good." He looked around as he followed her. "Ben here?"

"Up in New England with a Goldman Sachs analyst. Why? Is that who you came to see?"

"I came to see both of you."

"Well, he'll probably be here tomorrow, if you can stay over."

"Stay over, here?"

"Of course not."

While the coffee brewed, they moved to the living room. A book was open, face down on the coffee table, by a vase of carnations and hydrangeas.

"The spring flowers are nice," said Dragan.

"You want to give me a clue what this is about?" she asked, flopping down on the couch, placing a pillow on her lap both to rest her arms and, perhaps, as a shield. Dragan chose an armchair across the room.

"You look good," he said, hesitating before he got to the uncomfortable part. "Are you still doing yoga?"

"Thank you. Yes, I am. Are you stalling?"

"Perhaps, a little. This is awkward."

"Oh my. Is this official?"

"Partly."

"You and Julianna doing your things, then? Occupying the gray areas? Why am I not surprised?"

"You know Ivan, the older man who manages Sergei Golubev's art collection?"

"You introduced us."

That was a reminder of his own peripheral involvement, he noticed. She either knows what's coming, he thought, or is laying the groundwork in case the news is bad. He said, "It seems Ivan has fallen in with a dishonest Georgetown gallery dealer. The dealer goes by the last name of Collins, but his real name is Kalashnik. Together they got involved in a couple of illegal schemes. One is that Ivan was stealing artworks from Sergei Golubev and selling them to Kalashnik."

Nina had become still. Brandy jumped onto the couch next to her, and she idly scratched the dog's head as she waited for the rest.

"I got involved to look after Sergei's interests," continued Dragan. "In the process I discovered a second scheme. Which is that you were working with Ivan and Kalashnik to launder a small fortune through phony art sales."

The silence was interrupted only by the coffeemaker going about its business in the kitchen.

"I wasn't looking for it," 'he added, "I stumbled over it. But here we are."

She said, "Is this where I strongly deny it?"

"Don't. I saw the paperwork. I talked with Kalashnik. You were cleaning money. I need to know what it was about, so I know if I have to intervene."

"Ben and I can handle it."

"Maybe you can, maybe you can't. But you still need to talk to me. You know how this works. It's not an investigation and my presence here may be off the books, but it's still official. If it gets ugly it will cause blowback up to Julianna and maybe back in Moscow. I have to know what to prepare for."

She looked at her dog and remained silent.

"Kalashnik is ethnically Ukrainian, for example, like your husband," he said, leaning forward a little. He adopted a more urgent, more threatening tone. It didn't seem to have any impact on her. "That will be noticed. The dots will be connected. If there's any Ukraine element there you need to tell me."

"Julianna knows all this?"

"Of course."

Nina nodded. "You were always such a good boy around Sergei and Julianna, and such a bad boy around me."

"Just doing my job."

"What a waste of who you are."

"Your opinion of me isn't relevant, so can we get on with this?"

She walked to the kitchen. Dragan sat, his hands clasped between his knees, uneasy in his core. He hated this and hated himself for agreeing to do it.

"What have you been up to since New York?" she asked, cheerily, handing him his coffee, as if she could simply reboot the entire conversation.

"Drinking and sulking, mostly."

"That's good. I'm glad you're moving on."

"You're changing the subject."

"There's no subject to change. Ben and I will take care of any questions that come up."

"Tell me about this mess you're in."

"Who says there's a mess?"

"Julianna ran into you at some event recently. Said you talked about having to work things out, that you had bitten off more than you can chew. How bad is the trouble?"

"I'm not certain we're in any trouble at all."

"Not certain?"

"Don't you have anything better to do than be an errand boy?" There was a flash of something in her eyes, anxiety, fear, or anger. Probably all three, thought Dragan.

"Again with this," he said.

"You're still lost, my love. You have no purpose. What do you accomplish in your job? You make sure there's enough supply of this and that. Manage things when VIPs come to town, coordinate events. Change a few details and you could be the assistant manager of a catering hall. You deserve more."

"I wanted more. I wanted you." He broke the seal, stepping into forbidden territory. The air in the room shifted.

"You wanted too much. You certainly wanted too much from me."
She stood. "I think you should leave."

He reluctantly got to his feet. They stared into each other's eyes for
a moment. He took two steps forward and took her in his arms and
kissed her, and she kissed back, her hands on his back and in his hair,
pulling him to her.

10

Push and Pull

A s Brandy watched from the couch, Nina stripped off her jeans and underwear with one hand, still locked in the kiss, and kicked them away. She reached for his belt and undid his pants and shoved them down. She leaped up, wrapped her legs around him, and slid down until she impaled herself on him.

She gasped. "My god it feels like you're up to my ribs," she said, smashing her mouth back onto his.

He stood there in the middle of the room, deep inside her, his hands on her ass, holding her as she slid up and down on him until her orgasm broke over him, her juices flowing over his thighs, like old times, like they were still meant to be. He exploded in her and for a moment lost track of where he was, when it was, and he felt like he was home. When his breathing calmed, she pulled away from him and dropped her legs to the floor.

"Your legs are shaking," she said, her hand still tightly holding onto his neck. "I thought you would drop me."

"They'll be shaking for a while."

She stepped away. He awkwardly pulled his pants back up, nearly tripping and falling, and he felt a little ridiculous. She gathered her clothes and tossed them onto the sofa, narrowly missing Brandy, and took their coffee cups back to the kitchen, naked from the waist down.

"I'm making us a couple of real drinks," she said over her shoulder.

He had to wash up, he was coated in her. He wandered to the bathroom off the entrance hall, but found it half destroyed, with tools and pieces of tile stacked on the floor.

"Use the bathroom upstairs," she called out from the kitchen. "We're redoing the one down here."

Upstairs he walked down the hall, past the bathroom, past Ben's room, to look into her bedroom. The disrespect for her privacy didn't concern him. Her bed was unmade, and a pocket-sized vibrator lay on top, by a book huddled in the sheets. He recognized the book, he remembered when she bought it. It was during a period that he later realized was the beginning of her breaking up with him, when she would unexpectedly become quiet, and do things seemingly out of character. They were in a large bookstore off Broad Street. She drifted away as he looked at the photography books. He later found her in the erotica section inspecting a contemporary bondage and discipline novel, a work of literary smut by someone with a French alias, which she announced she was buying. This startled him a little, he didn't think her tastes ran that way, which seemed to amuse her.

And here it was in her bed, giving every indication that she carelessly left it there after she masturbated to it, almost as if she expected him, displayed it for him. He picked it up and read a few passages, most of them dedicated to women being dominated and used as sexual objects, tied up and covered in semen, everyone dripping and gagging. How had he overlooked this part of her during their time together? Was buying that book in front of him, making sure he saw it, an intentional message for how he should behave? Was she telling him then, if he wanted to keep her, this was the roadmap he needed to follow, and he completely missed it? Good god, did she leave the book on the bed as inspiration, for him to find as a signal that winning her back started that day, in that way?

No, of course not, she didn't know he'd be there. He wasn't thinking straight. Maybe that performance downstairs was intended to keep him from thinking straight.

Back downstairs, she was still nude from the waist down when she handed him vermillion liquid in a tumbler.

"What did you make me?" he asked.

"A Negroni, strong, the way you taught me. I know you like them."

He took the drink. It all seemed confusingly normal and surreal at the same time. She had fucked him like she couldn't help herself, like she still felt the same passion for him. She stood in front of him, half naked – a taunt, or an invitation, or something else entirely? She had made a Negroni; it was just for him, she didn't care for them. Was all of this only for show? Was she trying to distract and confuse him, to blunt his questions about the money laundering? He genuinely couldn't tell.

"We can't do that anymore," she said. "You have too much power over me."

He didn't know how to respond. This was dizzying, the push and pull, the mixed signals, the get-away-closer of it all. He said, "It works both ways, you have that power over me, too, you know that. Isn't it a good thing? Isn't that the way it should be, for two people who...?"

"Don't say it." She held up a finger in warning.

He sat back, gathering himself. It was a mistake coming there, he realized. He felt sad and remorseful, and a little queasy. She strolled to the couch and casually put her underwear on, then her jeans. She asked, "What kind of trouble are we in with Julianna and such?"

He stared at her. That's it, he wondered, now we're back to talking business? "Not too much that I know of. It depends on what you've gotten yourself into. She's concerned about optics, and how it could impact her, you know the dance. You're guilty of financial crimes, but that doesn't mean anything to us unless you get arrested. Or if the source of the money will reflect badly on the organization. And we're concerned about the Ukraine coincidence, with the war happening. If there's anything in that, it could cause problems."

"I don't know about the Ukraine thing." She seemed to be weighing matters. He sipped his drink and waited. "The situation I was referring to when I made that comment to Julianna wasn't about the money, we can handle that. There are some people threatening us, and it isn't clear how serious they are. Benny feels they aren't serious at all, just making noise. But I'm not certain. If we talk to you about it, it has to be off the record, completely confidential, or he won't participate. And if he won't, I really can't. I won't do it without him."

"Okay. I can agree to that, but conditionally. I have to protect the organization I work for, you know that."

"Sure. Come tomorrow for dinner, he should be back. Get here late afternoon, we can have a drink and relax for a bit. Benny likes you but he probably won't like being forced to have the conversation, so be prepared for bluster and insults."

* * *

When Dragan walked back to his car, he didn't notice the man sitting on the steps of a townhouse across the street, like he lived there, smoking a cigarette. The man was dressed in clothes almost identical to what he wore when he met Mickey at the Chick-fil-A in Willow

Grove, the same loose-fitting brown leather bomber jacket and thin gold chain, with just as much product in his hair.

A phone chimed and the man answered with a grunt, listened for a few moments, then told the person on the other end, "The big guy isn't back yet, so hold tight. But something just happened: a tall dude came by, was in there for a while. Could be her brother, could be her lawyer, could be her priest for all I know. But I didn't like him, something about him makes me uncomfortable. There's stuff going on I don't know about. We need to move forward on this as soon as we can, I think. Be ready for when I call. A day or two, tops." He hung up, took a final drag on his cigarette, and flicked it onto the street.

11

— · —

NINA

The following morning Nina was watching television and folding laundry in the living room. The fireplace was lit, fighting an unseasonable morning chill, and Brandy the Lhasa Apso snoozed nearby. The Federal style townhouse looked best with the morning light streaming through the windows. When they first bought it, the building was in serious disrepair, with a grey marble fireplace painted over in black, damaged hardwood floors, and a kitchen that looked like something you might find in the rear of a youth center, all ancient appliances and hideous floral wallpaper. Two upstairs bedrooms were ruined by fake wood paneling, and the entire structure was a squandered opportunity, an historic architectural legacy betrayed. But over time they had brought it back to life as a genteel, inviting space. They added modern conveniences and smart storage, along with touches that evoked the home's history, including crown molding, tray ceilings with center medallions, and wainscoting on the walls. They loved their house, and Nina especially loved it on mornings like this one.

She wondered how dinner was going to go. Dragan was genial but willful, relentless when he wanted to be. Benny was secretive by nature and easily offended by people prying into his life. It could make for a tense evening, and she tried to predict its outcome, depending on what she might do to influence it.

In their marriage – part friendship, part business alliance, part theatrical performance – Ben was the impulsive, impatient one. He had big ideas and a personality to match, along with money to spend no matter if the idea was good or terrible. Nina balanced that with patience, analysis, and a willingness to play the long game. This was her nature. She had been that way all her life, along with the ability to be honest about who she was and what she wanted. What started as personality traits grew into a skill set. It enabled her to claw out of a soul-killing childhood in Penza, an industrial center and one of the poorest cities in Russia, to sitting in a beautifully restored colonial townhouse in a historic section of Philadelphia.

She carried few illusions about herself. She recognized most people saw her as the show wife of a wealthy gay man, a social dilettante, and she embraced the small amount of truth there. If people focused on the façade they weren't likely to pay any additional attention to her, and she was free to act as she chose. Because below that surface image lived a serial adulterer, a nascent criminal, and, almost as an afterthought, an embedded Russian agent. She recognized all of these identities when she glanced at the mirror. She was aware of her motivations just as well; she had no craving for power or influence, only for money and what it could buy, and in this she and Ben were aligned. They had both lived long enough in this corrupt world to know that if they acquired enough money they could purchase the rest, as needed.

She asked herself: What was the situation in which she now found herself? Complex, mainly. Things felt like they were closing in, from several directions. If it was just the money laundering, she wouldn't be too concerned. Ben could bullshit his way out of nearly anything, and he could always tap his father if necessary. For a family as wealthy as his, with as many sources of income, there were always ways to explain why you had a pile of extra cash of mysterious origins. Besides, it was his idea to work with those clowns Ivan and Kalashnik, let him clean up that mess.

However, it was bad timing, with the threats they were receiving from overseas. She hoped it was as Ben said, all bluster with nothing behind it. And if anything did happen, she was confident she and Ben could defend themselves, as long as they stayed alert and prepared. But it would be much better to deflect something before it occurred. An incident would bring a lot of attention from intelligence leadership, which would be bad. It might pull back the curtain on some of the things she and Ben had been doing, and they would be hard pressed to have convincing explanations for all of it.

She believed it possible Dragan could relieve some of the pressure, if she could convince him she was the victim. She and Ben could present a scenario that was about eighty percent true, true enough to be compelling for someone inclined to believe them – or at least inclined to believe her. If they could get Dragan to intervene somehow, just push things a little further off balance, it might work out in their favor. That eighty percent true story had to be good, however. She had to explain things to him without making herself sound like both a felon and a fool.

Poor Dragan. She loved him but he was too much. When he wanted her to leave the marriage and run away with him, she laughed and said there are rules in their world about that sort of thing. With distress-ing predictability, he said rules were meant to be broken. He didn't, couldn't, understand that yes, for brash, smart, passionate people like him rules stood ready to be shattered and reshaped. For most others, rules were meant to be followed; the masses needed those instructions for what to do and how to do it. For the few like Ben and herself, economic mercenaries with no ethical standards, the rules were there to be exploited for personal gain, according to circumstance. It was always thus, as Ben liked to say, we're all captives of our coding at birth.

Her train of thought was interrupted by footfalls on the stairs.

12

BENEDIKT

Ben Petroski, a tall and thick man who, in his jeans and faded red cotton sweater, looked more like a rural carpenter than the heir to a business fortune, trudged into the room.

"So he's alive," said Nina. "What time did you get in last night?"

"Late. Or early today, take your pick. I need a strong cup of black tea."

"And how's what's his name?"

"There was drama. He left halfway through the week."

"There's so often drama. Why didn't you just come home?"

"There were other people. I had to stay and show a brave face, to keep up appearances. I'm here now, that's the joy of it." He made his way to the kitchen, put the kettle on, and joined her in the living room. "What's new?"

"Quite a bit, actually. You might want to sit down for this."

With a scowl he dropped into the armchair.

"Dragan came by. Sat right where you are, in fact. Needs to speak with us both, so he's coming for dinner. I want your promise that you'll be here."

"You're kidding."

"No. And that's the most benign news I have to offer. It seems those idiots Ivan and Kalashnik were taken into custody by the security team the other day."

"What the hell for?"

"Remember when you wanted to work with them because you suspected they were corruptible?"

"I don't know if I would call them merely corruptible. More run of the mill crooked, in an amateur sense."

"It turns out they were up to more than you might guess. They were stealing works from Sergei Golubev's collection."

Ben's mouth opened, closed again. It took a moment. "That's insane."

"As you say, they're crooked. And Ivan, through his job, had opportunity. A bad combination."

"Point taken."

The kettle whistled and he went to the kitchen to pour his tea, followed by Brandy. As it steeped, he leaned against the doorway and ate a shortbread cookie. He said, "Well if there's guilt by association then it falls on Dragan, he's Ivan's pal."

"He doesn't seem concerned about that."

"It screws things up for us," said Ben, disappointed about the loss of the money laundering scheme. "But it still doesn't explain why Dragan is here."

"He was on scene as Golubev's delegate. He came across records for our thing with Crown Street. He knows his art history, Benny. He knows the works were bogus, and that we were cleaning money."

"Oh shit," said Ben, dipping his head in exasperation. "Why didn't you give me a heads up?"

"I just found out yesterday, and you weren't answering my calls anyway."

"You could have left a message."

"I thought it would be more fun to talk about this in person."

"Again, this falls on Dragan. He made the introductions. I think we can make that work for us."

It had all happened naturally. Ivan was coming to Philadelphia to see an exhibition at a non-profit gallery where Ben sat on the board. Dragan set up an introduction, and suggested Ben show Ivan around the space and its collection of local artists. Afterwards Ben, Nina, and Ivan had dinner, and a good deal of wine was consumed. Ivan, in a misguided attempt to impress the Petroskis with art world gossip, mentioned he was friends with a Georgetown gallery owner who sometimes dealt in black market works stolen from mansions and office buildings in the area. It was a piece of information Ben and Nina stored for later use. Sure enough, there came a time when Ivan and his gallerist friend came in handy.

"You're suggesting we set up Dragan to take the blame? Are you serious?"

He shrugged. "Who else knows?"

"Julianna, of course. Ivan and Kalashnik are being questioned by Sacha, so it's just a matter of time before he finds out too, if he hasn't already."

"Oh good, let's get all your ex-boyfriends at the party. Look, the war isn't going so well for Moscow right now, no one will care very much if we have a side hustle. I can handle this."

"That's what I told him."

"Then why is he coming here for dinner?"

"It's time we got ahead of Denmark," she said. "Dragan has that connection. He could be a wild card we play."

"I don't think there's anything to get ahead of, just a lot of noise."

"I'm not certain that's all it is. It seems serious."

"Who are we dealing with here? Al Capone? Blofeld? I'm pretty sure we are out of reach. If you want we can send a few dollars, that will shut them up."

"Nothing will shut them up at this point. In any case Dragan is coming. He's given me his word he'll keep anything we tell him confidential, and whatever his character failings might be, he keeps his word and does what he says he will. Let's feed him an abridged story and see if he can be of use, okay?"

Ben nodded. He returned to the kitchen, emerging with a steaming cup in his hand. "I let Brandy out into the backyard. She was yipping at the door."

"I walked her not long ago."

"You keep slipping her people food, it messes with her insides," he said as he started up the stairs. "I left the door open a bit for her to come back in."

"Make sure you're here for dinner," she called after him. "I want to sort this out tonight."

"There's nothing to sort out!" he shouted. Nina rolled her eyes and returned to folding laundry, when Brandy began barking frantically at the kitchen door.

13

SEASHELL KEY CHAIN

The day slid into afternoon, and Dragan stood on the stoop, looking at the green door leading to Nina's townhouse and preparing for what was certain to be an awkward conversation. He had debated whether to record the conversation but decided that it would appear hostile if he did it openly, while doing it secretly would be a breach of trust. He was gathering information, not evidence.

He rang the bell. They took their time answering. Cirrus clouds hung in the sky, and the handful of maple trees on Crown Street were leafing. He looked at his watch. He rang again, and listened for it this time, to make sure he heard it, that it was working. Then why wasn't Brandy barking at the bell? They might have taken the dog for a walk and would be back any minute. He phoned Nina, but she didn't answer. He texted Benedikt – who hated answering phones – and got no answer there, either. That all felt wrong. He still had the key to the house. He unlocked the door and stepped in, closing the door behind him.

The house was still, with a mix of odors drifting by. Something like iron, and faintly acrid. A broken ceramic mug lay in a puddle at the bottom of the stairs, with splash stains on the wall. No movement, no sound. He stepped carefully forward. The door to the basement was closed. In the dining room the drawers of the china closet were open, and several plates were broken on the floor. A pile sat on the table, valuables he recognized as belonging to Ben and Nina: Kindle ebook readers, iPads, a pair of laptops, clear kitchen storage bags containing jewelry, Ben's expensive wireless headphones, along with vials of prescription drugs. Someone had been busy.

He looked toward the kitchen and saw Brandy's body on the floor. She had been stabbed and her throat cut. Contents of a junk drawer surrounded her, rubber bands, odd screws and batteries, souvenir keychains. The door to the back yard was ajar; he closed and locked it. His vision was blurry from anxiety and rage, and a high-pitched buzz was deep in his head. Burglars was his first thought. They came in through the back, killed the dog because she was barking. That doesn't matter now, he told himself, that's not the important thing. His adrenaline was high. His heart rate increased, his breathing rapid, small beads of perspiration on his forehead. Now: where were Nina and Ben?

The living room was chaos. There had been a fight. Blood splashes on the grey marble of the fireplace. Cushions tossed off the couch, a basket of laundry scattered. Violet Converse sneakers peeked from under the overturned armchair. He tossed the chair to the side. He cried out and checked Nina's pulse but she was gone. She had been shot, twice, once in the chest, once in the side of the head. A nearby cushion had a single hole ringed by a scorch mark, the killer had used it to muffle the shot. Her left arm was offline, her ulna broken.

He held her and screamed, then sobbed, then let out a guttural noise that sounded like it came not from him but from the air around him. He closed his eyes, reminded himself that he couldn't stay there with her, not yet.

She was warmer than the room temperature, she had been killed recently, within a few hours. He cursed himself for not being there;

had he arrived earlier he might have protected her. Close to her right hand was the fireplace poker, with blood on it, so she defended herself. When he found the person who did this, they would have wounds, might be banged up.

He quickly ran through it again. The killers broke in, presumably to rob the house. They entered through the back, killed the dog to silence it, then fought with Nina. They grabbed what they could and dumped it on the dining room table. Why was it still there? Where was Ben?

Dragan grabbed a butcher knife from the kitchen and stepped quietly to the stairs. The broken cup made sense now; Ben had come down at the noise of the fight in the living room, saw what was happening, dropped his cup and ran back up. Why? Why not come to Nina's aid? Because it was too late for her.

Ben was running for the guns.

At the top of the stairs, looking down the hall, he saw Ben's body on the floor of the rear bedroom, in front of the gun safe. In the room he saw the safe was unopened – Ben didn't get to it in time. He had been shot. His arms were cut up, they looked like defensive wounds. There was another body on the floor, a slim young man with torn jeans and stained grey sweatshirt, dark curly hair on top of a head lying at an unnatural angle. A knife lay nearby, but no gun.

Dragan played it in his mind: the foolish kid, armed with the knife, had raced down the hall after Ben, to get to him before he armed himself. Ben fended off the knife attacks until he could get a good hold on the kid and break his neck. Ben was big enough, and strong enough, and mean enough to do that. But there was no gun, so someone else came in and shot him.

Now Dragan knew there were multiple intruders, and at least one was still walking around, armed. They weren't professionals; the kid on the floor looked like a punk barely able to rob a convenience store, and the killers didn't seem prepared for the resistance Nina and Ben gave them. But if it was a burglary gone wrong, why not flee when they found the house occupied? Why not run when the owners fought back? Why leave the stuff on the table?

When Dragan let himself in, or when he rang the doorbell, they must have panicked, ran out the back, leaving the door ajar. In their hurry they left their loot. That scenario felt right, for the moment.

Nina's bedroom had been ransacked, drawers emptied, closets tossed. The floor was covered with underwear, reading glasses, a half dozen books, a key on a seashell key chain, a small diary notebook, the television remote. Ben's bedroom was much the same, his sketchbooks and vinyl album collection thrown violently around. Shoeboxes were taken from the closet and emptied.

Standing in the middle of Ben's room something nagged at the back of Dragan's mind, something he saw. He realized what it was and returned to Nina's room. He picked up the key on the seashell chain and put it in his pocket.

As he carefully climbed to the third floor he thought he heard something below. He froze, listened. He was near a window and noises came faintly from outside: a truck nearby, laughter from a group of people, what sounded like repairs being done half a block away. But nothing from inside the house. He continued up.

The third floor was where Nina and Ben kept their offices. Their laptops were missing, taken down to the dining room, but a high-end workstation remained, too bulky to steal. Dragan pulled out his phone to call it into the security team, to bring in a crew to deal with the bodies, take steps to contain any loss of information, and get investigators tracking down the killers.

But there it was again, noises from below. This time there was no doubt. He was not alone in the house.

14

SOUTH STREET

He heard muffled voices – it was more than one person. He had been careless. The killers hadn't escaped out the back door when Dragan entered the house, as he assumed. They hid in the basement. Now that he was upstairs, they could emerge. Creaking floorboards told him they had made it to the second floor. Why were they coming for him? Why not grab the loot and run?

He considered his options. He was trapped on the top floor. They were willing to kill and were armed with at least one gun. He merely had a kitchen knife. He didn't know how many there were. His prospects looked grim if he took a stand in the house. He had to get out of there. He pulled up the sash of one of the small dormer windows. He cut out the screen and left the knife on the desk. He stepped out on the narrow roof section, scrambled up, crossed over to the townhouse next door, then to the next one. It had been turned into apartments, and was equipped with a fire escape. He descended as quickly and quietly as he could and dropped onto the patio in the back. The building had a breezeway, a narrow access channel between it and the next house, which he followed out onto Crown Street.

A man in a brown leather bomber jacket burst out of the Petroski's house in a hurry, looking anxiously in both directions. Dragan turned and started walking away. As he rounded the corner he allowed himself a single look over his shoulder, and was surprised to see that the man was following him. Whoever this guy was, he seemed reckless. Perhaps capable of firing a gun on the street, so he needed to be dealt with. Dragan picked up his pace and headed toward the shopping district on South Street.

When Dragan turned onto South he was only a quarter of a block ahead of the thug. He passed a shoe place, a souvlaki restaurant, then came to a dollar store. He stepped into it and roamed the aisles. He found a roll of duct tape and a set of long zip ties. He also wanted something he could use as a weapon. A collapsible baton would be terrific but they were illegal in Pennsylvania. Pepper spray could be found in some convenience stores but apparently not this one. He thought the killer might become impatient and leave, or worse yet enter the store with gun drawn. But before either of those happened Dragan found a carabiner large enough to fit all of his fingers, with a locking collar. That would have to do.

The young woman with green hair at the cash register looked at his items, then at him, raised an eyebrow, adjusted her winged glasses, and rang him up. As he paid, he saw the thug in the brown bomber jacket across the street, watching. Dragan didn't glance at him as he left the store and continued on. He was looking for a café he and Nina used to visit, and found it on the next block. It had a new name, and the picture window frame was painted a different color, but it was the same storefront; he hoped they hadn't remodeled in the back. Inside he ordered a latte and sat at a table, facing the front, close to the door leading to the bathrooms. He waited.

He saw the brown leather bomber jacket pass by the café once, twice, and on the third time the man entered. He sat on a stool at the high table by the front window, turned, and scowled at the room. It gave Dragan the opportunity to take the man in. He was five-nine, tops, built like a gym rat. He had a welt and a bruise on the left side of his head, with a fresh cut above his right eyebrow, remnants of his fights in the brownstone. The jacket, which was roomy enough to conceal a handgun, had a slash on the upper left arm. Slicked hair, black t-shirt, thin chain around the neck, a few rings on the fingers. Dragan wrote him off as low-level South Philly mobster, hired muscle. What could a thug like this, and the dead punk back at the house, have to do with Nina and Ben?

Dragan did some quick calculations. He heard multiple people in the house. One stayed behind to watch the loot, apparently, and perhaps continue looking for whatever they were after. The tough guy with the weapon came after Dragan. Why? To take out a witness? Buy more time? If they could, to make sure the job was done, they would have sent more than one. So chances were good it was just the two of them left: the one in the café, and one in the house. Dragan could work with that.

He abruptly stood, went through the door and down the narrow hallway past the restrooms, crossed a storage area, and exited the back door to a small, enclosed, cement-covered yard. There were a couple of chairs with cigarette butts scattered nearby, a few unidentifiable machine parts, and two plastic storage containers. He pulled himself over the stucco wall and landed on the shallow pavement of Rodman Street behind the café. Across Rodman was a fenced-in park with a ballfield, empty except for some kids and their mothers in the playground at the far corner. He climbed over the fence and put one of the large sycamore trees lining the edge of the park between himself and the rear of the café. He sat and leaned back against the tree and waited. In the dimming light and the shadows of the park Dragan was essentially invisible to someone on the street.

He heard the café rear door open, heard a storage container dragged across the patio to the wall. There was a shuffle as the thug stepped on the container to look over the wall, and a grunt as he hauled himself over and onto Rodman Street. The thug cursed and walked down to Seventh Street, and turned toward Crown. He was heading back to the townhouse.

Perfect, thought Dragan. Things were now flipped.

15

MALICE

Dragan stayed close to the line of sycamores, remaining on the grass to muffle his steps, until he reached a gate to the street. He walked as close to the houses as possible, keeping a half block between him and the thug, who never looked back. The thug turned onto Astor Lane, and Dragan smiled. Astor was narrow, more alley than street, and had several modern apartment buildings with semi-enclosed exterior stairs, perfect places to hide things for a short time. He slipped the carabiner over his right hand and made a fist.

Dragan picked up the pace, checked up and down to see where the closest witnesses might be, then broke into a run. He turned onto Astor and towards the thug at full speed. The thug slowed at the sound of footfalls behind him, and turned to look, freezing in surprise. Dragan put out his left hand and hit the thug's upper arm, preventing him from reaching for his gun, while slamming his right into the thug's throat and jaw. The force lifted the thug off his feet and he hit the cobblestones, hard, on the back of his head and his shoulders, Dragan on top of him. Dragan pulled his arm back to strike, but the thug was already unconscious.

Dragan grabbed his feet and dragged him into the nearest apartment stairwell, leaving a smear of blood where the head had hit the stones. The thug began moaning. Dragan reached into the bomber jacket, removed the gun, cracked the man across the temple with it, then put the gun in his coat pocket. He flipped the thug over and bound his hands tightly together with the zip ties, and did the same to the man's feet, then zip-tied the man's hands to the stairwell banister. He wrapped duct tape around the bottom half of the man's head, covering the mouth, leaving his nose open to breathe but not being all that careful about it. He removed the man's wallet and shoved it into a pocket for later.

Dragan got to his feet and walked down Astor. He looked and listened for any observers, ready to run if needed, but the street was quiet and quickly becoming dark. He phoned a special emergency number, and to the abrupt young woman who answered in Russian he gave a verbal code, along with the identification of Philadelphia, and he was quickly routed to another woman, this one older and even less pleasant. He provided a quick summary, gave the address of the brownstone, and the location of the secured thug.

"You need to hurry to Astor," he said. "The guy is in bad shape, and someone will discover him soon."

"Understood," said the woman on the other end of the line. She had a voice seasoned by cigarettes and hard living. "A team is already on its way. Is the house on Crown Street secure?"

"No," said Dragan. "I'm heading there now to close it down."

"Advise to keep your distance until the second security team arrives at the house."

"No time for that," he said, and hung up before the woman could object.

A few minutes later Dragan was at the entrance of the townhouse, ringing the bell, his hand on the thug's gun in his pocket. He thought he heard a voice on the other side of the door. "It's me!" he barked in a half-mumble. It was apparently convincing enough, as the door was open by a ferret-like man in a red Phillies tracksuit and a five-day beard.

Dragan swung forward and up with the gun handle into the man's face, cracking his cheekbone and his nose and sending him staggering two steps back into the house. Dragan stepped in, kicked the man backwards and onto the floor, and shut the door. He pointed the gun at the man, who was squirming and whining, his right ear covered with a bandage, his left arm resting in a teal pashmina shawl used as a makeshift sling, an ugly red wound across his right forearm peering out from a tear in the tracksuit.

"You broke it," the man cried, blood seeping between the fingers of his right hand covering half his face.

"I recognize that shawl," said Dragan. He kicked the arm that was in it and the man yelped.

"Fuck you," the thin man said.

"You don't have much time," said Dragan. "Why did you kill them?"

"Fuck you." Dragan kicked the broken arm, harder this time. The man screamed.

"Robbie killed them not me."

"Is Robbie the one with the brown jacket?"

"Yeah. Where is he?"

"Who's the dead guy upstairs?"

"He lives here!"

"The other one, with the hoodie, you moron."

"Some nasty kid Robbie knows, a druggie. I never saw him before."

"Why did you come here? Why did you break into this house?"

"We got paid," said the man, tears mixing with the blood on his face. He was focused on the gun, not Dragan. "Robbie asked me to come along. He might need a third guy, he said, and we could keep anything we found in the house. I was supposed to look for cash, there was a lot of cash here Robbie said. And help him look for some computer thing. Nobody told me the owners would be here. Nobody told me anything about people getting hurt. This is the truth."

"What computer thing?"

"I don't know. Robbie fucked up, I think, it wasn't here. There wasn't any cash either. Robbie knew what to look for, but he didn't find it."

"Why did you kill them?"

"Robbie was the one said we had to kill the owners. He planned that going in, I could tell, but he didn't warn me, man, or else I wouldn't be here. Where is he?"

"You were paid to kill them?" Dragan moved the gun closer to the man's face, panicking him.

"Not me! Robbie. He said some archfiend paid him to do it. I don't know, I just came along, we were going to find some cash and get out. Me and the kid, the druggie, we were just hired help."

This was really all the man had to offer. Dragan kicked him in the head just for fun, zip-tied his hands and feet, then zip-tied him to the thick newel post. The man complained, and moaned, and made threats, so it was a relief to tape his mouth shut. Then Dragan sat on the floor of the living room, overcome with fury and grief. He held Nina's lifeless hand and cried as he waited for the security team to arrive.

Until he decided he wasn't going to wait any longer. He got another knife from the kitchen. His left hand holding the knife, his right on the gun in his jacket pocket, he returned to the thug tied up in the foyer. He pulled the tape off of the thug's mouth, then cut the zip tie attaching the thug to the stair newel, then cut the tie around the thug's wrists. He let the thug see the gun as a warning not to act up, then handed him the knife.

"Cut your legs free," Dragan told him. "I'm moving you to the basement."

With his remaining good arm the thug cut the zip tie around his ankles, then awkwardly stood, stiff, in pain from the beatings he received that day. Dragan stood a few feet away, watching, his eyes red but bright with malice.

It occurred to the thug he was on his feet, unbound, with a knife in his hand. "No," he said, "Don't."

Dragan shot him, and the thug collapsed where he stood. Dragan gathered up the tape and the zip ties, took them to the kitchen where he cut them into tiny bits with scissors, and shoved them to the bottom of the trash bin. Then he sat on a kitchen chair until the security team arrived.

16

NOSFERATU

They came in vans marked as cleaners and home renovators, with uniforms and caps to match. The idea was to blend in, but how well that worked in Society Hill on a Friday evening was open to debate. They moved about the house collecting electronics, documents, and personal belongings. They used crates to move the bodies out of the house so that prying eyes wouldn't recognize them for what they were. After Dragan gave his initial statement he was asked to remain for a senior inspector. He needed to relocate multiple times, to get out of their way, until finally he was told to go to the third floor and wait.

The office had been stripped of nearly everything, leaving just two desks, a lamp, and several chairs. Dragan sat by the window, the same window he had escaped from earlier, and looked out onto the darkness beyond. It was after midnight when he closed his eyes. He opened them again as the sun began to illuminate the overcast sky. A thin, balding man with remarkably long fingers and a sour expression was standing in the entrance to the room, watching him.

"Are you Nosferatu?" asked Dragan.

"My name is Viktor," said the thin man, in Russian. "You are Dragan Pavelovich Markov?"

"Yes."

"Good. Shall we begin?" Viktor pulled a chair around so he could face Dragan and use a desk. He took off his charcoal blazer and draped it over the chair back. He placed his bound notebook on the desk in front of him, reached into his grey sweater vest to retrieve a pen from the pocket of his shirt, and opened the notebook in preparation.

Viktor looked up and smiled. "Dragan is a Serbian name. Are you Serbian?"

"My mother was."

"She married a Russian?"

"Yes."

"A wise choice," Viktor said with a nod. "Russian men are more robust."

"He was a drunk who beat her, and me, and abandoned us, then died in a car accident."

Viktor looked at him blankly, made a note in his book, and asked, "I understand you are a project manager?"

"Associate director of operations at the embassy in Washington D.C."

"So yes, you are a glorified project manager. This is an important role?"

"There are things that need to be done and done well. I'm tasked with doing them."

"Do you enjoy it?"

"There's variety in it. I have a lot of autonomy."

"Some friends in high places too, I hear."

"That's just talk."

"Fair enough." Viktor scribbled something down and turned to a page filled with notes. "I see you have lived in the United States a long time."

"Since my mid-teens, yes."

"There's a comment here about basketball."

"Yes. I played when I was young."

"You are tall but not so tall as the professionals I see on television."

"I was tall enough for a shooting guard at a mid-level division one school."

Viktor looked at him, again without expression. "I don't know if I understood anything you just said to me, but that isn't important. You attended college here, became an art history professor. Surprisingly you left that to become a project manager." His voice carried the merest hint of skepticism. "You were able to best two American gangsters who had already murdered seasoned, trained Russian agents. Most art historians are not able to do that. Even the ones who become project managers."

"I was fortunate."

"No doubt. Why were you here?"

This man Viktor knew the Petroskis were embedded agents; he and the team downstairs would have to know that in order to do a thorough cleanup. It wasn't clear if their relationship to Dragan was known so he needed to be cautious. "I know the Petroskis socially, from their activities in arts organizations. They invited me up for the weekend. I was going to have dinner, then go to the museum tomorrow before I returned home."

"There are rumors that you were having an intimate relationship with Nina Petroski."

Okay, there it is, thought Dragan. This was where things were headed. "There's no truth to that. Do you normally pay attention to rumor?"

"Rumor is often an excellent source of insights. So you deny this?"

"Of course."

"Did you have a reason to think the Petroskis were in danger?"

"No."

"Do they, did they, have something in the house of special value?" Among Russian security circles, the phrase "special value" was highly charged and flexible. Dragan had heard it used to refer to anything from a pouch of diamonds to a stash of classified documents to a kidnapped courier.

"Not that I know of."

"Did the killers tell you anything?"

"As I explained to the others, the one in the house said they were looking for money, and a 'computer thing' whatever that means. And that an archfiend paid them to break in."

"An archfiend? Like in American comic books? Did he appear to be hallucinating, on drugs?"

"It's hard to know that."

Viktor nodded. "He managed to say this before you shot him?"

"Yes, of course. We faced off for a while. I asked him questions, he answered a few. I told him to drop the knife. He was begging me to let him go, but he was just looking for a chance to attack me."

"I see. This all sounds very exciting. He attacked you then?"

"Yes."

"Even though you had that gun."

"He didn't know I had it, that I took it from his friend."

"He must have forgotten you smashed his face with it. Where did he get the knife?"

"From the kitchen, I guess. He had it on him when I forced my way in."

"The other man, the one on the street, he said nothing?"

"He hit his head hard. He wasn't conscious."

Viktor put on a sad face. "They inform me that he may never recover. He had a terrible wound on the back of his head" – he reached back and touched there – "and a severe bash on the side, here" – he touched his left temple. "This man in the street, he was the 'Robbie' the other spoke about?"

"His name was Robert, you have his wallet."

"And 'Robbie' was the one who had all the information, all the answers. Unfortunately, you bludgeoned him into a coma, and you shot the only man who could confirm what you are telling me."

"We do the best we can in the moment."

"And the third man, upstairs?"

"He was already dead when I found him."

"Yes, so you said earlier." Viktor referred again to his pages of notes. He reached into an envelope and withdrew a postcard with the national flag of Ukraine on one side. "We found this under the body of Benedikt Petroski," he said, setting the postcard on the desk to display it. "Do you know what it means?"

Dragan did not conceal his surprise. "Someone wants us to think it has to do with Ukraine."

"So it would appear."

"I know Ben is ethnically Ukrainian."

"He is a Cossack?"

"I don't know that much about it."

"Did he talk about Russia's campaign against fascism in Ukraine?"

"He mostly talked about food and traveling, and gossiped about other rich people."

Viktor nodded again. "I understand there was some excitement recently with the art collection of Sergei Golubev."

"I don't know much about that, either."

"I appreciate the discretion. Although two agents are now dead. And those two agents had business dealings with the two men who were stealing from the Golubev collection. A theft you were investigating. And now you are here today. This is all a remarkable coincidence, don't you think?"

Dragan recognized at that moment Sacha was the one feeding information to Viktor.

"The gallery dealer who was part of the Golubev thefts was also of Ukrainian background," said Viktor. "A second coincidence. You are half Serbian. The Serbs have a long history of supporting Ukraine territorial integrity."

"Do the trash who killed the Petroskis look like they would care about any of that?"

"Yet another interesting coincidence," said Viktor, ignoring him, "is that Ivan Bortnik, one of the men involved in the art thefts, was an acquaintance of Nina and Ben Petroski because he was introduced to them by you."

"How could you know such a thing?" Dragan was impressed by the thoroughness of the man's preparation, and a little intimidated. Viktor was not the usual bureaucrat. He was mostly asking questions he already had the answers to, looking to see where Dragan lied or tripped up. The man was good at his job, which made him dangerous.

Viktor spread his palms open in a gesture that said he was just the messenger. "Many people are alarmed about the murders. They are eager to provide whatever information they can, to help determine what happened."

There was nothing in it for Dragan to reply. He understood the performance unfolding in that room. Viktor was not there to negotiate or argue. He was there to gather information and present that information back to his keepers in whatever way he saw fit. All Dragan could do was hope Viktor was not completely corrupt, and had at least a little desire to determine the truth.

"Can I go now?" asked Dragan.

"I think that would be acceptable," said Viktor. "We will speak again."

Before Dragan made it out of the room Viktor reached out and caught his sleeve.

"I'm not sure about you, Dragan Pavelovich Markov," said Viktor. "You are lying to me about the woman being your lover, this I know. But the rest of it, I am not sure. Take care, the light is harsh on you at the moment."

They stared at each other, neither one certain if the other was an ally or an enemy.

17

BEACH HOUSE

The morning sun threatened to pierce the cloud cover as Dragan drove west into New Jersey. He had too much time to think and too much to think about, and the music he blasted through the stereo did little to drown out the clatter in his head. The Atlantic City Expressway to the Garden State Parkway to an exit that put him on a road heading straight towards the Atlantic Ocean, past bushes and reeds, past a shuttered farm stand, past the line of cottages backed up against the canal. It was still the off-season, and traffic was light as he entered Stone Harbor, a vacation home community north of the Wildwoods across the inlet. In the summer the town was filled with white, moneyed families, the kids wearing Ivy League college sweat-shirts, but as Dragan drove through the two-block business district only a handful of people were on the pavement, nursing coffees and walking dogs.

He parked at the end of a street where the dunes rose up and curled around the pavement. The summer home owned by Nina and Ben sat quietly looking out across the sand toward the water, a lean modern building with plenty of windows and beachside porches on both the first and second floors. The air was colder here than it was in the city, with a steady breeze. Dragan pulled out the key on the seashell keychain he found in Nina's bedroom and opened the door.

His footsteps echoed on the wood floors. The house was cool, the thermostat still set for a maintenance minimum. The water had been turned off so the pipes wouldn't freeze over the winter. Ben didn't like opening the house for the summer until May, but when Dragan and Nina had been together they liked coming down in the off-season to walk on the sand in bare feet and parkas.

He started at the top, working his way through the bedrooms, opening drawers, examining closets. He didn't know what he was looking for, and there wasn't much to see, mostly linens and a few sets of clothes.

Downstairs he considered the credenza in the dining room. He smiled sadly at the replica of the shore house in LEGOs, complete with the two decks and entrance patio, and blocky approximations of the furniture. Ben had put it together, "as a bit of fun," he claimed, a project of cute whimsy not really in keeping with the big man's personality. There were also two cream-colored porcelain sculptures, and a short stack of novels. Inside the credenza was a mix of serving dishes, a few bottles of liquor, and tablecloths. The kitchen cabinets held dishes along with canned and packaged staples; in the drawers were utensils and cookware.

He stood in the middle of the living room and wondered if he was overlooking anything obvious. The house was uncluttered; people tended to bring their own clutter when they visited. There were no computers, no hard drives. No files, no stash of money. No attic to hide things in. Whatever the killers were looking for in the townhouse on Crown Street didn't appear to be here, either.

He flashed back to an afternoon in the summer, when their plan was to rent a powerboat and take it offshore to drink and make love and swim, pretending that would be their life forever. He had told Nina he needed her license for the rental paperwork, so they could both drive the boat. She told him it was in her purse, in the closet upstairs, on the third shelf, on top of a box. He retrieved the license and for the first time saw her official date of birth. Four years older than Dragan, even older than Ben was, not at all the age she had originally claimed. Later, as the boat skipped south over the water toward Cape May, he asked her why she would lie about her age. Because that is what people do, she said, as if explaining something simple to a child. He asked her: but why lie to me? She only looked out onto the water, pretending not to hear him.

That incident meant nothing to him now. What caught his interest was the box in the closet her purse had been sitting on. He remembered it as a small, flat, vintage document box of thin wood with brass fittings. The kind of thing a woman like Nina would turn into a keepsake box. Running back upstairs he found it on the same shelf in the rear of her closet. He expected a collection of items from her affairs, memories of lovers more important to her than he was. He was surprised to find only mementos related to him, and their travels. There were notes he had left for her after weekends together, theatre and concert tickets, a strip of photos taken in a booth at a craft fair in the Pocono Mountains, and an envelope.

In the envelope was a photograph. It was a color snapshot of a modern, five-story office building shaped like a cube, surrounded on three sides by water, like a moat. To the left was a parking lot with a handful of cars and a few trucks at the far end. In the foreground three people stood on a stone bench by the water with the building behind them. Two of the people were Ben and Nina, smiling broadly. He turned it over. On the back was a hand-written Gmail address, a string of numbers.

He looked again at the photo. He recognized the building. It was in Copenhagen; the photo was most likely taken a year or so ago, when the Petroskis went on a Scandinavian holiday. He identified the building; it was the work location of the third person on the bench, a man with a surprised look on his face as he seemed to lose his balance. Dragan knew him. His name was Paul Koslov. He was an embedded Russian agent in Denmark who worked in finance. Paul's intelligence role was tracking trends and attitudes in commodities markets, especially focused on European supply chains. But his real value to his Russian masters was his skill in money laundering.

18

HUMILIATION

That night, in his apartment in Washington D.C., Dragan stretched out on his couch and examined the photograph of Paul, Ben, and Nina. There were so many questions, and the most important were how did they know each other, and what were they up to?

Dragan met Paul Koslov years earlier, during a cleanup operation after the French financial institution Pécy Bank was discovered to be laundering billions of euros and rubles out of Russia. Russian intelligence had one of their own in a highly placed position at the bank who disrupted the security processes, so the standard kinds of anti-fraud mechanisms were not functioning. It was elegantly done and the agent disguised his involvement, but when the US and UK sounded the alarm it was only a matter of time before smart auditors found a trail that led to him. He would be brought up on charges of, at the very least, criminal negligence and put under tremendous pressure to talk about the network behind the scheme. So Russian intelligence needed to get him out of there.

It had to be low key with plenty of obfuscation. At Julianna's suggestion they tapped Dragan as the lead. He was based in America and wasn't connected to finance, so wouldn't be on anyone's radar

and could come at the project sideways. He was paired with Paul
Koslov, who was one of the finance people scattered around Europe
who had helped keep the laundering machine running through false
accounting practices. Paul held a legitimate, responsible position in
financial advising in Denmark, so he provided cover as needed. When
the two of them traveled from Copenhagen to Paris, Paul brought
his girlfriend Lily with him so the trip looked like a holiday. And
ninety-eight percent of it was a holiday, except the part about getting
the Russian banker out of France before anyone realized he was gone.

But none of this explained the connection between the Petroskis
and Paul. When the Petroskis returned from their Scandinavian holiday, Nina didn't mention connecting with him. For that matter, going
back a little earlier, when he told Nina about what had happened
with Pécy Bank, and mentioned Paul and Lily, she didn't say she knew
them.

And there it was, of course. What an idiot he had been.

Sprawled in bed with Nina, under the sheets, probably a little drunk
on wine and woozy from the sex, after she went down on him until
he didn't know what planet he was on, Dragan himself had told Nina
about the Russian ex-pat money launderer in Scandinavia. She du-
tifully put that information away for later when she and Ben might
need it. Just as he had introduced them to Ivan and, by extension,
Ivan's dishonest art dealer friend Kalashnik. The Petroskis didn't need
a network of criminal references for whatever shenanigans they got
up to. They had Dragan, under Nina's spell, handing them all the
connections and opportunities they needed. He felt humiliated, and
angry.

***

While the investigation into the Petroski murders continued, Dragan was forbidden to travel outside of the United States. Viktor, or another equally chilly figure, would periodically stop by with questions Dragan had already answered. In the process they sometimes mentioned a few theories they were working on, without much enthusiasm.

The war against Ukraine continued, marked by drone and missile strikes on both sides. Putin talked about "taking back and reinforcing" while citing the actions of Peter the Great in the Great Northern War as precedent and supposed inspiration, thereby tacitly acknowledging his imperial ambitions. Chatter at the embassy was performatively supportive of the war, but when in small, private groups they shook their heads in dismay. The Great Northern War was in the first two decades of the eighteenth century, someone would say, does Moscow know what year it is? The success of Russia should be based on technology and industry, someone else would say, not in geography. They would despair for Russia's future as it isolated itself from much of the rest of the world, and shake their heads some more.

One positive was that after a cluster of sudden and unexplained deaths of Russian business executives during the first third of the year, no such supposed accidents had occurred for months. Everyone hoped this was a sign that pressure was lifting, but privately assumed it only meant the loudest contrary voices had been silenced.

Dragan waited. He did his job, kept to himself, worked out at the gym, tried new restaurants, read books, and thought about the murders. Nina had been worried about a threat, which suggested they were assassinated. He had to consider the possibility they were killed because of their intelligence work, but that would be a stretch. Their intelligence value was not particularly high; they were primarily cultural observers watching trends among the upper crust, one step removed from gossip columnists. And what intelligence professional would hire low-rent local gangsters to kill Russian agents?

He told no one of the photograph he found in the beach house in Stone Harbor, which he slipped into the nearly seven hundred pages of a Frank Lloyd Wright biography kept on the top shelf of his bookcase. If the official investigation failed to find an explanation, which he expected, he would use that photograph as the start of his own mission. He was just waiting for the right moment.

19

LEONID

"We understand Kalashnik a bit," said Dragan. "But we're never going to understand why Ivan got involved."

He and Leonid were in a Chinese restaurant in Brentwood, just beyond the D.C. border in Maryland. The place specialized in hand-pulled noodles, and they selected it as much for the food as for its distance from downtown.

Leonid shrugged. "People do crazy things." He was a security agent and had seen his share of inexplicable behavior.

"I know. But Ivan had the life he wanted, at least the one he told me he wanted. Why throw it away?"

"I have neighbors, the wife works at one of those big pharmacy stores with everything in it. She says they catch people all the time shoplifting two-dollar bags of candy or a five-dollar hairbrush, and every time the person has plenty of money with them. They don't need to steal the candy or the brush. Yet, they do it. Ivan makes sense the same way."

"Could be true."

"Did Ivan say why he did it?"

"He wanted to take things away from Sergei. Said Sergei had too much and should have less."

Leonid slurped noodles and nodded. "Sergei Golubev does have too much and should have less."

"You and I can say this over lunch, but Ivan did something about it."

"A hero of the modern revolution. I hear he's doing okay, by the way. Everyone was right, with the war going on no one cared about a few stolen paintings. They sent him back to his family. Kalashnik, I know nothing about. We scared him enough he took off, apparently."

"Has the investigation into the murders finished?"

Leonid shrugged again. "No, but they're running out of fuel. There are currently three layers of explanation. Top layer, the one most commonly told to family and such back home, is that it was a robbery gone bad. That's simple and easy to believe, there they always talk about America as a cesspool of crime. Second layer, the story the intelligence and government people embrace, is that there is a pro-Ukraine cell in the US that killed them because they saw Benedikt Petroski's father as a traitor. It conveniently fits everything. It places the blame on Ukraine and makes Benedikt a martyr and confirms his father as a pro-Russia Ukrainian, and therefore a true patriot. It explains the card with the Ukraine flag found at the scene, and eventually they'll figure a way to work that Kalashnik mess into it."

"What's the bottom layer?"

"Some people think you did it. It's now an open secret that you and she were having an affair and she ended it. The idea is you were scorned by a woman and it blew the roof off your head."

"Fucking Sacha."

"Probably. He and I are the same rank and I can shut him up if he talks like that in front of me, so of course he doesn't. Instead it's all quiet conversations, here and there. Unfortunately it lays groundwork for making you the scapegoat if they decide they need one."

"They didn't get anything out of the guy in the alley?"

"He never came back to normal. You scrambled his brains good. Unfortunately, that feeds the rumor about you. If the killers were your guys, the logic goes, you wouldn't want them caught alive."

Dragan ate a bite, thought for a moment. "I didn't kill the Petroskis."

"I didn't think you did."

"I read about three bodies found by the railroad tracks in a chemical plant in Philadelphia."

"If there is some Ukraine cell, it was a message for them. But to me the big puzzle is why men like these? Not professionals, not trained. But that seems to be a thing these days, doesn't it? Yevgeny Prigozhin is recruiting inmates from Russian prisons to fight for his Wagner Group in exchange for their freedom. He's getting thousands that way."

Dragan leaned forward. "I think what it really looks like is they were hired because whoever hired them didn't care about the job."

"What does that mean?"

"This is a thing that comes up in business, I see it sometimes dealing with vendors at the embassy. You have some dirty job someplace that needs to be done, a box needs to be checked, but it's ugly or dangerous or there are so many regulations it's a giant pain in the ass. So, you contract it out. Your contractor wants your money but doesn't want to do the job either, for all the same reasons. He subcontracts it out to someone even cheaper and less professional than he is. The contractor keeps a piece of the money, and he looks the other way while the subcontractor does a sloppy job, but at least the thing is done. The box is checked."

"They were amateurs who were lucky the Petroskis didn't kill them instead," said Leonid.

"That's bothered me. It could have gone either way. Those punks weren't prepared. They didn't know who the Petroskis were. Consider if it didn't matter how it turned out. If the Petroskis were killed, that was success. And if the thugs got killed instead, then the attack would serve as a message – look how close we got to you this time, we can do it again whenever we choose."

"Then how do you explain the card with the Ukraine flag?"

"I don't know. But I know those two men I dealt with in Philadelphia couldn't find Ukraine on a map, if they ever even heard of it."

20

SACHA

A few days later Dragan was walking out of the embassy and nearly collided into Sacha coming in. The security officer looked immaculately groomed, as always. He ignored Dragan as he walked around him, but Dragan caught his sleeve and pulled him to the side of the entrance foyer.

"I want you to stop talking behind my back," said Dragan, trying to keep his voice low so everyone didn't hear their business. "If I need to I'll move it up the chain until someone eventually steps on you."

Sacha was unimpressed by the threat. "The only source of information we have on the murders is from you, conveniently. We don't even know why you were there."

"I was invited to dinner."

"Unlikely. She broke it off with you."

"How would you know something like that?"

Sacha removed his sunglasses, an uncommon move. He wanted Dragan to see his eyes as he said, "You don't think we still talked?"

"She chose me and you're angry? That's why you're spreading bullshit?"

"The bullshit you talk about is all over this building, everyone is concerned about the murders. Some will wonder about your responsibility. It's natural."

"That makes you happy."

Sacha shook his head, as if despairing that Dragan just didn't get it. "Why would I be happy if the people responsible are still walking around? If I find out who did that to Nina I'll kill them myself." He put his sunglasses back on.

"If that's true, then consider the possibility that the formal investigation will get no further than it is now. Someone alone, below the radar, will get further than your team stomping over everything."

"Someone alone? Like you?"

"Not me. I don't need the additional attention, and they won't trust me to do it anyway."

"But people wonder if you had anything to do with it. I'm sure you'd like the chance to find out the truth before they cart you away."

"There's that."

Sacha thought about it. "Be careful what you wish for."

It took until mid-August for the seed to sprout. Dragan was playing basketball in a pickup game at his gym, mostly ex-high school and ex-college players now in their thirties trying to recall lost youth and not injure themselves. After the game he came off the court, wrapped a towel around his sweaty neck, and saw that he had received a text from Julianna. She wanted to meet.

21

VESELKA CAFÉ

Dragan and Julianna maintained an uneasy relationship. There was affection and respect there, but also a buffet of darker feelings, including bitterness, disappointment, and resentment. This had been the case from the very beginning, when she plucked him from his adolescence and dropped him into a planned career in espionage. It was something he neither asked for nor fully embraced; Julianna and Russian intelligence had chosen him, not the other way around.

Orphaned at a young age, he had been placed by relatives in an academy with military ties. He was tall, athletic, smart, perpetually angry, and seen as having strong potential. His lack of self-discipline and open resentment of authority were deeply embedded, however, which made a normal military career unlikely, at least not without a lot of effort to change him, and no one believed he could change. What he was clearly suitable for both physically and emotionally, however, was basketball, and finding success on the court was the only place where he seemed either comfortable or something close to happy.

A senior faculty member became intrigued by him and started paying attention, asking about him discreetly among students and other teachers. He learned that Dragan had influence over his peers, a ringleader who was happy to stay in the background after he set other students down a path. He had a way of not doing things he didn't want to do and getting away with it, and liked disrupting the status quo without leaving a trace that he was behind it. He had an excellent memory but often barely passed tests because, apparently, he didn't care. He could be generous with his time, and trained smaller, weaker students in fundamentals of self-defense and encouraged them to stand up to bullies. He flirted with girls but didn't pursue them, until eventually the tension hit a turning point and they pursued him. In other words, he was a charismatic, manipulative weasel in the guise of a star athlete. The senior faculty member was also a recruiter for the foreign intelligence service, and he recognized Dragan's talents as suited to that world.

The man contacted someone, a woman who had recently married a filthy-rich Russian businessman, moved to the United States, and was building a network of intelligence agents deeply embedded in everyday American life. So it was that Julianna Titovna Golubev, at the time a strikingly attractive up-and-comer eager to make her mark, recruited Dragan into her little corner of the Russian intelligence empire while he was still a teenager. Under her guidance he was placed with a cooperative, and compensated, Russian émigré family in the Baltimore area. He joined an elite youth basketball program that played tournaments throughout the eastern part of the United States. He attended a top private school where his team made it to the state finals. This exposure led to an athletic scholarship at a university in western Pennsylvania, where he received a bachelor's in business and a master's in art history. He was working on his doctorate when, through some intervention by the Golubevs, he landed a tenure-track assistant professorship at a college in New York State.

This was a nice victory for both Dragan and Julianna, an illustration of how to place Russian agents in the everyday working life of western countries. Until Dragan started pushing against the constraints on his life and made some spectacularly bad decisions, showing that he remained in many ways the same angry boy with a barely contained urge to violence. Julianna had spent plenty of time and money molding Dragan into the person she wanted him to be, and from her perspective he had failed to provide a return on that investment. After she pulled him from the New York college town and into the D.C. embassy, she and Sergei treated him professionally enough, but behind it they believed they owned him.

This history hung in the air between them as they sat at a table near the far wall of the Veselka Café, a no-nonsense eatery a few blocks northwest of Mt. Vernon Square. It featured good food, chandeliers, and Eastern European decorations, with a wait staff that sensed when to check on you and when to leave you alone.

"This place is usually more crowded," said Dragan.

"It's always catered to both Russians and Ukrainians," said Julianna. "In the current climate everyone is a little anxious about who they are seen with."

A short waiter with spiked blonde hair came by. Julianna had black tea, Dragan a double espresso and a glass of ice water.

"You've been avoiding me," he said when the waiter left.

"I've been furious with you. I still am. You killed that man in the house in cold blood. You think I can't read a story in the details? I thought you were over that sort of behavior. I thought you had learned to mind your manners and be a professional."

"I'm passionate about my work."

"Don't get clever with me, you smug prick. I'm the one who has to clean up your messes."

"It was self-defense."

"Stop. Just stop. It was terrible field work. You've embarrassed yourself, and embarrassed me, again, for putting trust in you. Now everyone is focused on the remarkable coincidence of the murders happening right after you discovered the money laundering."

"I'm willing to bet they had a dozen side hustles. All of them concurrent with the murders. No causality there."

She considered that, reluctantly. "You make a good point. We know about at least one back-room operation Ben was running, trolling or a sales scheme or something, but by the time we got there everyone was gone along with the equipment. The Petroskis were very good at keeping secrets and minding the details. The business with Ivan and that gallery dealer was a bit sloppy, a rare misstep it seems. We still have no idea of the source of the money they were laundering. In any case, you are the common factor right now, and it is unfortunate for you."

"I hear some are putting me forward as a convenient scapegoat."

"Rubbish, of course. Most of it can be ignored."

"Most of it? Where's the genuine threat?"

"Benedikt's father. Being Ukraine-born, he's under a lot of pressure because of the war. He wants the investigation wrapped up soon so he can focus on all the other things that are stressing him. He's making a lot of noise about the murders, about you, about me, and he has enough wealth that certain types of people listen to him. I'm afraid he'll move to take this entire thing away from us, bring in his own private group, and after a short investigation conclude you were responsible, and that I've been utterly incompetent. My career will be over, and you'll be in prison. Let's order some food."

Julianna had borscht, Dragan had mushroom soup, and they split plates of smoked salmon, small stuffed peppers, and potato cheese varenyky.

She said, "If it makes you feel any better, I doubt anyone seriously believes you were behind it. Even your enemies admit you're too efficient to have put this mess together, although they would be happy for you to take the blame."

They ate in silence. Dragan saw what was coming next. It was what he expected all summer, once it became clear the investigation was getting nowhere. It was why he gave Sacha the little shove to move it forward. Julianna was going to throw him alone into the woods, where he would either kill the wolves and save them both, or be devoured and take the problems with him. He knew it, and she knew it, and she knew he knew it, so she waited for him to bring it up.

He said, more a statement than a question, "You want me to look into it."

"I think you want to look into it," she said, turning it back on him. "Don't you?"

"I want answers."

"We all want answers. Sacha actually suggested this to me. He seems to like the idea of you trying to save yourself from drowning. Said it will motivate you."

"If I do this, I'll need backing."

"Sergei and I are eager to put this behind us, so we can personally provide funding, but that is all."

"You want me to take all the risk."

"It has to be unofficial."

"While you contribute the one thing you can most afford, which is money."

"Money opens a lot of doors, you know that."

He understood very well. Her money made Julianna essentially his beneficent jailer, and he would willingly tolerate it only so far. Which was why he didn't tell her about the photo of Ben and Nina in Denmark. Nor did he let her know he was leaving the country as soon as possible, or where he was going. The target was on his back not hers, after all, regardless of how much she felt exposed.

It was possible he could solve this mystery, or not, but the stakes were high and the risks were truly borne only by him. He was on his own.

22

PAUL

Dragan took Iceland Air to Copenhagen, entering Denmark with counterfeit paperwork. He thought it was a good idea to leave a false paper trail in case anything turned awkward; it also came in handy for leaving the United States without anyone being able to trace him.

He checked into the Hotel Frederik in the Gammelholm district and asked the desk to send up a few items. He took a hot shower, and found a bottle of Reyka vodka, a bucket of ice, and a selection of fresh fruit waiting for him on the table. He wrapped the terry robe around himself, poured himself a large drink, and sat by the window. He used the hotel's phone and when a woman answered he asked for Paul Koslov.

"Who is calling, please?"

"Denis Sobol, of Infocon Solutions," said Dragan. She asked him to hold on. A few moments later appeared a man's voice, suspicious, cautious.

"Yes, this is Paul," he said.

"Hi Paul. Denis Sobol, Infocon Solutions. We met in Paris a few years ago, on the Pécy Bank financial restructuring."

There were a few silent moments as Paul pieced things together. Then, an anxious, "Yes, how are you?"

"Terrific," said Dragan. "Business is strong, can't complain. I'm in Copenhagen visiting clients for a few days, I thought we could have dinner."

"You're in the city? I guess we could get together. When did you have in mind?"

"How about tonight?"

***

Murstenshus, near the Grand Teatret, was an adequate steakhouse with an adequate waitstaff, one of those mediocre restaurants that managed to maintain loyal customers and a significant tourist trade for no discernable reason. But Paul Koslov seemed happy enough to be there.

"It's been a few years, hasn't it?" asked Paul, adjusting his fork. "You here on business or holiday?"

Dragan considered the man across the table. Physically much the same as when he saw him last: well-dressed, average height, a little thick, with the air of a salesman. But now there was something off about him, different from the man who kept his cool as they spirited that banker out of Paris.

"Unfortunately, I'm here on assignment, no time to relax," said Dragan, with a regretful smile. "I'm looking into a pair of murders, I'm afraid. A couple of our own. You didn't know Benedikt and Nina Petroski, did you?"

For half a second Paul froze, then nervously took a sip of his beer. He shook his head. "No, I don't think so. Were they the victims?"

Well there's the first one, thought Dragan. Not even in Denmark for an entire day and the lies have already begun. "Yes. Married couple, in Philadelphia."

"That's terrible. Professional consequences, you think? Not that anyone really cares what we do in our section, not even our people. But still, there are risks."

Dragan thought Paul seemed a little on edge. Possibly under the influence of something. "We're completely in the dark," he said. "But it's likely to be connected to something they were working on. There was a card with the Ukraine flag left with the bodies, so related to the war."

"How could that be?"

"The father of the husband is a prominent businessman, Ukrainian by birth but pro-Russia by choice. The thinking is that a Ukraine unit in the United States did it to send a message."

"That's a tough one, all around. So what brings you to Denmark, then? So far away from Philadelphia. Some Scandinavian connection?"

Dragan nodded slowly.

Paul fidgeted with his tableware. "Is there something specific you're looking into?"

"No not really."

"If it's related to their more private activities," Paul said, referring to their work as embedded agents, "does it impact me? Do I need to look out for anything?"

"Most likely not." Dragan started in on his tiger prawns with chili and lime, letting Paul think whatever he wanted to think. Then he asked, "And how is Lily?"

"Oh... not sure. We were always a little on and off. Off now. For a while, actually."

"Sorry to hear that. I thought you two were pretty strong."

"Nice of you to say so. Not really strong, though. The way I remember Paris, she spent more time with you than she did with me."

There was nothing in that for Dragan, so he let it go. The rest of the dinner was mundane, and Dragan kept the conversation focused on Copenhagen weather and shopping and recent movies. The further they drifted from the murders the more comfortable Paul became, until talk shifted to Danish Superliga football, which Paul discussed with enthusiasm.

After dinner, standing outside the restaurant, they buttoned their coats against the falling temperature. Paul put his hand on Dragan's shoulder and gave it a squeeze meant to be reassuring and empathetic. "Best of luck with your investigation," he said.

"Thanks. But there's probably nothing here to investigate. I expect to leave in a day or two."

Paul waved and headed toward the taxi station. Dragan watched him for a minute, then turned to walk the kilometer and a half back to the hotel, to think about the dinner. Not only did Paul lie about knowing the Petroskis, Dragan was certain he was lying about Lily as well. The big thing on his mind, however, was that Paul wasn't surprised to hear Ben and Nina were dead.

23

LILY

After he left Dragan standing in the square, Paul took a taxi to Café Syv, a small restaurant on a corner in a mixed residential and industrial neighborhood to the southwest. He asked the driver to wait. As he neared the front door he saw a woman with a bicycle come out from the alley behind the building.

He gestured to the taxi driver to stay and ran to the woman. Lily Sandersen was tall, taller than Paul, with unnaturally black hair in bangs, her calm and distant eyes ringed by nearly theatrical eyeliner.

"What are you doing here?" she asked. Her voice was flat, neither hostile nor friendly.

"To talk to you. Why are you leaving your shift early?"

"I have things to do. What do you want?"

"Do you remember Dragan Markov? He was with us in Paris?"

"Your friend?"

"He was a colleague, but yes."

"You told me he was your friend."

Paul waved it off. "It doesn't matter. He's here."

"Okay."

"He's interested in Nina and Benedikt Petroski, about their visits."

"Okay. What did you tell him?"

"Nothing."

"Good. I need to go." She started off with the bicycle.

Paul jumped into her way. She glared at him. "He's investigating their deaths," he said in a strained whisper, with a backward glance at the taxi.

"Okay. The only thing I know about that is what you told me. Does he want to talk to me?"

"No, God no. Don't do that."

"It's settled then. Go back and focus on getting our money," she said as she left.

Paul watched her go, clenching and unclenching his fists. He spun once all the way around and looked at the sky.

***

Lily pedaled deeper into the neighborhood. She considered how Paul had an uncanny ability to show up at the wrong time for the wrong reason. At some point he needed to stop being a nuisance. If he didn't fix himself someone else would do it, but only after they got that money. Until then she needed him, but at arm's length. She needed those funds to continue her work. She wasn't going to subsidize social change through a waitress gig.

She drifted to a stop in front of an old factory structure that had been converted into apartments. She locked her bicycle at the long rack in front and searched the bell buttons until she found "Lorca" and rang. A few minutes later a thin man in his late forties appeared and nodded to Lily.

"Hey, Fedde," she said.

He wore a dark brown parka with a dark brown scarf, old wool pants in a chocolate brown and charcoal check, and ugly, scuffed brown shoes. Wisps of hair popped out from under his brown watch cap and dangled over his ears.

"You should consider adding a little brown to your wardrobe," she said as they jammed themselves into his tiny coupe.

Lily first met Fedde Lorca in the theatre world. He was a writer of earnest plays that were little more than didactic screeds based on historical incidents of political injustice. Fedde thought himself a revolutionary, and he was only too happy to help Lily change the world, with whatever it took. He was infatuated with her, but he was also a little frightened of her. She encouraged both perspectives.

They drove to a poorer neighborhood in the Sydhavnen district, with many residences in need of structural and cosmetic repair. They pulled up in front of a shuttered laundromat, where the lighting was poor. A man materialized from the darkness. Lily got out of the car and walked up to him.

"I am Amsu," the man said. It was a fabricated name, just something she could call him while they did their deal. He asked, "You are the buyer?"

"Yes," she said.

Fedde walked around his car to stand next to Lily.

Amsu gave him a look equal parts annoyance and amusement and said, "You're not the buyer."

"I'm the playwright, I'm the one who contacted you."

"I know who you are," said Amsu. Turning to Lily he said, "In this work it is important who you surround yourself with." It sounded like professional advice, and a warning.

"He's harmless," said Lily. Amsu didn't look so certain.

"What about you?" asked Fedde, pointing a finger at Amsu. "What are your credentials?"

"I own a coffee shop," said Amsu, answering Fedde's question but looking directly at Lily. "I am happily married with two lovely children. And I can create an effective device in a backpack per your request if you supply me with the list of ingredients, which I will give you, and you pay me the fee we agreed upon in two installments. Half at the beginning of the project, and the rest upon delivery."

Lily agreed.

Amsu handed her the list. "The key items are common and easily acquired," he explained. "They are often combined for construction blasting. Settle for agricultural grade ammonium nitrate, the kind they use as fertilizer, it is good enough. Attempting to acquire the military type will just draw attention."

"Yes," said Lily, "makes sense."

Amsu also suggested nails and screws from a hardware store for enhancements, if Lily was interested, but warned her it would mostly increase the bomb's damage to people nearby rather than to property.

"I'll have to think about that," Lily said.

They agreed on the next meeting, at a different location. Lily returned to the little car with Fedde, who gave Amsu one final glare meant to be intimidating, and the car sputtered off into the night.

Fedde droned on about how rude Amsu had been. Lily tried to block it out. She wasn't surprised Amsu was annoyed, Fedde had that effect on a lot of people. He was a poseur, taking Lorca as his last name after the Spanish poet and theatre director Fedrico García Lorca. He was a creep who had lost two jobs because of the way he treated women. She tolerated him because he had a car, had unexpectedly good underground connections, and was willing to throw some money her way to make things happen when she was short. She needed a co-conspirator and Fedde fit the bill, as long as she controlled him.

But that night he surprised her. When they returned to his apartment and she moved to retrieve her bicycle, he felt the flush of excitement at what they were planning and attempted to kiss her. She gave him a quick knee to the groin, a look of warning, and she pedaled off into the night as he sat on the front stoop recovering.

24

CHRISTINA

The September weather in Copenhagen was normally mild, but things had taken a turn for the chilly, with an overcast sky. The outdoor seating areas of restaurants were running space heaters in the evening. Dragan sipped hot coffee in front of a café on the edge of Plaza Amagertorv, watching a young man busking with his guitar by the stork fountain. People strolled along Strøget, looking sharp in jackets accented with huge scarves offering splashes of color.

He recognized Christina Filippovna Koumba as she walked toward the café, and he waved to her. They had met once before, and again he found her distractingly attractive: petite and pretty, with black hair, brown skin, and deep green eyes. She smiled as he stood.

"Ms. Koumba, it's a pleasure to see you again," said Dragan, shaking her hand.

"Welcome to Denmark."

Dragan sensed she was guarded. He told himself it was normal, for someone in her position: an African-Russian intelligence agent embedded in a prominent organization, conducting social research. She would be curious why he was there, and what he wanted from her.

"Thank you for meeting me on such short notice," he said as they sat at the small table. She wanted hot chocolate, and he ordered one, and another coffee for himself, along with a pair of scones.

"I often take a walk around this time, to get air," she said. "My office is not far. You said on the phone that we met in London. I think I recall, now that I see you."

"There was a group of us, and I was purposefully keeping a low profile, so don't feel bad about not remembering."

"You said you needed my help?"

"More your advice," he said. "I need someone who understands things in Denmark at a deeper level than I do. I may reach out occasionally with questions."

"That will be fine, I imagine, as long as the time demands are modest." She had a clipped formality in her speech, with an accent that reflected time in London as well as Copenhagen. "You said you were looking into something?"

"Security is tight on this. The fewer people who know what I'm doing, where I'm going and when, the better."

"I understand. Also intrigued."

He gave her a highly edited version of the murders, leaving out the fake art sales, his relationship with Nina, and the photograph. "We're letting everyone think it was a robbery gone bad, just terrible luck," he said. "Meanwhile, in house, everyone worries it was an act of terrorism by Ukraine extremists. But I don't believe either of those are true, and neither do my superiors. My part is to look more closely at the personal travels of the victims, and I think there's a connection with Copenhagen. Although I have no idea what it might be."

Her eyes rested on him. "But it could be professional, part of their agency work?"

"Yes."

"Am I at risk, just being here and talking with you?"

"I have no reason to think so."

"Then how can I help you?"

He took a breath. That morning he had debated with himself how to play this conversation, whether to be reserved and roundabout with her, or to kick open the barn door to see what happened. He had decided to kick. "What are your thoughts on your colleague here, Paul Koslov?"

She was visibly surprised by the question. Normally it was considered inappropriate to discuss other agents. "I know him just a little," she said, with hesitation. "He works in finance. We're supposed to be part of each other's support system if anything happens, but things are quite routine here."

In areas where Russian intelligence only had a few embedded agents, like Denmark, they served as a flimsy kind of network, in lieu of a more substantial one such as Julianna led in the US. The idea was that colleague agents could provide information or other help when needed.

"Just a relaxed relationship, then? No old KGB fake couple tactics?"

"They would prefer if we pretended to be lovers, yes. They think it makes us blend in better."

"But you didn't do that?"

"I didn't want any part of it. Is this why you're talking with me first? To check on him?"

"Actually, I had dinner with him last night."

She stiffened a little. She offered a slight smile and said, "Good to know where I sit on the priority list."

He ignored it. "Do you trust him as your back up at least?"

She frowned. "I'm not sure I would rely on him if something came up."

That was a provocative statement and he waited for her to continue, watching the midday shoppers pass by. She looked away toward the square, then said, "That was harsh, I realize. I don't think I've met him more than a few times, and each one of those was by chance at some event or another. The last time was half a year ago at a reception in the Great Hall in Christianborg Palace, the big room with the tapestries. Have you been there?"

"Yes, of course."

"We were both attending as part of our organizations. He was there from the financial services company Innoveria, I think it's called. I was representing the National Institute of Public Health, where I work. I had the impression he was under the influence of something. He was distracted, nervous, and when I said hello he was unpleasant."

"To you?"

"To everyone, really. He seemed stressed. He was stroppy, arguing with the waiters and the woman he was with."

"Can you describe her?"

"Tall, dark hair with bangs, dramatic eye makeup. She seemed remote, or just angry. At one point I noticed them across the room, in a spat. They left soon after."

"This upset you?"

"Of course. I know in America and England my counterparts have someone who coordinates, keeps them informed and safe. We don't have such a person here, my closest resource is in Amsterdam and I rarely speak with her. Here in the city Paul and I are on our own, essentially. The idea, on paper, is that we have each other, but he is too unprofessional for my taste. I don't see how he could be useful."

"You don't have contacts in the Russian embassy?"

"They know I exist, if that's what you mean. I'm sure I'm in some kind of register there. But they don't know much about me, and certainly not about all my activities. What we do is an anachronism from the old days, I realize that, and they don't care about it."

"So you can't rely on Koslov. It sounds like you feel outside of the structure, isolated."

"You make it sound dismal. My situation is far from that." She hesitated, looked at her hands, then started again. "I have a job I love, working for the Institute. I do research in health behavior and lifestyle."

"Yes, I remember."

"I also serve in an editorial capacity for their publishing arm, reviewing manuscripts, contributing to white papers and thought pieces. Sometimes I get a byline in Scandinavian newspapers and periodicals. The Institute is associated with the University of Southern Denmark and twice a month I travel to Odense to teach a seminar there."

"You have stature and reputation."

She grimaced. "I'm not sure if you're complimenting me, or being condescending."

"I'm complimenting. You've put together a good life."

"I'm not telling you this to be chuffed about it, I'm just explaining my situation."

"I get that."

"I can't afford to be associated with someone like Paul Koslov if he's erratic and unreliable, which he seems to be."

"How would anyone know you have a connection to him?"

"Of course they know, sooner or later. People like him have a way of intruding. If he thinks I'm a lifeline for him and he stumbles into my professional or personal life, people will assume he's an ex-lover. They'll question my judgement. If he's abusing drugs and our organization decides he is detrimental, I may be tainted if they think we spend time together. My reputation will suffer. I need to stay on my side of the street. I'm sure you understand."

"I do."

Christina stared at him, looking through him, thinking. "Are the police back there handling this?" she asked.

"They don't know. We're keeping it in house."

"You can do that in America?"

"Circumstances were in our favor. It rarely happens that way."

"Our people are all over it then, I assume," she said. "And yet you are here, alone, looking for scraps of assistance. I think there is a lot you are not telling me, Dragan Markov." Mild annoyance passed quickly over her face. "I should get back to the office."

Dragan thought her a little imperious, and nonetheless found it appealing. "I'll walk with you." He said it as a statement. She reluctantly agreed, and they strolled down Strøget.

"Then tell me this at least," she said. "If you think there is a connection in Copenhagen to those murders, why are you here confiding in me and not Paul Koslov?"

He smiled to himself. "It didn't take long for him to lie about something at dinner. This greatly concerns me. It tells me he's hiding things and knows more than he says he does. There's an old-fashioned American slang phrase I like: Koslov feels hinky to me."

"Hinky?"

"Yeah. It means there's something wrong there. There's corruption there."

By the front gate to the National Institute for Public Health she turned, and said, "Good luck with your investigation. I'm available to lend a hand as best I can, within the limited time and resources I have available. But understand, if you're going to cause trouble, I can't afford to be associated with you, any more than I can with Koslov."

25

REAL

At the same moment that Dragan and Christina parted, Lily and Fedde returned to the city in his car, the tiny trunk and the space behind the seats full of the ingredients from the list Amsu had provided. The passenger seat was moved all the way forward, and Lily's long legs were drawn up nearly to her chest. Neither was talking.

They drove to a section of Sydhavnen filled with light industry – auto part merchants, storage buildings, truck garages, machine shops, and hardware yards. They pulled up in front of a flat, squat, brick building with two large roll-up doors the color of dirty bathwater.

Amsu had been watching for them and came out a side door with a dolly before Fedde and Lily left the car. Fedde opened the trunk, took out two boxes, and placed them on the dolly. Amsu removed a black heavy-duty trash bag from behind the seats, its contents sagging and stretching the plastic. Lily handed Amsu a beat-up canvas backpack in black and grey camo.

"The money is in the bag," said Lily.

Amsu opened the backpack, removed a white envelope, tore it open and riffled through the cash, counting it. Satisfied, he folded the envelope and put it in his back pocket.

"I'll text you when it's finished," said Amsu. He wheeled the loaded dolly back to the side door and disappeared inside. Fedde and Lily returned to the little car.

"Here we go," said Fedde a few blocks later. "It's real now."

"Who's doing it, you or me?" asked Lily. "We never settled that."

"I've been thinking about it. There's a street guy I know a little. Unstable, like most of them, but he'll do it for us for some weed, money, and booze. We can stay out of it. Sound good, baby girl?"

And that's why I keep you around, thought Lily. "That might work. Take me back to my place so I can get changed," she told him. "Then drop me off at the café, I have a shift. And don't call me baby girl again."

26

—·—

GALERIE STRID

As the train glided above the water on the lower deck of the Øresund Bridge heading to Sweden, Dragan looked again at the list of bogus artworks he had found in Ivan Bortnik's desk, the ones Benedikt and Nina claimed to sell through Kalashnik's gallery in order to launder money. The list included the supposed sources of the artworks, and nearly all of them were said to be purchased from private collectors. There was only one source named, Galerie Strid in Malmø, which according to Ivan's records sold three pieces to the Petroskis. It was the earliest acquisition date on the list, and corresponded with the period of the Petroskis' Scandinavian trip.

Dragan was certain the artworks never existed, even though an original bill of sale was in the file. He also believed whatever Ben and Nina were up to that got them killed probably started in Copenhagen, and the Galerie Strid was part of it.

Three quarters of an hour after the train left Copenhagen, Dragan walked out of Malmø Central Station into a cool, bright day, and he set off south on foot. The gallery turned out to be a pleasant, light-filled space at street level, with a show of imposing, contemporary abstract paintings visible through large front windows. Dragan walked through the exhibition, and as he made his way he glanced into the back offices area where he saw early twentieth century works on the wall. A man in his late forties, in a sweater and tortoiseshell glasses, was working on a computer. Seated at a nearby table was a young woman with Down syndrome sorting paperwork into several piles.

Dragan stopped and gazed at one particular painting, lingering in view of the man in the back, waiting. It only took a few minutes. The man drifted over and spoke to Dragan in Swedish.

"I'm sorry, I don't understand," said Dragan in English.

"Ah," said the man. "British?"

"American," said Dragan. "Russian-American, actually." He looked to see if there was a reaction. There was none.

"My name is Anders Strid," the man said. "This is my gallery. Do you have any questions?"

"The artist is very good," said Dragan. "These give me the feeling of industrial spaces."

"You have a sharp eye," said Anders. "She's German, and these are inspired by factory locations in Essen. She gives clues through color and some details half-hidden." He pointed to several places on the canvas to prove his point.

The young woman walked from the back to show Anders a document. As he skimmed it, she looked at Dragan and smiled warmly, as if, even though he was a stranger, she was happy to see him there. He smiled back. Anders handed the document to her, they chatted briefly in Swedish, and she returned to the back, then disappeared through a door into another room.

"You have an excellent assistant," said Dragan.

"My daughter Linn. She'll be going to college soon."

"Really? She looks so young."

Anders nodded. "Her condition does make her seem younger than she is," he said, referring to Down syndrome. "Right now she is taking a class – not for official credits, to get her ready, to make sure she is comfortable there and can do the work with minimal assistance."

"I'm sure she'll do fine. She does well here, obviously."

"She keeps me in line," said Anders, with a laugh. "She sometimes thinks she is my boss, I believe."

"Is it expensive, raising her?" asked Dragan, pushing a little.

Anders' smile dimmed. "No, not especially. There are some needs, and many things can take more time. It was better before my wife passed away, now it is the two of us. We make it work."

There was a moment of quiet. Anders frowned. "Many here in Sweden terminate a pregnancy if they discover Down syndrome, but my wife wouldn't hear of it," he said, as if he felt the need to explain himself to this stranger. "She was right. Linn is a wonderful person, a good worker, exceptional memory and good with numbers. She's the joy of my life."

There was defiance in what Anders said, as if Dragan had challenged why his daughter was there. Dragan pulled out his phone and showed him the photo of Nina, Ben, and Paul standing on the bench outside of Paul's office. He said, "Do you recognize these people?"

Anders, confused by the turn in the conversation, shook his head. "No. I don't think so."

"These two," said Dragan, pointing to Nina and Ben. "You sold them three Gustav Klutsis photocollages." He gave Anders the exact date.

Anders' eyes gave it away: he remembered. "Perhaps, it was a long time ago."

"They were here, at this gallery," pressed Dragan. "Was it all three, or just the two?"

Anders looked again at the photo. "The woman and the big man only, perhaps. I never saw the other."

"Which one proposed the scheme to you?"

"I don't know what you mean."

"You didn't sell them any Klutsis pieces," said Dragan. "You just gave them an invoice that said you did. Tell me about that."

A darkness came over the gallerist's face, mixed with anxiety. "Who are you?"

"The woman and the big man have been murdered, back in America," said Dragan. "I'm trying to figure out why, following their trail. I think it had something to do with things that happened in Denmark, and I know they visited this gallery. They arranged with you a fake bill of sale for artworks that don't exist. I just want to know about that."

Fear and anxiety were in Anders' eyes.

"You're not in trouble," continued Dragan. "You and your daughter are safe. If you'll allow me to make a gift to help her in her studies, please take this."

Dragan handed an envelope to Anders, who looked inside.

"You are not the police, or Interpol, they don't usually give money for information," said Anders. "This is a lot, just to talk." He looked over his shoulder, to make sure she was not nearby. He put the envelope in a pocket inside his jacket: they had a deal. "The man and the woman came in and said they heard I sometimes had early twentieth century avant-garde art to sell, which is true. I have a few contacts who feed me pieces to put out on the market, and some eager buyers. It is mostly Russian and German artists, occasionally Polish. They also knew about my daughter, and that my wife had recently died; I don't know how. They offered me money, a lot more money than you just gave me, to help them hide profits from something."

"They told you that?"

"They were surprisingly candid, but since I didn't know their names, or where they were from, they probably thought there was no risk telling me. Or they didn't care. They wanted me to draw up an invoice for three expensive Klutsis works. They had names and dates for them I didn't recognize, of course since the works weren't real. They had a silly cover story they gave me, full of details: that I bought them from the grandson of an elderly private collector who had the pieces for decades. The money I received was to be disguised as my percentage of the sale."

"And you did this?"

"Yes. I needed the money at the time," said Anders. "I was still in grief over my wife, and worried about the future with Linn. They chose the right moment to approach me."

"Did they come back again later, with another deal?"

"No, I told them not to. Also, I told them they were doing it wrong."

Dragan frowned. Before he had a chance to respond, Linn reappeared carrying two espressos on saucers, each with a cube of sugar on the side. She smiled as she handed them over, and lingered, curious about the conversation. Anders spoke gently to her, asked her something, and she relocated to his desk.

"What were they doing wrong?" asked Dragan.

"I took the money," said Anders. "I'm not proud of it but I did. I didn't want to get in trouble with the authorities, though. These two, they didn't seem to be gangsters, or criminals. I'm not naïve, I understood they had gotten this money illegally somehow. But they behaved like amateurs, like it was a hobby for them, and they were running an experiment. If they kept doing it that way they would be caught, and I didn't want police at my doorstep someday, I had Linn to think about. Also I liked the woman, she was charming and funny. Pretty. I spoke mostly with her, the man seemed like he couldn't keep his focus on the conversation. I didn't want her to end up in jail. It is very sad, what you say happened to them."

"It is sad," said Dragan. "What did you tell them?"

"I told them I recognized what they were doing, and it was good they came here and not some other gallery that might turn them in. I warned them, if they insist on using art dealers this way they are certain to talk to one who will call the police. Plus, it is expensive, and some dealers will want extra money, to blackmail them. The man acted hurt and defensive, like I was criticizing his idea, but the woman wanted to know more. I told her the other mistake was to use famous artists like Klutsis. They were lucky with him, he was disappeared by the Stalin regime in the 1930s and his earlier work repudiated, so there could be many pieces still to be found. But most better-known artists have better documentation. I told them to focus on the less-known artists, the ones in the margins."

"The artists where the records are the worst."

"Exactly. They didn't need paperwork from a dealer like me, that makes it complicated. I told them, just say they bought them from private citizens. They were traveling, met people who had works to sell, recognized their value, that is fine. No one is really keeping track. What about provenance? the man asked. I explained if they tried to sell a fake to a real person, then yes, they would want documentation. But if they acquire imaginary artworks from imaginary sellers and pass them on to imaginary buyers, who's going to complain? Who will care?"

Dragan held up his phone to give Anders a final look at the photograph. "And you are sure this man did not come with them?" he asked, pointing to Koslov.

"No," said Anders. "It was just them. As I said, they seemed new to this sort of thing, and in a hurry, like the money was going to be coming soon and they needed to get the scheme ready. You say they were killed. That is a terrible thing. I hope you catch the people who did it."

"That is the goal," said Dragan.

27

Café Syv

D ragan had the BBC news on the television as he dressed. A
Russian telecommunications executive and his wife had been
found stabbed in the garage of their estate near the border of Finland.
Russian authorities were quoted as saying the wife killed her husband
in a jealous rage because he wanted a divorce, then took her own life.
The news reader only mentioned, in passing, that the executive was
born in Ukraine. Much was made of the coincidence that earlier the
same day the body of the president of a Russian mining company had
washed up on the rocky section of the coast near Nakhodka on the
Sea of Japan. The official statement from Moscow was that the man
had fallen off his yacht and disappeared in the water. His death, the
statement said, was a tragic loss.

Dragan was ready. Under his coat he wore a patterned cashmere
scarf the colors of terra cotta and moss. He had packed it specially. The
hotel desk called a cab, and he set off on his search for Lily Sandersen.
He began at a place known to him, on the Knabrostræde, where Lily
was working when he first met her, when she was openly the girlfriend
of Paul Koslov and they were preparing how to execute the escape
from France of the agent in Pécy Bank. The restaurant was seedier
and less popular than it used to be, he thought, but he found one of

the wait staff who remembered Lily. A blonde woman with tired eyes, she reluctantly provided three other restaurants where Lily might be working.

"She's been on staff at all three of them at one time or another," the woman said. "I know because she used to gossip about them."

"She complained?" asked Dragan.

"All the time. She gets bored and restless, likes to move on. But she doesn't like being someplace unfamiliar. She just goes round and round to the same places, if they'll have her back. She's worked here four separate times that I know of. I'll be happy if there are no more."

The first two possibilities were dead ends, no one at either location remembered her. But he got lucky with the third, where the bartender, a curly-haired man with a beard and a smirk, claimed to remember her well.

"Yeah, of course I know Lily," said the bartender. "You'll probably find her at the Café Syv, that's where I last heard she was working." He gave the address, taking Dragan's tip and shoving the bills into his pocket. "Tell her Theo sends his regards." There was an intense sparkle of mischief in his eyes.

***

Dragan took a seat at the end of the bar. The crowd at Café Syv was younger and more energetic than he expected. A Dutch indie-rock band came out of the speakers. He asked for a Tuborg and pretended to take a look at the menu as he scanned the room. His eyes rested on Lily Sandersen working tables at the opposite end. She still had the dark straight hair with bangs that he remembered, and the eye makeup. Her tall, lean, athletic build still moved smoothly through a crowd.

However, her face seemed changed, somehow. Older than Dragan remembered, a little more roughly treated by life perhaps. He thought of her in Paris, with an interior glow and an easy laugh, qualities that seemed completely missing in the woman across the room.

She looked up and caught him staring at her. There was a hardness and resentment in the set of her mouth. A moment later she recognized him. Her eyes became blank as if her mind was roaming, deciding. Then it was as if a switch had been flipped – a huge smile crossed her face and her eyes took on the same internal flame he remembered. The woman he spent the day with shopping in the ninth arrondissement had instantly returned, looking years younger, and delighted to see him. Dragan did not read this as sincere, however, but as a performance. He smiled back. A minute later she worked her way to his table.

"Hello," she said in English, touching his arm. "I didn't recognize you at first."

"It's been a long time."

"How did you find me here?" There was just the slightest edge of irritation in her voice.

"A lucky coincidence."

"Lucky, I'm sure," she repeated, her eyes flaring. "Listen, I can't talk. But we close in about an hour."

"I'll have a bite to eat then."

"Try the squid ink linguine," she said, and crossed the room. She barely glanced at him the rest of the evening.

***

At closing he waited for her on the sidewalk.

"Nice coat," he said. She wore a three-quarter length wool coat with brocaded plants on the sleeve. It looked expensive. A little more than a bistro waitress and sometime actress would be expected to afford.

"Thank you. My place is walkable if you don't mind a bit of a hike. We can talk."

He agreed and they set off.

"You should have been here a few months ago, I was in a play over at the Teatret Rød Auk," she said. "It was well received."

"You got good notices?"

"A few."

"I'm glad for you. Sorry I missed it."

"Right after that run ended, I chained myself to the Hans Christian Andersen statue near city hall. You might have liked that performance better!"

"That sounds interesting. Was it an art piece, or a political statement?"

"Good public theatre tends to be both, don't you think? Unfortunately, when someone like me does something like that, they say it is subversive."

"All art is subversive," said Dragan, paraphrasing Picasso.

She laughed. "Well, with his money and fame it was easy for him to say that."

They had fallen quickly back into the easy, layered pattern of their conversations in Paris. She looked him over. "I like your scarf."

"You should, you picked it out."

This surprised her.

"Paul was busy one day and we walked around the city. You chose this for me."

"I remember," she said, without much conviction. "That was a good trip. You and Paul had something important to do together. Have you talked with him yet?"

"Yes, I did. He seemed a little stressed."

"He's always been wound tighter than he needs to be."

"He told me you two had broken up. I was sorry to hear that."

She nodded. "True. It was when I was doing that play, which is probably not a coincidence. I think he wasn't getting enough attention from me, or he was jealous, or I don't know. But it was time for it to end. His gambling is worse, and he isn't any good at it. All for the best, I think."

Dragan noted that she placed the breakup less than six months ago, while Paul said it was before the Petroskis' visit. They weren't comparing notes for their lies.

They continued for a few minutes. She asked, "What brings you to Denmark?"

"I'm retracing the steps of two colleagues, a married couple, Nina and Benedikt Petroski. They came here on holiday, and I think they may have spent some time with you and Paul."

"Benedikt was the big man, loud, liked boys? She was the pretty Jewess? I met him first. He would come through, get together with Paul, I'd see him to say hello to. He was full of himself, sort of thought the world owed him special favors."

Dragan was surprised to learn Ben had a relationship with Paul Koslov for a while. What were they up to?

"I only saw them a few times. I was in rehearsals for something back then, a musical revue in Tivoli. A silly thing. I remember the man Benedikt making fun of me for it, and his wife laughing."

"That doesn't sound very nice."

"It wasn't." She gave him a glance. "What did Paul say about it?"

"About their visit? Not much."

"And how are they, this couple?"

"They were murdered." He watched her reaction. She turned with a look of sympathy that was surprisingly unconvincing for a professional actress. She already knew.

"How horrible," she said.

"Robbers, probably, who didn't expect to find them home."

"What bad luck. I saw some of the jewelry she had, it was lovely, and expensive. The kind that attracts attention."

They walked in silence for a block. They passed a tiny wine bar open late, and stepped aside to let a clutch of bicyclists pass. The clouds had broken up, and the air was cool enough for them to see their breath.

"They seemed like a couple that had traveled a lot and had all kinds of adventures," she said.

"They were."

"Not good people, though. They still owe me a lot of money. Bad things like that happen to people who aren't good."

They walked down a narrow cobblestone street to an intersection. She pointed to the second floor of the corner building.

"My apartment," she said. "Why don't you come up?"

Dragan wasn't sure where this was going, or why. "Okay," he said.

28

ROSA LUXEMBURG

The building was old, and he thought of ghosts living there as they climbed the wide steps to the second floor. The door to her apartment was thick, with wire mesh glass panels. Beyond was a short entrance hall with a coat rack on the wall. Straight ahead was the bedroom with a full-size bed and a framed poster for an Italian production of Brecht's *Threepenny Opera*. She led him to an L-shaped main space. There was a small sitting room with a compact couch, a couple of armchairs, and a coffee table. The furniture was a hodge-podge, like a graduate student lived there. Two low bookshelves lined the wall and on the top was a small collection of partly emptied liquor bottles. Beyond that, in the corner of the L, was a small round dining table seating four, then a compact kitchen in the short leg.

"This is a nice apartment," Dragan said, although it was not.

"Thank you," Lily said.

She walked down a short hall to the bathroom. Dragan looked around. On the wall beyond the dining table was a large original painting based on the style of a 1950s paperback pulp crime novel, but with British law enforcement figures terrorizing black and brown families who appeared to be refugees. There was scattered reading material on the coffee table: a French *Vogue*, a copy of the book *Contemporary*

European Theatre Directors, an English translation of *The Letters of Rosa Luxemburg.*

Music began playing quietly through speakers somewhere in the room, and Lily reappeared. She poured akvavit for the two of them and handed him one of the glasses.

"To reunions," she said, clinking glasses. They both took a sip and sat down.

He gestured to the book on the table. "You're reading Rosa Luxemburg's letters," he said. "Are you interested in political history?"

She smiled. "I'm interested in rebellion."

"You're giving up acting?"

"The arts are often the best way to drive social change. I think of myself as dancing to the revolution, like Emma Goldman."

This is all a performance, Dragan said to himself. Out loud he asked, "Are we in a revolution?"

"Society is always undergoing a revolution. Sometimes it moves so slowly people aren't aware of it, if they're not paying attention."

"But you pay attention."

"I try. I can smell change in the air. Look what's happening in Denmark right now. The mistreatment of immigrants, and fascists burning Korans in public. The riots last year were the start."

"I don't remember you talking about revolution the last time we met."

She moved closer to him. "I was just Paul's girlfriend to you then. You still only see me as a waitress, and if you feel generous as an actress too. But I have a part to play in this, a big part. I can make a difference where others can't."

He couldn't figure out what was going on. This was the same woman he had met years earlier, but different. Was she sincere about any of it? Was she just a dilettante, or actually capable of serious actions? And if the latter, would there – could there – be any connection to what happened to the Petroskis? Would she consider them friends or foes of her cause? There was nothing to do but feed the performance and see where Lily went with it.

"I always thought of Goldman as an anarchist, not a revolutionary," he said.

"Anarchy is liberation, if you do it right."

They sipped akvavit and smiled at each other.

"I've always liked you," she said. "You should stay here tonight with me."

"I don't think that's a good idea."

"Are you concerned about Paul? Not important. He has no hold on me." She started slowly moving toward him, parting her lips. She wanted him to look at how pretty she was, at the fullness of her mouth and the way her hair framed her face. But what he saw was a disturbing quality to her eyes, like something else was in there looking out.

A key turned in the front door and heavy footsteps were in the hall. Two men entered the sitting room and stood there, looking at Dragan and Lily on the couch. She cursed under her breath and closed her eyes in frustration. Dragan got to his feet in a show of politeness and, depending on how things progressed, to be ready.

The man on the right was thick, with close-cropped dark hair, olive skin and a four-day beard above the tattoos on his neck. He wore a black leather jacket, and on the left breast was a Germany coat of arms patch, black eagle on a yellow field, and above that a horizontal patch that read "Tinhanhem M.C." Beneath the jacket was a black tee tucked into heavy-duty jeans that ended at the bottom over rugged black work boots. His eyes were lidded and there was a dullness in them, like a man who didn't think too much before he acted, and not much afterward either. Dragan chalked him up as a brute, the kind of man who had always been a brute and saw no reason to change.

The other was a different sort entirely. He looked like a biker who had gone to a stylist, wearing a cream-colored waffle-weave pullover with two thin gold chains around his neck, over black worker pants and hiking shoes. He held a thick hooded black sweatshirt under his arm, and a thumb was hooked over a thick black tooled leather belt. Crudely executed tattoos could be seen on the back of his hand and the base of his neck, almost certainly acquired in prison. He was tall, nearly as tall as Dragan, lean and sinewy. His long, premature gray hair was carelessly pushed back from a face dominated by sharp cheekbones and a strong nose with a bend that told of being broken at least once sometime in the past.

Despite the nose, or perhaps because of it, the man had a distinctive and stunningly handsome face. When he was younger that face would have drawn the attention of both men and women. The boyish attractiveness had been roughed up by bad years and several scars, however, which probably heightened the appeal for certain crowds. There was something deeply unsavory about him, and he had the air of a man who might be even more dangerous than the brute standing next to him.

"What do we have here?" asked the gray-haired man in Danish. He flashed a smile, his eyes focused on Dragan.

"This is Dragan Markov, a friend of Paul's from America," Lily said in English, signaling that to be the language to use. She turned to Dragan and said, "The pretty one is my brother Viggo. The other is his friend Anton."

Viggo and Dragan nodded to each other. Dragan thought he saw the faintest look of recognition pass over Viggo's face. Anton, the brute, remained still, watching the proceedings.

"Don't mind the scowl on my friend here," Viggo said in English. "He's German, he scowls about everything. His Danish is passable, but his English is terrible, I'm afraid."

"We were about to fuck," said Lily. Anton and Viggo turned to stare at Dragan.

"No, we weren't," said Dragan.

"Don't be embarrassed," said Lily. "They don't mind." She looked at Viggo and smiled.

No one smiled back.

"Viggo is between places," she continued. "He's staying with me for a little while."

"It's good to have a sister with an apartment of her own," said Dragan, who immediately recognized that Viggo was no more Lily's brother than he was. He looked down at the couch. "It doesn't seem very comfortable though, your head and feet must stick out of the ends."

Viggo's pale blue eyes were cold, and watchful. "It's not very comfortable, but what can you do?"

Lily seemed to be enjoying herself. She said to Viggo, "You and Dragan will become best friends, I'm sure. You're both big deal athletes."

Viggo looked at her, then at Paul. "Is this true?" he asked.

"No," said Dragan. "I played college basketball in America, that's all. How about you?"

"A little football," said Viggo.

"Not a little," said Lily. "He was a professional goalie."

"I was with the Aarhus Fremad club for about one minute," said Viggo. "In the Danish second division, a long time ago. More of a semi-professional."

"But still something," said Dragan.

Viggo shrugged. The tension of a few moments earlier had dissipated. Boys and their games as the great common ground.

"I should go," said Dragan. He gave Lily a polite hug. He told Viggo and Anton that it was a pleasure meeting them. Dragan squeezed past the two men, and as he did he had the impression that at least one of the men was fighting an urge to sucker-punch him. But that would be absurdly hostile, why would they want to do that?

29

—·—

RESPECT

Lily, Viggo and Anton stayed where they were and listened as Dragan walked down the stairs, opened the entrance door, and left the building.

"Schlappschwanz," said Anton. Viggo laughed.

"No, he's not," Lily said.

Viggo grabbed the whiskey bottle and a couple of glasses from the bookshelf and put them on the coffee table. He asked, "What does this man want?"

"He's sniffing around about Nina and Benedikt Petroski," she said, topping off her akvavit.

Viggo raised his eyebrows. "How did he find you?"

"I don't know. He wouldn't say."

"He knows something, or he wouldn't be here." Viggo poured two drinks. "He's also motivated; he was in love with Nina."

"How do you know that?" asked Lily.

"She told me."

"This is not good," said Anton.

"A Russian spy man with a Serbian name who talks like an American," said Viggo. "That sounds like too many people at one time. And yet... Nina told me playing basketball was the peak of his life, now he is just what they call a middle manager."

"What does that mean?" asked Anton, who had never come close to working in an office.

"He's a glorified file clerk who has some people to push around," said Viggo, and the two men laughed.

"Paul was always a little scared of him," Lily said, leaning back on the couch. She was enjoying their anxiety.

"Why?"

"I don't know. You'll have to ask him."

"I'm not talking to that klaphat." Viggo poured himself another. "Did basketball boy say where he's staying?"

"The Hotel Frederik in Gammelholm."

"I don't like him asking about things."

"He'll find out nothing and leave on his own in a day or two," said Lily.

"Maybe," said Viggo.

Anton finished his drink and left without saying goodbye. The apartment was quiet except for the music coming through the speakers. Viggo rolled a cigarette of tobacco and crushed hash, and glanced over at Lily who was sitting on the couch looking annoyed.

"You are angry," he said. "What about?"

"I told you not to let yourself in without calling ahead. You have to respect my life and my privacy."

"Sure," he said without conviction. "It's no big deal."

"I wanted to find out information from him. He probably knows where the money is, if he was with that bitch."

"There's no money anymore, Lily, I keep telling you that."

"Paul says there's money."

"Paul doesn't disagree with you when you say there's money, which is not the same thing. He knows perfectly well there's no money. I'm telling you, Paul's American friends took it all."

"I could have learned something important," she said, ignoring him.

"More likely he would have gotten information out of you."

"Oh, you think I'm not smart enough to handle things?"

"If you were half as smart as you think you are."

Lily's eyes narrowed. She picked the French Vogue from the coffee table rolled it into a thick club and hit him with it. Then hit him again. Then again, and again, as Viggo held up an arm to deflect the blows.

30

DRUG TRADE

"I need your advice and insight," Dragan told Christina, who listened politely while focusing mostly on her lunch. She had walked into the café with a sour look on her face and he could feel the chilly antagonism floating off her. Something wasn't right. In response, he ignored his food, focusing instead on her, trying to understand what was going on. "Can I run down what I know and think I know?"

She nodded.

"The couple who was murdered, the Petroskis, came here on holiday. I know they met Paul Koslov, although he lied to me about that. He also lied about his ex-girlfriend Lily, at least about the timeline and whether she had ever met the Petroskis. Sometime during that holiday visit the Petroskis came into a lot of money, or were expecting to, and explored ways to launder it. Meanwhile, Lily is connected to someone she claims is her brother who is clearly a member of a motorcycle gang. Although I have no evidence for it, my gut tells me that whatever the Petroskis were up to, it involved one or more of those three people."

"Okay, that sort of holds together, if you ignore all the other possibilities," she said, realizing some sort of response was expected. She still wouldn't meet his eyes. "It's a string of guesses."

"Fair enough but hear me out. I tried to think of schemes that would generate a lot of illicit money quickly, would involve some dangerous people, and if things turned ugly could get you killed. When I started playing with scenarios I assumed the key person was Paul, which meant the finance world. What would fit the bill? Embezzlement, or fraud of some type."

"In that case, why would Paul need the others?"

"Exactly. I could see Ben Petroski getting involved in something like that, but what would be Lily's involvement?"

"Is she actually part of it do you think? Or just in proximity to what was going on?"

"She said the Petroskis owed her a lot of money. She's involved somehow, independent of Paul. Then I thought, she's an actress. How could the theatre world fit in?"

"Blackmail?"

"Somebody famous she has dirt on? Could be, though it feels like a stretch to me. Again, why involve Ben and Nina Petroski? They didn't know people here. What did they bring to this?"

"Capital."

"And you don't normally need capital for blackmail. So, it brought me to the Petroskis, their apparent lack of ethical restraints, and their money, around which I suspect everything pivoted. I thought, what if it was all of them: not just the Petroskis and their cash, Paul and his finance knowledge, and Lily, for some reason, but also Lily's supposed brother Viggo? That guy and his friend seemed like outlaw bikers, genuine criminals. That made it click into place. The need for capital, the potential for violence, bikers, money laundering. In my mind it pointed to one thing."

"Drugs," said Christina, her eyes flashing with interest despite her sour demeanor.

"Nothing I can think of fits as well," said Dragan, nodding in agreement. "I need to learn more about the illegal drug trade in Denmark. You're the expert."

"Not an expert, but at the Institute we do track these things."

"Just start telling me about it."

"What are you looking for?"

"I don't know. Give me a little lecture."

"Cannabis is the most popular, next is cocaine, then ecstasy and amphetamines. The young people indulge, as it is in other countries. Mostly between the ages of fifteen and twenty-five, then it drops sharply. By the age of thirty-five most people are finished with the drug thing. Older users exist, of course, but they barely register in the data."

"A lot of people using coke and speed."

"Yes. The good news is amphetamine consumption is going down. The bad news is cocaine and ecstasy are on the rise."

"And it's big business."

"By its nature the illegal drug trade keeps its numbers a secret, obviously. A big study from ten years ago put the annual market value in Denmark well over a billion krone, and it's only gone up since then. But no one knows the numbers for sure."

"I've heard motorcycle gangs are the big distributors."

"True," she said. She was warming to the conversation, since it pulled from her expertise, and she could hold court. Dragan just wanted to keep her talking, to try to build a better bond with her. "Outlaw gangs are the key importers and distributors of cannabis, amphetamines, and ecstasy, no question, and they get their hands in cocaine and heroin as well."

"How do bikers handle the import and export part?" asked Dragan.

"If you look at news reports you'll read criminal enterprises in the Netherlands, Serbia, Germany, Poland, and so forth all play a role in getting drugs into Denmark. What you need to remember is most biker gangs in Europe have chapters in multiple countries, certainly the countries I mentioned, so the gangs and the distribution networks map the same. Denmark often serves as a gateway to the rest of Scandinavia, again through the bikers. Everywhere you look at drugs in Denmark there will be a man on a motorbike."

"Bikers have the capital for this?" Dragan asked.

"There are money people behind them, usually well hidden. I wouldn't be surprised if some famous, respectable people add to their income by investments in the illegal drug trade. But it isn't like anyone is doing excellent bookkeeping, tracking all of this. The money trail is extremely complicated."

"Lucrative."

"But ugly and dangerous," said Christina.

"Until I learn something new, this is the thread I'm pulling."

"Then I hope you like being a target," she said. "Because that is where it will end up."

31

—·—

OBLIGATION

Dragan frowned and looked at Christina. There was a sadness in her eyes, but she also seemed far away. "Drugs feels right to me," he told her. "Whether that makes me a target or not. One thing I'm sure of, no one will be happy if that is what it turns out to be. Drug running will reflect badly on the victims, and the organization. Leadership won't want it to come out. Benedikt's family is prominent; they'll push back against any accusation like this."

"You need to be cautious," she said.

"A puzzle is how the Petroskis would have become involved. A Russian-American couple can't just come into Copenhagen and knock on doors looking for a drug ring. Some sort of opportunity presented itself."

"These gangs don't encourage involvement from outsiders."

"Perhaps something that altered the landscape back then."

"I'm a researcher and analyst," she said. "I work with data. That sounds like a question for someone with more of a street perspective."

"There's a dealer in Christiania I've been acquainted with for a long time, under various circumstances. If he's not dead or in jail, or in some other part of the world – all of which are possible – he might be able to help me. I think I'll drop by."

He looked at her, saw her withdrawing, with her mask of detachment falling back into place. He decided to clear the air. He said, "You're upset about something. Frankly, you seem angry with me."

She chuckled slightly. For the first time she met his eyes. "You led me to believe you were still an agent in good standing and were here on assignment. Neither of those are true, I've learned. I contacted a few people; they told me you left the service."

"It's complicated."

"In disgrace, I'm told."

He gently shook his head. "That's not an accurate way to describe it."

"Then you describe it."

"What does it have to do with this situation?"

"I want to know who I'm working with."

"At the college where I was teaching, I became involved with one of my students."

"The one and only time?"

"No."

"It never is, is it?"

"At a party the young woman was raped and roughed up by a local boy. I was furious. I tracked him down, which wasn't difficult, it was a small town. I wanted to give him a dose of his own medicine, as they say, but I took it too far. I was drinking a lot in those days and taking speed. I lost control and he ended up in the hospital. My handlers swooped down. The boy was a known problem, a punk, no family other than an elderly uncle, and it wasn't his first sexual assault accusation. The local authorities were made to understand it was a case of self-defense, I was just protecting myself. There was also the idea that the boy had it coming. Bribes may have changed hands, I don't know. Certainly, the uncle was given enough money to not make a fuss. But they had to get me out of there."

"Is this the true story?"

"Essentially. There might be a few details I skimmed over."

"So now I know," she said.

"Yes. And for what it's worth, I actually am on assignment. It's just what Americans call on the down low."

"They couldn't say that, it sounds silly."

"Well, a lot of them say it."

"I don't know if I believe you, actually. Not about the phrase, about the assignment. I have no reason to think anyone authorized you to do anything. Is it true the woman who was killed was your lover?"

"That's not relevant here."

She nodded, satisfied that her worst expectations of him were fulfilled. "I promised to provide whatever help I could, but that was before I understood the reality of your situation. After today I'm available to answer an occasional question, but that's all. Don't ask too much of me, however. I'm not your partner here."

"I didn't ask for a partner. An ally would be good."

"We don't even work for the same organization, it turns out. I'm not sure who or what you are."

"I hear more fear in your voice than anger."

That rubbed her the wrong way. She said, "The other day, when I attempted to explain my situation, I don't know if I made myself clear. So let me try again, a different way." She finished her tea, folded her napkin and placed it in front of her, clasped her hands. "My father was one of the bright African students who came to the Soviet Union to study engineering. He married my mother, but it didn't stick. I think the racial attitudes in the provincial city where we lived were too much for him. He moved back to Gabon, and I never saw him again. My mother and I moved to Saint Petersburg, which was more accepting. But still, growing up a Russian of color was disorienting. Though Black people have been in Russia for a long time there aren't many of us, it was difficult for me to find ways to connect with others my age. With a single parent there wasn't a lot of money. But I was smart and ambitious, and others noticed. When they recruited me, with their open doors and material support, I jumped at the opportunity."

"I've heard similar stories. My own, for example."

"Everything I have now was hard-won and represents a genuine career. I'm grateful for the help I received. In return I'm happy to complete reports and give my insights. I'm an observer and a researcher for them as well as for the Institute, and I imagine my work has genuine value. I'd like to keep all of it in place, do you understand?"

"Yes, I do."

"As far as I'm concerned, you're jeopardizing it," she said. "I was resigned to helping you when I believed you were official; I felt I was obligated. But you are not official, and I am not obligated."

A few minutes later, when they stepped outside the café, she paused and touched his arm, which seemed to him an oddly affectionate gesture at that moment, right after she told him off. Christina walked briskly away with barely a goodbye. As Dragan headed off in the opposite direction, he noticed a young man loitering in a doorway across the street. The man was dressed in a hooded sweatshirt and jeans, and wore his long blonde hair long under a watch cap. Dragan's first thought was one of the bikers was following him, but this kid looked more like a skateboarder. As he continued down the street, Dragan had the strong feeling the kid was watching him.

32

—·—

DEWI

Dragan crossed the Inderhavnsbroen, the pedestrian bridge taking him to Christianshavn, the residential neighborhood in the eastern part of Copenhagen. He walked until he spotted the black and gold external winding staircase on the spire of the Vor Freisers Kirkea, the Church of Our Savior, and used it as his marker. He made his way to Prinsessegade, and to the graffiti-covered converted brick building and rough-hewn sign marking the entrance into Pusher Street, and Freetown Christiania.

The site of Christiania was once a military base and was defined by the ramparts protecting Copenhagen from eastern attacks. After the military moved out in the late 1960s, squatters, hippies, anarchists, and homeless young people moved in. Over time, somehow, the city and the squatters made peace, and Christiania remained a more or less self-sufficient community where police and cameras were not welcome. Tourists were tolerated, and one of the main attractions were the booths openly selling marijuana and hashish. It looked something like a high school crafts fair, except for the wares on display. But no hard drugs – keeping out anything more serious was part of the deal between the residents and the city. Homes and shops and restaurants were in the abandoned military buildings, their outsides painted in bold colors, with additions quite obviously built using the guiding principle of "architecture without architects."

Dragan walked down Pusher Street, past the café and a ramshackle version of a small shopping plaza, and into the gauntlet of weed purveyors. There were plenty of people, and more than one tourist family – mom, dad and the kids checking out the cannabis on display. He made his way to the end looking for his old acquaintance Dewi, but he was nowhere to be found. Perhaps he had moved on, or been arrested, or fallen ill. Dewi was not the kind of person to send out annual updates during the end-of-year holidays.

Disappointed, Dragan turned to leave. Another street source would be hard to dig up. Considering the way the dealers were eyeing him, wondering if he was an undercover cop, it wouldn't be easy to even get one of them to talk with him.

"Hey there, captain!" came a voice with the remnants of a strong Yorkshire accent. In front of him stood Dewi, a pale man in a newsboy cap, ambling along, heading back to the stalls while eating a falafel sandwich.

Dragan smiled. "Good morning, sir. It's been a while."

"It surely has. Is the visit pleasure or business?"

"It's always a pleasure to spend time with you, of course."

Dewi laughed. "Business it is, then. Walk with me back to the stall. If I'm gone too long Bassel will run off with my goods."

They made their way to the final stall, where a thin bearded man greeted them with a wave.

"This handsome fellow is my partner Bassel," Dewi said with a quick little point of his finger. He turned to Bassel and made the same gesture toward Dragan. "This is an old friend. He's from America right now but he doesn't really have a country. I think he should move here to Freetown, but he won't have it. Keep an eye on things, will you mate? We'll be over here." He gestured for Dragan to come join him about fifteen feet away, so Dewi could keep an eye on his booth.

"What can I do for you captain?" Dewi stuck out his hand and Dragan shook it, old friends reconnecting, except that a wad of krone passed from one to the other in the shake.

"Same again if you can give me the information I need, okay?"

"Depends on what it is," said Dewi. "I have to live here."

"What time do you pack it up today? We need a little time to do our talk."

"The sun's dropping and it hasn't been a great day. Give me thirty minutes – make it forty-five – and meet me over at the hardware barn."

"Okay." Dragan nodded. "Here's what I want you to think about. A few years ago, more or less, something out of the ordinary may have happened in this part of Denmark. It would have had something to do with the street drug business. Whatever it was changed things or created an opportunity. Someone probably made a lot of money, or lost it."

"Could you be more specific?"

"No. I don't know what this thing was. Possibly a drug shipment was hijacked. Organized crime took over an operation. Some big dealer was arrested, or killed, or a politician kidnapped."

Dewi cocked his head, like a spaniel. "Well, that's an interesting assignment. Why ask me? Why not go to the library, or the internet?"

"I wouldn't know where to start. I might not recognize what I'm looking at. Whatever it was may have happened behind the scenes, but people in the know, people like you, would have known, or least heard. Speculated, gossiped about it. I need your insight, your memory, and your instincts."

"You think flattering me will get better results?"

"It might."

"Could be you're right." Dewi considered. "See you in a little while. Let me get back to the booth before Bassel shoves all my product into his knickers."

***

Dragan took the time before they met to visit a market. As he walked out carrying a canvas tote, sagging at the end of his arm, he caught sight of a dark hoodie and long blonde hair under a watch cap, and thought it might be the kid he saw earlier outside the café. But when he stopped and turned to get a better look the kid wasn't there.

When he returned to Christiania the sun was low, and the buildings were draped in an unflattering grey. What were vibrant murals and bold unexpected house colors during midday now looked tawdry. There was loneliness here, he thought, but perhaps he was just projecting.

A big building, half hardware store, half salvage yard, was nestled near the southeast corner. It carried all manner of dry goods, from seeds to tools, along with building parts for those looking to add to their cottage. Dewi was chatting with a man at the T-shirt stall next door, sipping tea from a large paper cup.

"Let's go to the fire pit," said Dewi.

Dragan followed him around the building to a path that took them through a thin cluster of trees. In a clearing sat a roughly built, roofless structure like a decaying pergola, with benches and a small fire pit in the center. The official flag of Freetown Christiania, three yellow circles on a red field, hung off one of the vertical posts. They gathered wood off a nearby stack and got a modest fire going. Neither said a word during the process. They sat on a bench. Dragan pulled a couple of Carlsberg pilsners out of his sack and handed one to Dewi, who pulled out a joint.

"MI6 would disapprove," said Dewi, "but different rules for us contract freelancers."

They shared a joint in silence and watched the glow from the fire in the last vestiges of dusk. Dewi was an eccentric in his fifties who looked and acted like an unreconstructed hippie, but he was sharp and observant and seemed to know all sorts of helpful people. His origins murky, along the way he began doing work for British intelligence as an informant, scout, and street-level liaison, and then branched out to do similar work for the Americans, the Israelis, the French, and eventually the Russians. He never gave any agency dirt on any other, and he never divulged secrets. What he offered was street-perspective information: where does one go to find this, or who does one talk to about that? What is the background of a situation, and how is it likely to end? He called it "bespoke journalism."

Dragan and Dewi had known each other for a long time, if not very well. They first crossed paths in a hotel bar in Lima, both of them looking to meet an informant who, it turned out, had already been dead for two days. They bonded over ceviche and pisco sours. Over the years they sometimes found themselves in the same place at the same time, and got along, supplying each other with information and gossip. Their relationship was not easy to categorize; they weren't friends, they weren't enemies, they weren't colleagues. The big question for Dragan, this day as with any other day, was whether Dewi could be trusted.

33

STREET WAR

"**I** hope you have something for me," said Dragan.

"I think I might. For this to make sense I have to go back a ways," Dewi said, with the weed curled inside him and the words starting to tumble out. "Long before I got here, Scandinavia struggled with biker gangs and the drug trade. Things became tense in the eighties, right here in Christiania. A biker gang moved in and took over the drug business, the whole place really. They were violent, causing all sorts of problems. Picked fights with other gangs and people got killed. It was ugly. Kudos to the residents of Freetown – some of them still living here by the way – they came together as a community and kicked the bikers out. You can draw a line from those days to the rules we have here today, about no hard drugs, no weapons, no fighting, no biker colors, and the rest."

"They actually kept the bikers out?"

"So far so good. But periodically gang battles crop up in and around the city, sometimes building up to what you could call a war. They're always – supposedly – about the drug trade. But let me tell you, it's almost always more about turf and honor and respect, who gets to piss on what section of the pavement. There was a big fight in the mid-nineties, across all of Scandinavia. Bikers somehow got hold of army-level weapons, I'm talking about machine guns and hand grenades and the like. Gang headquarters blown up, it was crazy. Eventually came to a truce since even bikers get tired of stepping over bodies to buy booze at the off license."

A young man in a knit poncho came down the path, tentative, drawn by the smell of the weed with the intention of joining them, but Dewi gave him a little head shake meaning no, not this evening, and the young man shambled away.

"I think you get the idea," said Dewi. "Fast forward to a few years ago. Now, I was here at the time, so some of what I'm going to tell you I know first-hand, or I had mates who knew first-hand, or there was so much talk on the street it wasn't rumor, it was true, even if nobody could prove it in court. You know how it goes."

"I do."

"This most recent dustup, the one happened in the time period you asked me about, was mostly in the Nørrebro district, and spilling over into Østerbro and Nordvest. Nørrebro is multi-cultural, artists, young professionals, but also a lot of immigrants. Full of young people looking for action. Various bikers have territory there in different parts of the district and sometimes they get in each other's way, but it isn't normally an issue. Well, for some reason, it started to become an issue between the Brothas motorcycle gang, and a bigger group called Loyal To Familia. There were something like forty or fifty shootings over there, half a dozen people killed including some civilians and, I think, a kid or two, and a bunch of people injured."

"Jesus."

"Yeah. All of Danish law enforcement swooped down to put a cap on it. The whole city stank of a police state, tell the truth. They did not want this to turn into another madhouse like in the mid-nineties. As you can imagine, this started to impact the other gangs: the Bandidos,

Satudarah out of the Netherlands, Hells Angels, Gremium out of Germany, they were all getting jostled, and they were pissed off. The Brothas and Loyal to Familia came to a truce after about nine months, but there were occasional incidents over a year later. Even with the truce the Danish Politiet were crawling all over the city, a rozzer inside every closet."

Dewi drank from his beer and thought back on it, shook his head as editorial comment on the madness of it all.

"Nasty business, by nasty people," continued Dewi. "London was pressuring me to find out everything I could. They were worried about economic destabilization and other stuff that they get paid to worry over even though they can't do shite about it. I was asking so many questions people started looking at me funny, which is not what I want happening. I have a personal brand to maintain. I submitted many extraordinary expense reports, as compensation, which they paid. Since then, things have been stable." He stopped and considered Dragan in the flickering firelight. "This sound like the something you were looking for?"

"Yeah," said Dragan. He held out some folded euros.

"I'll take this now, thanks, but I haven't earned it yet. This has just been the introduction."

34

Opportunity

Dewi lit another joint, taking a few deep pulls in preparation for the next phase of his story.

"Everything I told you, you could look up on your own," said Dewi, handing the joint to Dragan. "Pretty common knowledge for people who live here. Like always, politicians and the media outfits were talking up a drug war, because it makes people extra scared, and scared people vote and follow the news, but it wasn't no drug war. It was just another johnson-measuring contest, and the law and the community leaders focused on getting the gangs talking. Nobody was focused on the drugs because it was about other things, but the attention impacted business anyway. There was a lot of pressure. Heroin sales were down, you couldn't get supply in. Weed sales were probably thirty or forty percent lower than normal for a while, and believe me we all struggled, us independents. A lot of motivated bikers were leaving the area, going over to Sweden and connecting with chapters in Malmø or up in Gothenburg, some going up Norway to Oslo, to make some money and get away from the hassles."

"This left a vacuum." Dragan began to see where this story was headed.

"Exactly. There was this one biker gang, they're called Tinhanhem Motorcycle Club. Vietnamese for "brotherhood" – it's three words squished together into one, as people do these days. The brotherhood idea, they mean it. They're a lot like the Satudarah, they let people of all races and religions and nationalities into the club, but they take it a step further, encouraging members to get to know people in the communities, eat meals with them, learn their customs. And they claim to have a policy of negotiation over violence, that they'd rather make money than settle scores, although I can't vouch for that."

Dragan thought of the "Tinhanhem M.C." jacket patch on Anton, the German biker in Lily's apartment. "You say they're Robin Hoods?"

"Don't get me wrong, captain, they run guns as well as dope, they do extortion, they're scary as hell and I don't want anything to do with them. But I do admire them a little, if you know what I mean, because they're smart."

"They're here in Copenhagen?"

"Mostly based in Amager and down in the seaport of Køge, but they're in pockets in the city and farther west. They have chapters all over, in Europe, and southeast Asia. Like I said, they're smart, and when they looked at what was happening they saw the opportunity."

"This great story earns you another beer," said Dragan, handing it to him.

"Thank you, sir. Tinhanhem recognized they could take over a giant chunk of the Copenhagen drug trade because the competition fled town and authorities weren't paying any real attention. Supply was down, customer demand was high. The situation invited an entrepreneurial approach to fill the gap, so to speak, and whoever did that could become a big gorilla before anyone had an idea what was happening."

"Easier said than done."

"Tinhanhem was in a good position, because through their chapters they had connections in Singapore, Thailand, and Australia for getting some fine product, and enough club members to serve as a sales and collection and protection force. They emerged as a strong player. The other gangs still have a share of the trade, not much different from before. But it was a big boost for Tinhanhem, which was nowhere in dope five years ago."

Another man came down the path, he was thin and bearded, wearing a denim jacket and a black and grey keffiyeh curled around his neck. Dewi nodded for the man to join them and embraced him, and Dragan recognized him as Dewi's friend Bassel. Dragan shook his hand and handed him a beer.

Dewi said, "I was telling my mate here about the mess in Nørrebro."

"A mess is putting it mildly," said Bassel, in heavily accented English. "Fucking oppressive. Coming to our neighborhood to harass us."

"What?" Dewi took a second to sort his brain out, lighting a joint and handing it to Bassel. "No, I was talking about the biker gang war, a few years ago."

"Oh. I forgot the gang thing," said Bassel. "I was talking about the riots last year."

That got Dragan's attention. He said, "I was talking to someone the other day, she was going on about the mistreatment of immigrants and how those riots were just the beginning."

"Riots might be overstating the case, mate," said Dewi. "Though I know everyone calls them that."

"She talked about being able to smell change in the air," said Dragan, watching Bassel. "Said she might have a role to play in the coming revolution."

"She did, did she?" Bassel laughed. "I don't think we need more weekend troublemakers, and we don't need a revolution, that wouldn't do anyone any good. We need real change in how the country treats us on an everyday basis."

"What's going on?" asked Dragan, taking the joint from him.

"Denmark is making it hard for Muslims," said Bassel. "It's bad enough with the politicians and the television, but sometimes people come into our neighborhood and insult us, condemning Islam, saying we need to leave. People get upset and angry, the police step in, and it can go crazy. Last year cars set on fire, people hit with tear gas, and of course it's our fault."

"I forget, where was this?" asked Dewi.

"Blågårds Plads," said Bassel. "Near the lakes."

"You were there, right?" Dewi asked.

"I was there, sure, my family lives there."

"It spread all over," Dewi said to Dragan. "There were protests in Østerbro, in Nordvest, and there were even some incidents around Christiania, a car was set on fire out on the street, over there." Dewi pointed in the direction of the gate Dragan had entered through earlier.

"Denmark has a reputation as a happy country," said Dragan.

"True if you are a Dane," said Bassel. "But immigrants are not so welcome. They call us 'non-westerners' and say we don't take responsibility for ourselves. We are treated like outsiders and then we are criticized because we haven't integrated ourselves. We are trying! It isn't because we don't want to be! My family and my neighbors try to learn the language, but Danish is hard. English is better, you can use it in a lot of places in the world, if you leave here. You have a lot of people talking Danish in America?"

"No."

Bassel held his arms out for emphasis. "No, of course not."

"Tell him about the ghetto package," said Dewi.

"Oh my god," said Bassel. "Where immigrants live, especially Muslims, they call them ghettos. I thought ghettos were run down, poor, but these are good neighborhoods – still called ghettos. Twenty places in Denmark…"

"Twenty-five," said Dewi.

"…twenty-five places in Denmark, because of immigrants, children have to go to special centers to learn 'Danish values' which I don't know from anything."

"I don't know what 'Danish values' are either," said Dewi, "and I've been here for over ten years."

"The worst," said Bassel, "is if they think you did something illegal in those places, the penalties are higher, like twice the punishment. Completely unfair."

"Why not move?" asked Dragan.

"Takes money a lot of people don't have," said Bassel. "And now that all the prejudice is out in the open, could be there isn't any place better. They say we should assimilate but it isn't what they really want. They want us to have lighter skin, dress like them, not be Muslim. They'll never be satisfied until we're gone."

Dewi nodded his head in agreement. "Politics in Denmark are not good with Muslims," he said.

Bassel sipped his beer. "I'll tell you this," he said to Dragan. "If you know someone talking revolution you should be careful. There are people around ready for violence. Some of them are angry, some of them are crazy. Some of them are both. Stay away from them if you can."

"He's right," agreed Dewi. "We all know there's one important rule: never turn your back on crazy."

35

NAUGHTY

Dragan sat in his hotel room alone, in the dark, looking out the window onto the city while sipping iced vodka, when a call came in. It was Julianna. Not the first time she called since he arrived in Denmark, but the first time he answered.

"You're alive," she said. "I thought you fell into a well."

"I've been busy."

"You disappeared. Where are you?"

"Not talking about that yet. I'm pulling at threads, looking into people who had dealings with the Petroskis. I want to keep a low profile."

She was quiet. "It's a trust issue, then. With me."

"I have a trust issue with everyone these days. I'll work on correcting that when I find the time."

"You're not in the United States, are you?"

"No." He gave her that much.

She was quiet again. "You wouldn't be in Denmark by any chance, would you?"

It was his turn to be quiet. He sipped vodka. "If that were the case, how would you know that?"

"Well, isn't this game fun? Okay, I'll give you something – I'll tell you how I guessed that correctly. Some additional forensic work into the Petroski's financial records turned up some significant things. Remember Ben's call center we learned about? Not abandoned, it turned out, relocated. When they heard about the murders they packed up and moved elsewhere, taking over the business since Ben was out of the picture. We found them in Lithuania, and had a serious talk with the young computer punks running it. It's a social media and email operation, but Ben and Nina weren't doing political disruption or anything respectable like that. They were running identity theft scams."

Dragan was surprised; such an operation was bold even for Ben. It broke a few unwritten rules. Moscow was fine with causing societal chaos. If Ben had been running a troll farm to disrupt an American election, that would enhance Russia's reputation as having eyes and ears everywhere. It would be good for the brand, in other words, and Moscow would be happy Ben was doing it. Setting up an illegal scam on the side, however, was asking for a reprimand or worse, because if a Western country somehow identified and arrested an agent for using the internet to steal pension money from grandmothers it would be no good for the brand at all. It would look cheap and tawdry, making Russian intelligence appear small-minded and desperate. The intelligence bosses would be angry about that.

"That's naughty," said Dragan.

Julianna agreed. "If Moscow found out they would have stepped on him hard."

"How hard?"

"Certainly not an assassination, if that's what you're suggesting. They might slap him on the wrists and take away his toys."

"Why would he bother with an operation like that?"

"Because he could, I assume. For his own amusement, knowing him. But here's the important part for you. That phishing mill generated hefty income, which needed to be hidden from Moscow, from American law enforcement, and professional colleagues like me and you. Our analysts in the basement followed all the trails they could find, and more than once they came across the name of someone who served as an agent when money was moved around. Turns out he's one of ours, located in Copenhagen."

"Paul Koslov," said Dragan.

"I take that to mean whatever threads you're pulling are connected to him as well. Confirming you were withholding information from me."

"It was just my turn to guess correctly."

"Of course, he's the man you worked with a few years ago on a project, if I recall. It pains me to point out that he's yet another direct connection to you. For someone who prefers to keep to himself and doesn't appear to like people all that much, you are everywhere in this carnival."

It would get him nowhere to explain how Nina used what she learned from him. A fine line existed between accomplice and useful idiot, and in matters like this the line was often treated as if it didn't exist. He could hear it in Julianna's voice, that layer of suspicion and doubt beneath the surface. She wasn't ready to write him off yet, but she was close.

"My understanding was Koslov knew money laundering," he said. "How did they pick him up so easy?"

"The analysts tell me he's good but not as good as he thinks he is," she said. "He left little fingerprints all throughout the suspicious transactions."

"He's abusing multiple substances. Can make a person sloppy."

"Presumably he had enough cash left over to hire a low-class American hit squad. He was coloring outside the lines with the Petroskis. Now they're dead, which puts him in our sights."

"He's an attractive villain candidate," agreed Dragan. "But not the only one."

"Will you explain?"

"Not now." He paused, thinking. "What you're telling me raises another mystery, and it feels important. If Ben and Nina already had a partnership with Koslov to clean their dirty money, then what were they doing setting up that laundering scheme on the side with amateurs like Ivan and Kalashnik?"

"You think they were cutting out Koslov?"

"Looks like it. I learned that during a holiday trip the Petroskis took out here, they were actively exploring new ways to clean money that didn't include him."

"Which might be a motive."

"Does any of this news take pressure off me?"

"Possibly it makes things worse. You know how people are. If they thought you were involved before, your history with Koslov just makes you more guilty. You seem to be the common denominator."

"The Petroskis are. I'm just adjacent to it." "And they're dead, aren't they? You're not. There are those who will see your presence in Denmark as trying to clean up loose ends."

"You're not making me feel more comfortable. What about Ben's father?"

"Well, that's something else again. You're not going to like this at all. The father has been calling for all of our heads, yours especially. Sergei even reached out to him – they travel in some of the same circles – but got nowhere. He even threatened Sergei if he got in the way, and you can imagine how Sergei felt about that. Shortly after, however,

Petroski senior disappeared. He'd been under pressure because of the war, and was quoted in several places saying Russia needs to back off from the attacks on civilian locations. He's Ukrainian, after all, his family back home was being affected. He said, and I quote, 'We need to remember we are soldiers not terrorists.' It was not well received."

"What drove him underground?"

"An old friend of his, a construction and shipping executive, was found face down in the pool at his estate outside Saint Petersburg, shot. Official verdict was suicide, though it is extremely hard to shoot yourself in the back of the head. It frightened Ben's father into going low profile."

"That should take some pressure off."

"No, it won't, and that's the really bad news I need to tell you. Before he hid himself away, he put out word he is looking for you, and offered a reward. He used intelligence channels to alert agents throughout the system. You're a hunted man, by your own colleagues."

"Fuck me."

"I would have told you earlier, if you answered my calls."

"They'll find me eventually," he said, thinking of the young blonde man trailing him.

"Of course, we can consider the possibility that Petroski senior already knows why his son was killed. That it has to do with some shady off-the-books operation they were both involved in, and this bounty on your head is his way of diverting attention. But it won't mean much to you if they haul you away or kill you in an alley before you know they're there."

After the call ended Dragan grabbed a jacket and left the hotel. He didn't have a lot of time, based on what Julianna told him, so he needed to stir the pot a little.

36

PHOTOGRAPH

Paul Koslov sat at his computer in the second bedroom of his apartment, the one he used as his office. According to his banking statement he could no longer afford to make the bets on Danish Superliga games, but he embraced the argument that he couldn't afford not to, either. How else could he climb out of the financial hole he had put himself in?

It had gone well for him in the beginning, and gambling winnings aren't taxed in Denmark, so bonus points. He failed at the time to recognize he was at the top of the Ferris wheel and was about to experience the inevitable correction. Like so many gamblers he expected the winning streaks to last and the losing streaks to be temporary. While he was waiting for his luck to change back, he sank deeper into the hole. To finance his bets he redirected from investments he managed at his firm. It was a temporary loan, of course, he told himself.

He continued to lose but couldn't stop. If he was going to recoup those losses he had to move forward, taking slightly bigger risks as he proceeded. His plan was to get back to where he had been, with luck a little more than that, and quit. Yes, this time he was serious, he would quit if he could just level off. He took another hit of cocaine to clear his head and boost his energy and help him concentrate on the betting site on the screen.

Someone knocked on the door to his apartment. He frowned. He didn't really know his neighbors, certainly not well enough for one of them to intrude like this. He opened the door to find Dragan Markov standing in the hallway with a fresh bottle of very good American whiskey in his hands.

"I wanted to surprise you," said Dragan with a smile. "I hope you don't mind."

"How did you find me?"

"You're living in the same place you were during the French bank thing."

Paul nodded sheepishly, waved him in, and brought a couple of glasses from the kitchen. Dragan put the bottle on the low table in the living room and looked around. It was a clean, orderly rectangle, with a living and dining area in the center, a kitchen at one end, and two bedrooms on the other. There were no books, and little ephemera of any kind. Dragan examined the handful of photographs on the wall. In one Paul stood waving by a cottage with ochre walls and a dark red roof in a dune-covered landscape near the ocean.

"What's this place?" he asked, pointing.

"I picked up a remodeled fishing cabin on the North Sea, out near a town called Ribe. A getaway retreat." He cracked open the whiskey and poured them both a drink. They clicked glasses and drank. "What brings you around?"

"To chat a little more about Nina and Benedikt Petroski."

Paul's expression immediately soured. "I told you everything. There's nothing I can help you with."

"Perhaps."

"What do you mean by that?"

"It means I think you have more to tell me."

They stared at each other for a bit. Paul's face was flushed. He cursed in Russian under his breath.

"You're agitated," said Dragan.

"You're accusing me of lying."

"There are loose ends, that's all. For example, the photograph."

Paul looked up sharply. He started to say something, thought better of it, then asked, "What photograph?"

"A picture of you with Nina and Ben in front of your office building. Taken when they had a Scandinavian holiday a few years back." Dragan pulled out his phone, found the photo he took of it, and showed Paul. "You said you didn't know them, but there the three of you are."

Paul became still. The righteous anger was gone, replaced by wariness. The beginning of panic entered his eyes. "You weren't being honest with me," he said, trying to build up some indignation. "Setting a trap, seeing how far I would go with it. Not playing by the rules I think." He bared his teeth in something resembling a smile without being one. "So much for our friendship."

"We're not friends. I'm investigating two murders."

"That's why I said I didn't know them. They were murdered, and I didn't want to get involved. You can understand that. I have enough troubles."

"How did you meet them?"

"They reached out. Someone said I'd be a good contact."

"You look like you knew each other well."

"It was a snapshot. Nothing unusual."

"Something odd about it though."

Something like fear entered Paul's eyes. "What do you mean?"

"Nice picture of the three of you."

"It was a good day."

"With you all in the shot, who took the picture?" Looking at Paul's startled face, Dragan almost felt sorry for him. "Lily Sandersen was the photographer, right? Yet you told me you had broken up with her before then."

"I don't remember who took it. A passerby, I think. Not Lily, though."

"Oh, I think it was her."

"No, it couldn't be."

"Yes, it could be. I talked to Lily."

Dragan paused and waited. Paul pursed his lips and stared at the floor.

"She didn't tell you, obviously," said Dragan. "If you expect someone to lie for you, make sure they get the details settled. She doesn't seem interested in covering for you, by the way, I don't think you have much influence over her. Are you still with her, or not?"

"We're done." Paul looked a little sweaty. "You're checking up on me?"

"No. Checking on a few loose threads related to Nina and Ben, as I said."

"Tracking down my ex-girlfriend is an invasion of my privacy."

"They were assassinated, Paul, you have no privacy as far as I'm concerned."

Paul, his eyes wide and darting about, took a healthy sip of whiskey.

Dragan picked up his own glass, and just before he put it to his lips he said, "Her brother appears a little dodgy."

The color drained from Paul's face. "You met Viggo?"

37

— · —

Exit Strategy

Dragan almost felt bad for Paul. The money launderer was drug addled, and so far on his heels he was flailing as he dropped off the cliff. "I did indeed meet Viggo," he said with a cruel smile. "And his friend Anton, a big German, doesn't talk much. I was in Lily's apartment when they came in. They look like they've done time. Am I right?"

"You met Viggo." It was said as a statement this time. Paul bit the inside of his cheek, his eyes searching the apartment for something to look at other than Dragan's face. "Whatever the hell you think you're doing isn't appropriate, leave my personal life alone."

"I've upset you."

"Viggo is trouble. Stay away from him."

"Good-looking, though, in a rough trade kind of way. Striking hair."

"You can't... Denmark is..." Paul hesitated, put his thumbs against his temples, and let out a low growl. "There's nothing to investigate here. I was trying to keep Lily and me out of this murder thing. She's a civilian, an actress, she doesn't deserve this. You might call it a lie – so then okay you have me, good for you, so what now, are you going to be a bastard about it? Nina and Benedikt came through, looked me up,

Lily and I had a drink with them, we gave them some suggestions on places to visit and the best ways to get around the country, and they were on their way. End of the story. You should be satisfied and go home."

"What are you mixed up in?"

"Nothing. I'm not... There's nothing going on."

"Paul, listen to me. You were working with the Petroskis for some time, laundering money."

"I hardly know those people!"

"During that last trip they started looking into other ways to clean income, ways that didn't involve you. You have a falling out with them?"

"I don't know what you're talking about."

"Yes, you do. You should talk to me."

"I didn't kill them if that's what you are getting at."

"You're in trouble then. I could help you."

"I don't need your help. You should leave Denmark. Get out of my life."

"I'm sorry to hear you say that."

"I'm sorry you made me say it. Is a little professional courtesy so much to ask? Who do you think you are, anyway?" Paul pointed his finger across the table in quick jabs and yelled in Russian. "Nina told me all about you. She said you're just an errand boy for rich people. You're a lowlife to come here like this and insult me. You have no authority over me, you have no authority here. I don't want to talk to you. Finish your business but keep me and Lily out of it."

Dragan put the cap back on the whiskey bottle and slipped it into his coat pocket. He paused at the front door, and said to Paul, "You seem under a lot of stress." He slowly, and quietly, closed the door after him.

Paul sat for a long time, considering everything. His life was not working out the way he had imagined. He felt it careening downhill. He considered jumping out of the window. Then he thought about his plans, all the plans for a full life. He had made notes. He had made drawings, with cars, and sunsets, and solitude on the beach. He had daydreamed. This was but a bump in the road.

He phoned Lily.

"You didn't tell me Dragan Markov talked to you" said Paul, struggling to remain calm and his voice in check, despite the anxiety and anger he felt. "How did he even find you?"

"Didn't you tell him where I was working?" asked Lily.

"Of course not."

"Then he's a clever little boy."

"He has a big-time focus on the Petroskis. He's being an asshole and I want you to stay away from him."

"Why is he here?" It was Viggo's voice. He was in the apartment with Lily, and she had put Paul on speaker without warning him.

"I just told you," said Paul." Looking into those murders."

"But why is he here, in Copenhagen?"

"He has the photograph. He showed it to me."

Lily and Viggo both cursed. "Where did he get that?" asked Lily.

"From Nina, where else?" Paul was frustrated as usual with these two.

"So, he has the money!" Lily was excited.

Paul closed his eyes in despair. "Just because he has the photo..."

"He has her photo! He has her photo it means he has the money!" Lily was almost screaming at Paul through the phone. "You need to get it back!"

"I can't... He won't give it to me..."

"Take it!"

In the background, Paul could hear Viggo say to Lily, "Tell Paul I'll handle it."

"Viggo says he'll handle it," said Lily into the phone.

"No! Jesus Christ no," said Paul. "Markov's not the kind of guy you can scare off. Unless you kill him, you'll only make him mad, and you can't kill him because Russian security will be all over us…"

"Paul says you'll fuck it up," Paul heard Lily tell Viggo.

"Yeah I got that," said Viggo. "I'll handle it."

"Viggo's going to handle it," Lily said.

"You have me on speaker, I can hear him," Paul shouted, increasingly desperate. "You don't understand people like him. Don't engage! If we do nothing and say nothing it will probably be over soon, and he'll go home. Don't talk to him, don't trust him. And for God's sake keep Viggo away from him. If you do — "

Lily hung up on him.

Nervous sweat clung to Paul's forehead and the back of his neck. He just wanted Dragan Markov to go back to America and for this to be over. If Lily had her way they would kidnap Dragan and torture him until he gave her what she wanted. And now Viggo said he'll deal with the situation, which could mean literally anything. If Paul ever had any control over things, that time was long gone. This was chaos, and he hated it. He hated his apartment with its modern minimal design, hated his tailored suits. He hated his job. He hated Lily and Viggo. He hated Nina and Ben, and now he hated Dragan.

He hated his life. He needed to get an exit strategy together. Like, yesterday.

38

VIGGO

The young man at the front desk phoned, telling Dragan in stiffly correct English that there was a gentleman to see him. It was late in the evening, and there was no one Dragan expected. Intrigued, he said he would be right down.

"Very good sir. The gentleman said to bring a jacket."

Viggo was waiting for him on the pavement outside, sitting on his motorcycle. He looked like a magazine photoshoot was in progress: thick work boots, heavyweight denim jeans, a wool pea coat, black leather gloves.

"We're going on an adventure," said Viggo.

"Are you serious?"

"Of course I'm serious. Hop on."

Dragan didn't know what to make of this, other than his visit to Paul's apartment was paying dividends. Viggo may not be a threat, he may not even be involved in what happened. Or he was deeply involved, and he was taking Dragan someplace to kill him and bury him in a bog. Against his better judgement, Dragan mounted the motorcycle behind Viggo and they headed out.

They crossed the Inner Harbor on the Langebro and headed toward the Amager East section. The night was cool but not cold, and a slight mist hung close to the ground giving the ride through the night streets something of a dream quality. They pulled into a corner kebob shop. They ordered coffees, Viggo got shawarma in a pita, and they sat at a small wooden table in the rear.

Dragan sipped coffee and watched Viggo eat for a bit. Finally, he asked, "Why are we here?"

"To talk."

"You drove me to a kebob shop to talk?"

"I hear you're upset that Paul lied to you." Viggo spoke English slowly, like a man wanting to be understood. "Paul is a liar all the time. Every day, all day. Do they train you to be like that, when you go to spy school?"

Dragan laughed.

"You think this is funny?" asked Viggo.

"It's funny you think someone trained him to lie. Because he's a terrible liar."

It was Viggo's turn to laugh. "You're right about that! He has many bad habits, and it causes him to lie to many people about many things in his life."

"Sounds exhausting."

"He can't keep it all straight. He gets in the way of his own lies."

Dragan took the measure of the other man. Viggo was confident, even arrogant, but there was an openness about him as well, a simplicity. Was he really a dangerous criminal, or a bystander to what happened? Both?

Dragan asked, "Why do you think Paul is a spy?"

"He told Lily he was. He said you were too, after you and he did some spy project in Paris. We didn't know whether to believe him or not, of course."

"You said he was a liar."

"Yes, but Nina also told me you were a spy. She said she and her husband were spies, too."

"When would she have told you that?"

"In bed together, at my old apartment. I was licking her fisse, and she was laughing, telling me stories about you."

The two men stared at each other for a moment. Viggo smiled. Dragan wasn't sure what to make of any of this. He wasn't as bothered about what Viggo had said about Nina, as he was about Viggo wanting to make Dragan angry. Usually when a man corners you in a strange environment and deliberately provokes you, it doesn't end well.

Things became tense.

"I see you are upset with me," said Viggo. "I tell you this for your own good. I understand you are angry they died, and now you are angry that I had my cock up your girlfriend's ass. You want to find an explanation. Sometimes explanations are not possible."

"Explanations are always possible."

"Sometimes you dig too much, and you find out things you didn't want to know."

"I want to know everything."

"You liked her, I can imagine you loved her, but you didn't know her very well."

"Who says?" Dragan's hand made fists. "You?"

"She told me so. I know all about you. She said you were good at sex but were like a little boy sometimes."

Dragan flushed and his eyes narrowed.

"She also told me you have a temper," said Viggo, "and you sometimes get violent."

"She said I was violent with her?"

"No. With people who make you angry. People like me, right now. If we are to fight let's not do it here, in a kebob shop."

The absurdity of that request somehow broke the tension. They both relaxed a little.

"Why are we talking about this?" asked Dragan.

Viggo wiped sauce off his cheek. "She was a criminal, she and her husband. She was also a liar like Paul, only much better. She was not a good person. If you keep going forward with all this, you may not get the answer you are looking for, but you will learn all about what a criminal she was. And then everyone will know."

"What do you mean she was a criminal?"

"She and her husband were working with Paul on some illegal thing, I don't know what. They talked about big money, a pile of it, they got Lily all excited. Either there never was any money, or they stole it all. I think they stole it."

"Paul Koslov was in it?"

"Oh yes, he was in it, but he doesn't have the money now, so I think they stole it from him, too."

"Are you suggesting Paul killed them?"

"Possibly, but I think he's too weak and frightened to do it. You never know about people, though. The important thing, my friend, is that they were criminals who cheated everybody. Someone, sooner or later, was going to get mad enough to make them dead."

Viggo was not delivering this opinion with any snark or taunt. He didn't appear to take any satisfaction at all. He seemed sincere, as if the two were old friends and Viggo had been tasked with delivering bad news. Despite that, or perhaps because of it, Dragan was still considering reaching across the table and punching him.

A shadow fell across the table and Viggo's German friend Anton stood there, looking at them. He was a big man, in a leather jacket, and he made everyone else in the shop uneasy. He pulled up a chair and sat in it.

"You didn't tell me it was a party," said Dragan. Viggo grinned.

"Two more, then we go," said Anton in heavily accented English, holding up two fingers on a right hand the size of a ham hock.

Two young Chinese men entered the kabab shop. Both slim and vibrant with energy, they looked very much alike, except one had long hair in a ponytail, while the other sported a shaved head and goatee.

"You know Anton," said Viggo. "These are the Chen brothers. They're twins, but they don't embrace that. Jin has the long hair, Alex has the goatee, not that you will remember."

It occurred to Dragan that all four men were wearing kerchiefs loosely around their necks.

Anton stood up, impatiently took Viggo's plate and the two coffee cups, and deposited them in the rubbish container on his way out the door. The Chen brothers followed close behind.

"Let's go," said Viggo.

39

CRIMINAL

Anton was already on his motorcycle. The Chens entered a white, battered panel van. Viggo and Dragan mounted their bike, and the crew continued east. Before they hit the strait between Denmark and Sweden, they turned, drove for some time, crossed a small bridge, until they reached a manufacturing complex.

The group split up. The white van moved ahead. Anton and Viggo pulled their bikes into a side street, obscured by trees. Dragan walked with them to a shadowed area by the brick wall surrounding the rear of the plant.

They waited in the darkness, with the city sounds in the distance.

"Do you have someone following me?" Dragan asked. "Young guy, lean, looks like a skateboarder, knit cap with long blonde hair."

"Not my guy," said Viggo. "If I have someone follow you it will be a short man with red hair and a long beard he keeps tied at the end. You'll see him, he is shit at following people, but he likes to do it, so I let him."

Anton lit a cigarette and walked ahead to look for activity. From where they stood Dragan could see the white van near the entrance to the plant, the brothers slouched down with a view of the warehouse doors.

"This is Hansen & Knudsen," Viggo said. "Machine and automotive engine plant. You have heard of this?"

"No. What are we doing?"

"A friend of mine worked the late shift here. He told me how management did some things off the books, mostly a cash business so no taxes. They arranged for a pickup of the extra cash the same day of the month, every month, same way every time. Today is that day."

"You're going to rob this place?" Dragan was astonished.

"My friend and I talked about how easy it would be. Four people is all it takes, just need to get the timing right."

"I make it five."

"You are audience."

"Why didn't your friend do it?"

"He got married and moved to Finland to work on a potato farm. This is mine now. Exciting, right?"

Anton walked back and spoke to Viggo in a sloppy mix of Danish and German.

"He said the security in this place is shameful," Viggo explained. "There's a fence but the gates are wide open."

"What are we waiting for?" asked Dragan.

"We are waiting for that," said Viggo, pointing to headlights coming toward the plant.

"An armored car?" Dragan almost burst out laughing, it was so ridiculous. "Do you even have weapons?"

"The guards won't be armed. It's illegal to carry weapons when moving cash, even for armored car guards. If they aren't carrying, we don't need to either. We just need to be fast. Stay near the gate and keep an eye out."

The Loomis truck came up to the plant, nice and slow, like there was all the time in the world to get the night's business taken care of.

It drove through the gate and pulled carefully up to the warehouse entrance. Two guards got out, one short and round, the other tall and thin. The short one entered the warehouse door to transport the cash. The tall one stood guard outside.

Viggo and Anton pulled their kerchiefs up over the bottom half of their faces and pulled watch caps over their heads. Dragan stayed near the end of the brick wall so he could watch things unfold and warn them if anyone was coming. Viggo said they needed to be fast, and fast they were. Anton, moving with remarkable agility and silence for such a big man, came up behind the tall guard and put him down with a blackjack, tied his hands, and taped his mouth. Viggo immediately took a position by the warehouse entrance, pressing his back against the wall. Anton took the guard's keys, unlocked the back of the Loomis truck, and with considerable effort lifted the unconscious guard into the back.

The Chen brothers pulled the panel van into the lot, turned it around, and backed up so the rear of the van was by the rear of the Loomis. Dragan could see through the van windows that they had also pulled their kerchiefs up and put caps on their heads. The van engine still running, the brothers hopped out and, with Anton, began moving bags and boxes from the armored car to the white van.

When the short guard came out, pushing a cart with two satchels, lost in his own thoughts, he walked half the distance to the armored truck before he realized anything was wrong. By then it was too late; Viggo put him down, too, and the Chen brothers came over and grabbed the satchels, throwing them in the back of their van. They closed and locked the back, hopped in the truck cab, and sped off.

Viggo took one last look into the Loomis truck; when he turned Anton was already gone. Viggo followed, walking quickly but not too quickly, out of the lot. He grabbed Dragan by the arm and they hurried to the motorcycles. Anton impatiently waited on his bike. Angry, he barked something to both Viggo and Dragan in Danish. Viggo said something back. Anton spit on the ground and roared off.

"What was that about?" asked Dragan.

"He said any longer and he would have taken off without us."

"What did you say back?"

"I told him, no, he wouldn't." Viggo laughed, and the two of them headed into the night, leaving an armored car empty of cash, with its rear doors open, and two concussed, groggy guards.

As they cruised the streets, listening for police sirens, streetlights passing by like meteors at the edge of sight, Dragan had the most unexpected memory, perhaps prompted by Viggo's nasty comments in the kebab shop. He remembered a winter night lying under a blanket with Nina in the Philadelphia townhouse, on the floor, in front of the fireplace. Her cheeks flush from the wine and the sex, the flames tossing shadows across the cornices above, she told him he was the one. She said she was sure he was going to rescue her from a life of quiet frustration as the trophy wife of a man who had no interest in her. If not him, she said, then no one. She made a sincere commitment that she loved him. That was the Nina he had been carrying with him, the one he had been seeking justice for. Apparently that person never existed, since it was hard to reconcile that memory with the woman happy to criticize and mock him when he wasn't there, when she was in someone else's arms. Not to mention that when he actually tried to rescue her from that life, she was appalled and broke up with him.

Who was she, actually? Was that question all he had left of her?

Twenty-five minutes after leaving the manufacturing plant, Viggo pulled up in front of Dragan's hotel. Anton was already there, sitting on a bench, smoking a cigarette, waiting.

"I've seen too many people become lost when they lose track of what is important," said Viggo, pulling a flask of liquor out of an inside pocket of his coat and handing it to Dragan. "They chase after fancy jobs, or a spouse, or becoming famous. But they're still miserable, even after they get what they think they want. Do you know what I mean?"

"Yes," said Dragan. He hesitated, then took a sip from the flask.

"Nina and Ben were like that," said Viggo. "They chased money, they got it, they were still miserable. You're like that, too, chasing information that won't help you in any way, and may make you unhappy. People like you and them, you've lost your sense of purpose."

"Lily told me she has a purpose, as a revolutionary." Dragan handed back the flask.

"She thinks so," laughed Viggo, taking a drink, "but she doesn't."

"And Koslov?"

"Paul is just lost and he's never coming back. You need to forget about him."

"What about you?"

"I'm doing okay, thanks for asking. I take every day as it comes, one foot in front of the other."

Dragan turned to enter the hotel, but Viggo grabbed his coat and yanked him back. He held Dragan's shoulders and pulled their faces close. Dragan could, for the first time, clearly see his eyes, the color of cornflowers flecked with grey. They were bright, like they emanated light.

"Nina and Ben were criminals," said Viggo. "And after tonight now you're a criminal too. Just go home to America, leave us be."

He kissed Dragan full on the mouth, holding his shoulders tightly, sticking his tongue halfway down Dragan's throat. He pulled away just as suddenly, then laughed. Dragan was stunned. He saw movement to his side, and there Anton stood, watching all of it, and he had a sour look on his face. Dragan stepped back, wiping his mouth with the back of his hand. Viggo laughed again, and he and Anton drove off.

40

FEDDE

Fedde Lorca imagined himself the poet of a revolution. What revolution? He would answer they were all the same struggle, from the depths of the past to the farthest future, always the same. And they were struggles! George Orwell said all revolutions are failures, but they aren't all the same failure, which Fedde liked. To him it suggested progression, in some perverse way. When he had a few at the pub, he would tell acquaintances that if revolutions learn from their mistakes and go on to make new ones, eventually revolutions will run out of mistakes and true change will occur. He said it the night he met Lily. He was drinking at a bar with theatre people, and she was sitting at the far end of the table.

"That suggests revolutions have finite mistakes," Lily had responded, shouting to be heard over the room noise. "But as long as people are involved there are endless possibilities for new mistakes no one has ever seen before."

He became instantly infatuated with her.

Fedde liked helping Lily. She was passionate and, in his estimation, a little emotionally unstable, a combination he found very arousing. He would prefer she paid more attention to him and perhaps shared his bed occasionally as payback for all that he had done for her, but he didn't want to rush her. She was volatile and not the kind to tolerate being rushed.

That volatility was part of the appeal, by the way, but also a major red flag. Fedde was no fan of restraint, but he didn't approve of carelessness, and not minding the details was one of Lily's defining characteristics. It would bring the roof down on all their heads one day, if she didn't become more careful.

This escapade with the bomb was an example. He was going along with it, but it made him nervous. The authorities seriously frowned on bombs, and the chances of innocent people hurt, or killed, were high. That was not how Fedde liked things to play out, but Lily didn't seem concerned at all. She was quite content as the two of them walked the streets surrounding Saint Paul's Church. They were in search of an indigent man who called himself Baldur and used the church as home base. She was going to arrange for this street person to be her bomber.

"Does he think he's the reincarnation of the god, or does he just like the name?" asked Lily.

"I don't know. He likely suffers from schizophrenia and an array of physical ailments real and imagined. He once told me he would do anything for money other than be unkind to children and animals."

"Then he's perfect, there won't be children or animals anywhere near the target." She took his cheeks in her hands and made his lips pout, as you would a toddler, and kissed him.

When they came across Baldur he recognized Fedde as someone who had spoken to him in the past, and had been kind to him. Baldur was a haggard man with grey hair and beard, swimming in multiple layers of overcoats, smelling of urine and mold. Lily handed Baldur a sandwich of sliced roast pork with red cabbage and pickles on a roll, a bag of potato crisps, and a small bottle of akvavit. They spoke for a while, and a deal was struck. Baldur said he was happy to do as he was asked, in exchange for the payment she promised. He pointed towards the spot where he would be sleeping.

"Ring a bell quietly, like a priest calling me to prayer, and I'll wake up," Baldur told her in his soft, wheezing voice.

41

—·—

In Plain Sight

In the café next to his hotel, Dragan pored over his digital copy of the photograph he found in Nina's beach house in New Jersey. Paul, Nina, and Ben posing in front of Paul's office; a routine, even dull photo.

And yet... Nina kept it hidden; Paul became agitated when he learned Dragan had it.

Something important was in this image. Something that didn't belong, or should be there but wasn't. He considered it might be inside the office building, but the resolution wasn't good enough to see any detail through the windows. He zoomed into the water surrounding the building on three sides, but there was no message in the reflection, nothing just below the surface.

He examined the three people standing on the bench, laughing. They were caught in the middle of a cheerful moment. Nina was leaning against Ben so she could peer around him at Paul, who seemed about to fall; her mouth was open like she was shouting something at him.

He scanned to the left, inspecting the cars and trucks in the parking lot next door to the office building, and then focused on the buildings in the distance. There were no hidden details in the bushes, nor did he expect there to be. He again scanned the parking lot, thinking some car might be a clue, when the trucks parked toward the rear of the lot caught his eye.

Something wasn't right.

They were routine Mercedes box trucks, Danish plates, parked side by side, facing him. He stared at the trucks for a minute, trying to recognize what his subconscious had picked up.

It was the license plates!

Now he could see there were three things wrong with them. First, they lacked the blue EU strip on the left side. Second, there were too many characters on the plates. But the important thing, the thing his subconscious mind picked up, was that he could read the lettering. At the resolution of the rest of the photo, he shouldn't have been able to identify individual characters. Before it was printed someone had gone into the original digital file and changed the characters on those license plates at a pixel-by-pixel level, to clean them up and make sure they were legible.

But why?

They were letters and numbers, nothing unusual. Then he considered the characters as a single line and there it was. He recognized what looked like a complex password. Random and long, which would make it very secure. It would open something locked, encrypted – the "computer thing" referred to by the man he shot in the townhouse. It could be for an online digital locker, a standalone hard drive, a USB drive, or a tablet PC.

This raised a host of new questions. Why get fancy with detailed manipulation of a photograph? Why keep a physical object at all, when there are so many ways to securely keep the password digitally? What kind of overkill was this? It was like the spy craft writers described in espionage novels from the sixties. Nobody indulged in that sort of thing any longer, if they ever actually did. It was like using a washboard to do laundry; it would work, perhaps, but why go to the trouble with all the better options available?

His enjoyment of this breakthrough was short-lived, however. He looked up, thinking about what he had found, and noticed that across the street, in the doorway of an apartment building, lounged the lean young man with the watch cap and long blonde hair, watching him. Dragan looked right at him, and the man brazenly looked back. There was no pretense of secrecy, no hiding. Short of walking across the street and starting a confrontation, there was little Dragan could do about this.

He pulled out his phone. It took four rings to be picked up. On the other end was his colleague Leonid, the FSB agent doing embassy security back in Washington; he sounded groggy.

"Did I wake you?" asked Dragan. "It's the middle of the day there."

"I was napping. Late night, there was an event. I spent the entire time standing by a door no one came in or out of. Where are you?"

"Travelling. I need you to do me a favor. The house in Arlington County outside of Washington – Ivan Bortnik's house. You know the one?"

"I helped Sacha make sure it was clean of tech."

"They haven't done anything with it yet, have they?"

"No, it's too early. You know how slow they work."

"I might need a shiny object, and the house could be it."

"A what?"

"A red herring. You know what a red herring is?"

"Of course, you think I don't know American phrases?"

"I'm only asking."

"You know how long I've been here?"

"A long time. Yet you still speak English with that accent."

"A lot of people have accent. It makes me sexy."

"Sexy to whom?"

"To everyone."

"Then please use your sex appeal to make sure they leave the Arlington County house alone. They can move Ivan's stuff out, if they haven't done it already. But I'd like the house and some basic furniture to stay the way it is. Disconnect the alarm, if there is one. And no for sale sign or anything unusual."

"This I can do. For how long?"

"For a while. I don't know. A month to start. Then we'll see."

"Too short. Turnaround time on the paperwork takes longer than that. I'll make it six months."

"Okay. Can you rig it inside with a motion-activated security camera or two? Connect them to the web. You can give me the link, but it would best if you keep an eye on it, too."

"When do you need this to happen?"

"Soon. Within the week, if possible."

"Of course it's possible."

"If you get any pushback let me know, I can get Julianna to intervene, but I'd rather not bring her into this if I can help it."

"She will not be necessary. I will handle."

"Thank you."

Leonid hesitated. Then said, "This does not sound like a red herring. It sounds like bait. What happens if something gets caught?"

"Let me know. What we do will depend on who it is." Dragan sighed. "I'm making this up as I go along."

"I think it's what you usually do."

"I try to be more of a planner."

"You want people to see you that way, sure. But it doesn't work out usually."

Dragan looked up. On the pavement in front of the café stood Lily.

42

CHOOSE WISELY

Lily stared directly at Dragan and waited for him to come out to talk to her, or invite her in to join him.

"Okay, this has been a delight," said Dragan into the phone. "But I need to go. Thank you."

"Of course," said Leonid. "Wherever you are you won't tell me, be careful."

Dragan disconnected the call, nodded toward the empty seat at his table, and said to Lily, "Would you join me?"

She sat. She seemed preoccupied, failing to flash her large, artificial smile. He glanced across the street and saw that the young man with the blonde hair was no longer in the doorway.

Dragan ordered two Negronis because he was in the mood and didn't bother to ask if she wanted something different. She didn't complain. They sat in silence for a few minutes.

"Viggo came by to see me, too," Dragan said eventually. "This place is becoming like a train station."

"I heard. You took an adventure together."

"He claimed to know the Petroskis pretty well."

Lily snorted. "A lot better than I did. He told you he fucked that Nina woman, didn't he? It's the kind of thing he would do, tell you something like that about your girlfriend."

"So, he was lying?"

"No, he was with both of them, her and her husband. This is what he does. He thinks it's the only thing he's really good at, so he leans into it. He'll go after you, if you stick around."

"I don't think he'll get very far."

"Lots of others have said the same thing, then were surprised."

"Including you?"

"He's my brother," she said, looking away.

"No he's not."

She looked away, then back. "I met him at university, it was that long ago. He was the smartest out of all of us. He read the most, knew the most. He was handsome, charming, and sexy and everyone loved him."

"What happened to him?"

"I don't know." She shrugged. "I think he got bored. I hated going to classes, so I dropped out when he did."

She seemed to go somewhere in her memory. He watched her eyes dim, then brighten again. She said, "Anyway, I wouldn't be surprised if he tried something with you already. He's a pig."

They paused there and took stock.

She said, "You're upsetting Paul."

"He knows things about Ben and Nina Petroski, and I need him to tell me what those things are. I'm asking him nicely now, but I'm running out of patience."

"You think he was responsible for them being killed?"

"It's certainly possible. What's your feeling on that?"

"You want to know about Paul?" she asked, tracing her finger around the rim of her glass. "He gambles and drinks and I think he wants to kill himself but he's afraid to, so he's doing it as slowly as he can. I couldn't stand watching it."

"So you left him."

"He's a loser. Do you really think a loser like him could kill those people in Philadelphia, from all the way across the ocean? How is he supposed to do it, magic?"

"Even losers can be angry and want revenge."

"Did he tell you he bought a fishing cabin? More of a shack, really. He tells people he uses it to meditate and work on his peace of mind. He uses it to drink, mostly, and I'm sure he sees it as a lonely, romantic place to die, like in a novel. That's where he's going to kill himself, I know it."

"That certainly sounds tragic. Or just dramatic." Dragan sipped his drink and looked across at her, assessing. He said, "You're not a loser. You have ambition."

"I'm going to make a mark. I'm not going to do it being a waitress, and I'm running out of time as an actress."

"You sound impatient."

"Why should any of us wait?"

"Wait for what?"

"For our place, for making things right, for stepping up and being..." She struggled to find the words.

"This is why you need that money?"

She clasped and unclasped her fingers. Her eyes were moist. "Those people and Paul had a business thing, and I was supposed to get a percentage. They haven't given it to me yet. That's all you need to know."

This was a new performance from Lily, a little deferential, a little sad.

He asked, "Can you explain what the photo has to do with it? Three of you in front of Paul's office?"

"It's mine," she demanded.

"What do you mean, it's yours?"

"It's a nice photo. I was the photographer. Therefore, it's mine."

"What's so important about it?"

"Nothing. I like it, that's all."

Dragan looked her in the eye, and said, "What does that password unlock?"

She looked startled at first. Her breathing was shallow. She leaned forward, and he was concerned about what she might do. He checked her hands for a knife. Instead of attacking him, she said, "How about if I suck your dick and you give me the photo? Right now, upstairs in your room?"

"I thought seduction was Viggo's thing."

"He'll just seduce you. I'm offering you a deal."

"I don't want you touching me."

"I want my money. If you won't give me the photo, then help me get my money back."

"How?"

"You already have it, or you know where it is."

"I don't have it, I don't know where it is. And I don't know what use the photo is."

"I don't believe you. But if you're telling the truth, and you don't know what it is, then just give it to me. You don't care about it anyway."

"But you care about it, which makes me curious."

"To get that photo I'm willing to suck your dick or cut it off. Choose wisely."

"You're not doing either one of those."

"We're going to gut you.," she snapped, her eyes blazing.

Dragan was happy to finally goad the creature into the open. "There she is."

Lily calmed her breathing, and the blistering flame in her eyes dimmed a little. She looked around the café, then above.

"The ceiling is ugly," she said.

"Listen, Lily, if..."

"You and Viggo really are a lot alike, you know," she said, turning towards him. "The sport thing. You're both tall, and I think you're both good looking but what do I know? Stubborn, vain, arrogant. You both act like you know what's going on but you don't. You want to be the boss but you're not really in charge of anything. Neither of you can control your woman. Plus, I'm becoming a little tired of both of you."

43

— · —

ASSET

Dragan left a message for Christina. It took her two hours to call back. When she did her voice was frosty, clearly displeased by having to deal with him again.

"What's this about?" she asked.

"I'm fairly certain Paul Koslov is in some way behind the deaths, though it looks more like it was from fear and panic than anything else. But it still doesn't fully make sense, because I don't understand what happened between them. Also, there are strange elements to this. I started looking for some kind of trail Paul might have left, something that could offer an explanation."

"Is this a long version of telling me you looked at his social media?"

"I tried that but he's nearly non-existent there, and he doesn't show up in media archives. But business records are something else. I got a huge hit on the public Danish Central Business Register. Koslov is a partner in two companies, a limited liability firm and a non-profit. In both cases his ownership partner is listed as Lucas Oliver Madsen."

"He's a real person?"

"Yeah, I checked on that. He's a college history professor who lives in Roskilde and teaches at the university there. The public records make those companies look legitimate, but it's all pretty vague, it reads like worldwide imports and exports stuff."

"A cover you mean?"

"More like a catch-all clearing house for whatever they get up to. If any of their activities were illegal, I thought Madsen, or the companies, might appear in your records."

"Not in mine, we don't keep an archive of that sort of thing. But I have a friend, she works for the police. She might be able to find something."

Dragan was concerned. Bringing in the police could expose him to risks. He had no desire to appear in an official report somewhere. He told Christina as much.

"She's not just an asset," Chrisina explained. "She's... much closer than that. She understands the need for discretion in the things I do."

"You are intimate, then?"

"If you insist on that, yes, though it is none of your business. We also help each other in our work, we both have information the other doesn't. The mutual trust works out."

"As long as my efforts aren't compromised."

"Are you questioning how I conduct my business? Are you really that eager to have me end this call? Not help you any longer?"

"I overstepped. I'm sorry."

"Give me a few days." She hung up.

44

SHINY THING

The threat from Benedict's father bearing down on him, Dragan was tired of the slow pace and wanted to prod things forward, see what came to the surface. He headed out to have some more fun with Paul Koslov. He walked past the lovely canals of Christianshavn, lined with boats, crossed the Stadsgraven on the pedestrian bridge, and down to the streamlined cube of a business office. By the time he passed through the rotating front door he was smiling. He nodded to the security guard at the reception desk and announced himself in English: "Denis Sobol, of Infocon Solutions, for Paul Koslov."

The guard looked him over once or twice, looked up a number in the directory, made a call, spoke into the phone. "Mr. Koslov will be down shortly," he said when he was finished. "Are you English?"

"No, American," Dragan said.

"Texas?"

"No. From Washington."

"Where the president is," said the guard, raising his eyebrows.

"Where the president is, yes."

Paul exited the elevator banks. He was in a sharp gray suit, crisp white shirt with a spread collar, and a burgundy tie with gold horses on it. To whatever extent Paul was unraveling, thought Dragan, he could still dress like a banker.

"Denis!" Paul said, a broad smile on his face and his hand out in greeting. "Wonderful to see you again so soon! Such a surprise!" Paul looked at Dragan sharply, held his hand a little too tightly.

"I have a meeting with Maersk later and thought I would stop by to say hello."

"Excellent!" All nice and normal, two business acquaintances, a performance for the benefit of the security guard.

"Do you have time to chat?" asked Dragan. "I don't want to intrude."

"Of course." Paul made a show of looking at his watch. "I have a few minutes before my next appointment. Let's step into one of the conference rooms." He led the way to a small rectangle in the back with a table and four chairs, windows looking over the water.

Dragan took the chair closest to the door, to intervene in case Paul tried to leave. Paul sat opposite, his back to the water, and glared at Dragan, trying to appear calm and disinterested.

"So, let me tell you what I know," started Dragan. "You've been working with Ben Petroski for some time, laundering the money he was making from his various cybercrime activities."

"No, that is absolutely..."

"Stop, you left a paper trail. I'm told you're sloppy. Can we agree you've been cleaning cash for them for years?"

Paul stared out through the glass of the room, down the hall to the front of the building. His nod was imperceptible.

"Good, we're getting somewhere," said Dragan. "Some time ago Ben and Nina came through here on holiday, and also to do some business. Around that time there was a small street war going on between motorcycle gangs and somehow you and they and Lily and her brother saw an opportunity in the regional street drug trade. I assume you put that deal together."

Paul slowly shook his head, denying it, but Dragan could see it was more of a stall tactic than a statement; Paul was thinking things through. "No," he said eventually, "it wasn't me. It was Lily."

"Oh really? You expect me to believe a waitress and occasional actress put together the plan for a multi-million drug deal?"

"She had the idea. She's clever. Viggo was talking about the situation, and she thought something could happen if there was capital. Then Ben and Nina showed up. The four of them developed the plan together."

"Not you? You weren't involved?"

"They didn't need me."

Dragan squinted and pursed his lips, folded his hands and leaned forward on the table. "Paul, you're the finance guy. You know how these deals are put together, and you know how to hide the profits. You're better at that than Ben is, which is why he needed your help in the first place. Now you're claiming you were completely shut out of a deal where you could have added so much value?"

"Viggo doesn't like me, and after Lily and I broke it off he had no reason to tolerate me being around. I guess Ben and Nina had to agree to cut me out if they wanted in on the deal, and the money was worth more than our friendship."

Dragan stared at him. He asked, "What's Viggo's gripe about you, anyway? I assume it has something to do with you and Lily?"

Paul rubbed his forehead. "He's protective of her. Technically they're married."

"How did you get involved?"

"Viggo was in prison. That's when Lily and I started up. He was still there when we were in Paris with you on that job. When he came out he saw Lily and I were a thing. He was angry, I guess, but not very. That was a relief, I thought he would break me in half, but Lily said no, he's not going to do anything, and she was right. There were a few threats, but nothing ever happened to me. With them, I'm not sure. Neither of them talked about it but sometimes I would see bruises on her, and sometimes the bruises were on him."

"Sounds like they have an intense relationship."

"Who knows what goes on between people, right? Anyway, Viggo got sent away again for a short time, around six months. That's when everything changed. He was convicted over something stupid and I'm pretty sure he thought either Lily or I set him up. Probably still thinks that. Also, at that time Lily broke up with me, and she took a turn into political activism; you saw some of that when you talked with her. That definitely made Viggo mad, and I know he blamed me for letting her get like that. As if I could stop it."

"More than just reading essays online and talking big?"

"She started associating with a Marxist playwright, a creepy little guy named Fedde, and they got involved in things. Actions she called them. Small stuff, vandalism and the like. She would call me in the middle of the night, talking on and on about how she had been chosen to make a difference in the world, about conspiracies, secret pacts in the EU. For a while she droned on about how the Freemasons were tied up with the spread of COVID, that the Freemasons really run Denmark. She wasn't the same, something happened to her. It was like she was sliding away, mentally. I was glad we broke up. Keeping her on the right side of sanity was becoming a chore. That's Viggo's job now."

"I don't know, I don't think anyone has that job. You really think she's mentally ill?"

"Not all the time. But the more you're around her, you'll see what I mean."

"So the money Ben and Nina are supposed to have stolen from her, it was money from this drug deal?"

"Yeah, I suppose. I wasn't involved."

"She crazy enough to have Ben and Nina killed over it?"

"Ninety-five percent of the time, no. That last five percent, could be."

Dragan pulled out his phone, opened his photos. "There's something they found when they burrowed into the Petroski's life after the murders. This house." He showed Paul a street camera view from the internet of Ivan Bortnik's house in Arlington. "Do you recognize it?"

Paul stared at the photo. He shook his head. "No. Is it in America?"

"It's near Washington D.C. I'll text you the photo, it has the address on it."

Paul's phone chimed when he received the image, and he eagerly stared at it.

"Did Benedikt or Nina mention anything about an additional house?"

Paul Koslov's eyes were bright with excitement. "They never said anything about it."

"It was a fairly recent purchase anyway. The odd thing is the location, in a suburb of the capital. It isn't a vacation home, no one would take a holiday there. It's not close to business. It looks like a safe house. More like a secret house."

"A secret house?" Paul asked, without looking up from the photo.

"To hide people. Or things." Dragan put his phone away. He was worried he was overplaying it, but Paul was captivated. "It's unusual for people in their position to do something like this. Against protocol.

It would concern the higher-ups, not as if that would stop Ben from doing anything."

"A mystery," said Paul. Then, hopeful, "Are we done here?"

"Yeah, I guess we are. I think what got Ben and Nina killed had something to do with the drug thing, but it turns out you didn't have anything to do with that. Which I'm glad about, to be honest, I would hate to take action against you."

"I wouldn't like that either." Paul smiled agreeably as Dragan stood. "Good luck."

"Thank you." Dragan pointed to the phone still in Paul's hand. "You have the picture and the address, so if anything turns up, or you remember something about it, you'll let me know?"

He headed to the door, then turned.

"One final thing," said Dragan. "I know you're lying to me. I think you're in the middle of that drug deal, and I think you either had the Petroskis killed or you know who did it. I'm going to follow the threads, and I'm going to work it out. You've already done enough to get in trouble with Moscow, and they're going to hear about what you've been up to. They can find out your connection to the murders by talking with you in a back room in the woods somewhere. You should consider telling it all to me, rather than wait for them to come."

Dragan walked out of there hoping his little performance would cause something to happen in response. He was both amused and appalled at the willingness of those three to throw each other under the bus and attempt to make themselves out to be little more than bystanders. If he could get them to take some kind of foolish action, especially if they turn on each other in the process, he might be able to step in and find the truth.

While he was certain that Paul Koslov was at least partially responsible for Nina's death, there were still holes and dangling ends in this story that bothered him. Paul's claim to be entirely cut out of the drug trafficking financing didn't seem plausible. On the other hand, it was true that Ben and Nina started looking for alternative ways to launder money while they were in Copenhagen, so a rift of some kind had opened between them. And then there were the murders in Philadelphia; motive remained elusive, as well as the method for someone in Denmark to connect with a hoodlum in South Philadelphia. What Dragan needed was a new piece of significant information, some trail to follow, that connected more of the dots. But where was he going to find it?

45

MESSAGE

Viggo, Anton, and Lily sat in her apartment. Lilly's phone sat on the low table in the sitting area, with Paul's agitated voice coming out of the speaker.

"Dragan knows about the drug financing thing," Paul said, loud and excited. "I don't know how."

"He's just guessing," said Lily.

"The guy knows too much, or guesses too good," said Viggo. "He's motivated."

"This is not what we want," said Anton.

"Why is he looking at that instead of the murders?" asked Viggo.

"He thinks they're connected," said Paul. "Don't be surprised if he burrows deep into the drug thing."

"What did you tell him?" asked Lily.

"Nothing!" said Paul. "What could I say? Also, he told me about a secret house the Petroskis owned."

That got everyone's attention. Lily asked, "What do you mean a secret house?"

"Some small place outside Washington. He said no one was aware they owned it."

"So what? Why is that important?"

"In our work, hiding something like that is a big deal, it's not done, not protocol," said Paul. "Like my place out west on the coast, I had to tell them. If I hid that and they found out about it they'd come by and ask me what I was doing with a secret house, what was I using it for? Who was I meeting there? They wouldn't ask me nice either."

"So why are you excited about a house in Washington?"

"Could be all sorts of things in there."

Lily was getting it now. Her voice rose and her nostrils flared. "Well they know about the house, so we're out of luck. Whatever is there they already found it."

"No, no, listen," said Paul. "Property rights and estates get complicated in America. It will take them a long time to deal with the house, to work through the legal stuff. Whatever is there is waiting for us."

"Your Russian security people will have gone over it already," said Viggo, waving his hand in dismissal. "They would have taken anything good."

"They don't have any reason to look for something," said Paul, "and even if they did, they wouldn't know what to look for."

"Send it to me," asked Lily. Paul protested, reluctant to share. She barked at him for a few minutes until her phone pinged with the image and address. "Don't share with V" said the text in the message. She immediately forwarded it all to Viggo.

"We'll talk soon," said Lily, as she disconnected the call.

"I don't like Dragan anymore," said Viggo. "He's not fun. He's trouble. As long as he was looking into the murders it was no problem, he would find nothing and go home. But now he's reaching into our business and that's bad."

"I always said he was trouble," said Anton.

"He'll leave on his own," said Lily. "But I need the photo first."

"He won't leave," said Viggo. "And he won't give you the photo."

"Let me try some more."

"No," said Viggo. He turned to Anton and said, "We need to send a message."

Anton nodded.

"Don't do it yourself, he saw you," Viggo told him. "Have a couple of guys who know how to be cautious. We need a light touch. We want it to hurt but we don't want to put him in the hospital, bringing the police. We don't want the authorities fishing him out of the canal either. A simple message delivered with emphasis, right?"

"We need him to go home, forget about things here," said Anton.

"Right."

"What about the photo?" asked an increasingly agitated Lily. "What about my money?"

"Line up a couple of guys today," said Viggo, ignoring her. "Get ready."

"I got it," said Anton.

"Fuck you, Viggo," screamed Lily. She threw her glass of akvavit at him, the glass bouncing harmlessly off the couch cushion, the liquid flying across the apartment.

46

— · —

Dilettante

Christina's lover on the police force turned up quite a bit more on Lucas Oliver Madsen than Dragan anticipated.

"My friend says the file on Madsen is surprisingly thick for someone they have never arrested," she said in a late afternoon phone call. "He's a history professor in Roskilde like you said. It turns out he has a hobby, dealing drugs on the side, often to his students. He'll get caught at that by local authorities eventually and fired, but right now he's walking the line and getting away with it. He's small-time but seems to know people. Copenhagen police leave him alone but keep an eye on him because he leads them to other, more important targets."

"So he is crooked."

"Yes, but peripheral. Not a serious player. He's been involved in some suspect construction deals too. His money he inherited when his parents passed. He has middle-class respectability and knows what fork to use, and gets thrills by hanging out with the criminal element. There's nothing in the file about any activities with Paul Koslov, but when I told my friend about those businesses you found she said it sounded like front operations to her."

"Thank you."

"You're welcome. I hope this is our last conversation. Now I'm even more concerned about being associated with Koslov, with you, with all of this."

"I'll try not to dirty your sidewalk. By the way, someone's been following me in town. Young man, lean, wears a watch cap over long blonde hair. Does that sound at all familiar to you?"

Dragan thought he heard a small intake of breath on the other end of the call, but perhaps he imagined it. Christina was quiet, until she said, "No, it doesn't."

47

BIG NOSE

Dragan headed west on foot, to dinner at a recommended place on Laksegade less than six blocks away. The brief, light rain earlier in the day left a fog on the city. The cobblestones on the side streets were slick, and people at a distance were little more than smudges at the edge of vision. He raised his collar against the chill.

He thought about Christina. He liked the way she looked, and he even found her independent, slightly contentious personality attractive, like one might with a pretty but mischievous cat. But she didn't seem to like him at all, and he wasn't sure how to handle it. Let it go? Wear her down through the force of whatever charm he might still have? The problem was he needed someone like her, someone who grasped things about Danish culture that he couldn't get from anyone else. It would be good if he could get her to relax a little and work with him more.

He picked up the tail two blocks into the trip. It wasn't the tall young man with long blonde hair. To make sure, Dragan took a couple unnecessary detours and the tail followed him. Dragan stopped to look into the window of a hat store and was able to get a good view of the man in the reflection: short, with red hair and a long beard tied at the end, just as Viggo described him. The tail didn't seem to care if he was spotted or not, and he didn't look interested in making an approach. There was really nothing for Dragan to do but proceed on to dinner.

The restaurant was outfitted in black, pewter, and off-white. He started with a glass of French pinot noir and focaccia while he checked his texts. One was from Julianna wondering how things were going. Dragan smiled and texted back that he was still poking around in the cave with a long stick to see what came out. He had beef carpaccio, pickled red onion and mild cheese, then chicken marinated in lime and roasted with rosemary. He ended with berries in cream and an espresso.

It was the first good dinner in a pleasant atmosphere he had enjoyed in days, and he was grateful for the quiet and solitude. He needed the time to think about next steps. Other than professor Madsen in Roskilde, which might be an interesting conversation but lead nowhere, he felt he was coming to a dead end just as time was running out. If something didn't emerge out of that Copenhagen fog to spur him forward he might be facing failure.

When he left the restaurant, it was dark with fewer people on the street. The fog had lifted but it was lightly raining again, so lightly it was more mist than rain, enough to give everything a sheen. He turned down towards the Havnegade; the wider area along the canal would make it easier to watch for a tail, and he considered confronting the man if he reappeared. Two motorcyclists passed him and drove on ahead, one of them with blue streaks in his dark curly ponytail and this grabbed Dragan's attention. It wasn't likely to have anything to do with him – not every motorcycle was a threat – but he was looking out for trouble. He reached the Havnegade and turned toward his hotel, walking along the pedestrian path by the water. He was on alert; the switchblade was a weight in his pocket, eager to be used.

The men made their move as he walked near the caged-in basketball court. It was a good choice on their part. The court fencing and nearby trees blocked the view from the street and the buildings. The men were able to wait for him around the corner of the court, where they were half-hidden by the fence, their dark clothing merging into the shadows of the trees. They stepped out and stood in his way. One man was dark-skinned, thin and wiry, with the long black curly hair streaked with a vibrant blue Dragan noticed earlier. He held a large wrench. The other was pale with a lazy eye and a nose a couple of sizes too big for his face, stuffed into a tracksuit a half-size too small. A couple of misfits doing an errand, thought Dragan. He wondered how this was going to go. He wondered where they had put their motorcycles.

Too late he remembered the man who followed him to the restaurant was on foot. He didn't hear him come quickly behind him and didn't expect the sucker punch in his lower back, or his legs kicked out from under him. He had a glimpse of the shaggy red hair and tied-off beard as he slid down. The men were on him in a second. He was pulled to his feet and his arms pinned behind him. The one with the big nose stepped forward and did the heavy work. He was professional about it. He hit Dragan in soft areas where it would hurt but nothing would be broken, and never hard enough to rupture an organ. The men didn't ask for money, they said nothing at all. They were careful not to seriously harm him, they were trying to scare him, and through his pain Dragan considered what advantages that gave him as he struggled to get free.

They paused. The one with the big nose slapped Dragan twice in the face, got close enough so Dragan could smell cabbage and herring on his breath, and said in heavily accented English, "You are harassing our friends. They need their privacy, same as you. You need to leave Copenhagen. You need to go home. You invade their privacy some more, we come back and invade your privacy, like now. More of the same. You bother our friends again, we notice you around, it will be a lot worse." He punched Dragan again under the rib cage, with extra force, knocking the wind out of him.

Dragan doubled over and turned away and vomited his expensive dinner on the pants and shoes of the man holding him. The man cursed and stepped back, loosening his grip. Dragan twisted free, turned, and shoved the base of his hand directly into the middle of the face of cabbage-breath and the huge nose cracked. He kicked the man between the legs, doubling him over in pain. The man with the red hair shoved him to the side and Dragan stumbled and fell near the edge of the canal. The wiry man with the blue-streaked ponytail took a few steps towards him, the wrench held back, ready to strike. Dragan struggled to get his legs under him, to rise up, and reached his hand into his pocket to grip the handle of his automatic knife.

A shout came from the path along the canal. The three thugs turned to look, and Dragan caught a glimpse of the lean young man with the long blonde hair under a watch cap, shouting at the bikers in Danish. The short man with the tied-off beard ran away to the southwest.

Dragan pulled out his hand and the knife was in it, opening with a satisfying click. He drove the blade deep into the wiry man's calf and pulled it out again. The man howled and flung himself back. He cursed and threw the wrench at Dragan's head. Dragan flinched and it hit high on his left arm, causing an explosion of pain. Deflected, the spanner bounced off the walkway and tumbled into the canal with a small splash.

The wiry man limped away. The man in the tracksuit, holding his broken nose, looked over his shoulder at Dragan and said in English, "We'll meet again, motherfucker." Motorcycles started and drove off into the night.

The young blonde man who scared them off had disappeared. Dragan pulled out his phone and dialed a number. "I'm hurt and need your help," he told the person on the other end. "On Havnegade by the caged basketball court. No, no police. Take a cab. Pull up to the curb, I'll come over to where you are." He hung up, and proceeded to vomit again, into the canal.

48

—— ∘ ——

KABOOM

When Christina showed up with the cab Dragan came out of the shadows of a building doorway, hunched over, holding his side. She helped him into the back.

"Are you bleeding?" she asked.

He shook his head no.

"Internally, the look of you," she said. "Were you robbed?"

"No. I fell." He glanced meaningfully toward the driver, and the two of them remained silent the five kilometers drive to the west, until they came to her apartment building.

"Nice neighborhood," said Dragan.

"It is Frederiksberg."

"Are we still in Copenhagen?" he asked.

"Yes and no," she said, getting out of the taxi. She didn't explain further.

She helped him into her building. She was quiet and composed on the elevator and didn't so much as glance at him. In her bathroom he carefully peeled off his clothing. He inspected himself in the mirror; he would have bruises, including on his face, and he would hurt for a few days. But no ribs appeared cracked, he didn't have a black eye, and when he urinated no blood came out. He took a long, hot shower, and when he emerged Christina directed him to her spare bedroom where she had a bed and a desk and storage boxes. She had provided a blanket and pillow. When he thanked her, she nodded slightly, turned and disappeared into her own room. Her anger and contempt left him feeling more isolated and alone than if he had been in the apartment by himself.

There was plenty of regret and self-pity for him to mull over, lying there in pain. He had done nothing but make mistakes. He no longer recognized who Nina actually was. He was careless, and had foolishly treated Paul, Lily, and Viggo with condescension; not an error he could repeat if he wanted to remain alive. Christina neither liked nor trusted him and he had no idea how to improve that relationship. He berated himself until the haze of exhaustion enveloped him, and his eyes closed.

He was soundly asleep when, hours later, Christina glided silently into the room to check on him. He had been shouting during a dream, and it woke her. She sat on the desk chair and watched him for a few minutes, to make sure he was okay.

***

That night, at approximately forty-five minutes past one in the morning, the street person who called himself Baldur took a surprisingly heavy backpack over to the editorial offices of the daily newspaper *Demokraten*, within two blocks of the formal gardens of Kongens Have, and five blocks from the Amalienborg, the home of the Danish royal family. He didn't know what was inside and he didn't ask the tall pretty woman and her odd little friend who had given it to him. Baldur left the backpack by the *Demokraten* front entrance, as instructed, and walked away, a wad of money and a cigarette pack full of marijuana joints in one pocket, a bottle of vodka in another.

About fifteen minutes later all the windows in the front of the *Demokraten* offices were blown out, along with the windows of two cars parked nearby. The surfaces of the lobby walls were shredded by the nails and screws that had filled the backpack, and the reception desk was destroyed. The night security guard had, by fortunate co-incidence, stepped to the rear of the building to use the men's room, thus avoiding injury or death. Questioned later he had no memory of anyone leaving a backpack near the front.

"People walk by all night," said the guard. "I don't remember any of them."

The authorities discussed with the media how the attack could be connected to *Demokraten* editorials of recent months. The spokesperson for the corporate owners of the newspaper back in Ger-many vowed to work with investigators to hold those responsible to account, and to "remain unbowed in our pursuit of journalistic truth in these troubled times."

49

LAST FAVOR

D ragan pulled himself out of bed, grunted in pain, and held his sides. He was wrapped in a throbbing ache. Waiting for him on the chair was a remarkably ugly tracksuit jacket in chocolate, sand, and olive. There were no matching pants, in their place was a pair of plain black sweats. They fit him well enough, though the sleeves and pants were short. He found Christina dressed in the kitchen, drinking tea and eating a scone.

"You're here," he said.

"Yes, I live here."

"I thought you would be at work."

"I couldn't leave you without knowing you would be alright. I took the day off."

"Kind of you." He held out his hands to model the clothes, to show the sleeves were inches too short, but the movement pained him and he winced. "Thank you for the fresh outfit."

"How are you?"

"Not great. Do you have coffee? And painkillers?"

She stood, pointed to a chair where she wanted him to sit. From her bedroom she brought several pills.

"These are not strong, just normal ones from the chemist's," she said. "It's all I have." She stood at the kitchen counter and made coffee in a French press. "How many were there?"

"Three. Bikers. Viggo sent them."

"Well now you know you're getting close. How did you win against three men? You some kind of superhero?"

"I didn't. I made it hard for them, but that would have only lasted so long. I pushed it so they would either have to leave, or kill me. I figured they didn't want to kill me or they would have done it right away."

"Not a smart tactic to test them, I think."

"Probably not. Best I could do at the time. Someone else came by and scared them off."

"That was fortunate."

"It was the blonde man I told you about, the one who's been following me."

She turned and looked at him. He saw in her expression both confusion, and curiosity. "At least you know he doesn't mean you harm."

"He didn't let them kill me, which is not the same thing." He gratefully accepted the coffee, wincing as he lifted it to his lips. "I need to find a new hotel," he said, reaching for his phone. "They know where I've been staying. Is there a good one near here?"

"There's the Grøn Engel, I hear it's nice. Three blocks." She pointed southwest. "Not modern, though."

"It will do, I'm sure." He called the hotel.

"I don't think you should get back out there," she told him. "You need to rest." She still seemed more angry than sympathetic.

He made arrangements with the hotel. He turned to her and said, "I can't rest. I don't have a lot of time."

"You didn't say anything about a deadline."

"At some point some wealthy people will overrun things, create a scenario that works for them. Some evidence will have to be concocted, some sworn testimony fabricated. I'll disappear in prison."

"That can be done," she agreed, frowning. She considered the implications. "What would it mean for me, now I'm helping you?"

"I don't know. Nothing, I hope."

"That's not good enough. You need to leave."

"Before I do that I have one final favor." He held out his hotel room key. "They're almost certainly watching the hotel where I've been staying."

"Why would you think they're watching the hotel? They already beat you."

"I did some damage to them, too. They're probably angry about it. Can you go to the Hotel Frederik in the Gammelholm district? I'll phone ahead to tell them I'm checking out; I'll explain I'm stuck out of town and a business colleague is getting my things. Go to my room, pack the bags – I only brought a few things, most still in the suitcase – drop off the key at the front desk and bring my bags over to the Grøn Engel where I'll get them when I check in."

"I know the Hotel Frederik." She barely looked at him as she took the room key from his hand. "I've cleaned your clothes as best I could. They're in the wardrobe. You'll probably want to throw a couple of things away."

She left him sitting in a quiet room so much emptier with her gone, her anger still hanging in the air.

***

The driver pulled the taxi to the curb near the entrance of the hotel, and Christina asked him to wait. When she stepped onto the sidewalk, she saw a man lingering nearby, watching her. He was wearing a blue tracksuit with the Gucci logo printed all over it, a cheap and illegal knock-off. A bandage straddled his large nose between two soulless black eyes. A little farther up the block two Chinese men leaned against a beat-up white panel van. They were watching her as well. None of the three looked like they belonged.

She entered the hotel and talked to the clerk, who was expecting her. Up in Dragan's room she was relieved it was so neat and organized, and he was true to his word that nearly all of his clothes were still packed in the small suitcase and duffle. She gathered his toiletries and his electronics, shoved the few remaining things into the duffle, and wheeled the stacked luggage down the hall.

As she waited for the elevator, she had a moment of anxiety that the three men from outside had followed her and would be waiting when the doors opened. It nearly panicked her, and she was relieved when she saw the elevator was empty. It cemented her conviction that her thoughts, words, and actions regarding Dragan and his mission were the correct ones. She needed to look out for herself, because no one else would.

She finished checking him out, and with the cabbie's help got Dragan's luggage into the taxi. As the driver was adjusting things in the trunk, one of the Asian men, with long hair in a ponytail, approached her slowly.

"Those your suitcases?" Jin Chen asked.

"Yes," she said without looking at him.

"Looks like a man's suitcases," he said, stepping closer.

She kept her face away from him, toward the taxi, and silently wished the cabbie would hurry. The other Asian man had come up and the two of them were speaking Cantonese to each other, in a mild disagreement. She sensed movement behind her and glanced over her shoulder to see the man with the broken nose and black eyes lift himself away from the wall and drift over.

The man in the ponytail had come to some kind of decision and turned to Christina. "Hey," he said. "Hey lady."

The cab driver didn't like the way this looked. He closed the trunk and walked around, putting himself between Christina and Jin Chen. A couple walking up the sidewalk to the hotel entrance stopped and stared a few feet away. The man with the broken nose stepped back against the wall, and Jin was pulled away by his brother. The driver opened the back door of the taxi and Christina quickly got in, locking the door.

With a last glare at the Chen brothers the cabbie got behind the wheel and pulled away from the curb into a sluggish line of cars. Christina looked back at the hotel. The man with the broken nose and the two Asian men were standing together in the spot by the curb where the cab had just been, watching her. They didn't follow, but she could tell they were thinking about it.

50

⸺ ✦ ⸺

Playing Hero

Christina returned to her apartment with soup, fresh crusty bread and Fontina cheese. Dragan, back in his own clothes, stood awkwardly when she entered.

"Your bags are at the Grøn Engel, waiting for you," she said. She held up the bag. "And I got takeaway."

The two of them wordlessly set the table, then sat and ate.

"Thank you," said Dragan, breaking off a piece of bread. "Especially for the food."

"We would both be hungry." Her tone was cold and angry. Dragan had been concerned about how he might improve his relationship with her, but had only driven her further away.

He asked, "Were they watching the hotel?"

"Yes." She told him about the man with the broken nose, and about the two Asian men with the white van.

"I didn't mean to put you in any danger."

"It was okay." She did not say this like she meant it.

"You must have been afraid."

"A little. It turned out alright."

She was not going to talk about it. They ate.

"Do you know who they were?" she asked eventually.

"The two Asian men are brothers, they seem to answer to Viggo," he said. "The other one sounds like one of those that attacked me. All part of the same gang, I assume."

She cut a slice of cheese and asked, "Did you break that man's nose?"

"Yes."

"And the blood on your pants was not yours?"

"No. The vomit was, though."

She frowned, and did not look at him when she said, "I still think you're not ready to go back out there."

"You may be right. Those men were sent to convince me to leave, eventually to kill me if I refuse." He watched her.

For the first time since she returned, she looked directly at him. Her eyes gleamed with anger. "You should leave," she said. "I've told you I didn't want to be involved, and now look what you've got me doing. Those men saw me."

"I'm sorry about that. It's not how I wanted it to be. I was hoping we could fix things between us. More than colleagues. Friends."

"You wanted to become my lover. I could tell from that first day."

"I won't argue that one way or another. It doesn't matter now. I just want you to know I feel bad about how this played out."

"It's not only about me. This is going badly for you. If last night was a warning, then next time it won't be. These gangs are dangerous. When I said you should leave, I mean leave the country. Go back to America."

Dragan ran his hand through his hair. "I coordinate some of the agents in the United States, and the Petroskis were my people. When your agents are murdered, you're supposed to take some kind of action. That I was having an affair with the woman just makes the need as personal as it is professional. It doesn't make any difference if they were involved in criminal activity, if they weren't nice people, that they lied and used me. Something still needs to be done about it."

"Not by you, though."

"It has to be done by me because I failed them. Yes, they lied to me and kept me at a distance. Nina breaking off the affair, I realize now, might have been to push me out of the way while they ran the scam that got them killed. But that doesn't matter. I was asleep at the wheel."

"Brilliant. You're playing the hero."

"I can't stop in any case, because of that young man with the blonde hair. He was probably sent by Ben Petroski's father. If they don't arrest me for the murders, that kid, or someone just like him, is likely going to kill me. They won't care if I'm here investigating or back in America eating lunch at a café, so I might as well be here. The only way out of this mess is to find out who killed the Petroskis, and why, and broadcast that information throughout the system before that kid steps out of the shadows somewhere."

He stood up, started cleaning up the remains of their lunch.

"Are you going to the Grøn Engel?" she asked.

"Yes."

"Don't come back," she said in a voice without inflection. "And don't call again. That was a nice little speech, but it only told me things will continue to become worse."

"I'll leave you out of it."

"I thought I made it clear, this sort of thing is not what I do. I'm a researcher and an analyst. Dragging you off the street bloody and disgusting, and parading you around for my neighbors and colleagues, is not what I signed up for. The police finding your dead body with my phone number in your pocket is not what I signed up for. You tell me you have a job to do, I understand that. But you can't drag me into your drama any longer, not like this."

"It wasn't my intention..."

"I don't care. If you go down in all this, you'll take me with you, I know it. They'll recall me. They always need people to blame. My mother is dead, I don't know where my father is, I have nobody back there. I'll be a half-black Russian woman yanked from an assignment because of failure, and they'll add corruption and theft on top of it if it suits them. What will my prospects be then, do you think? What will your intentions be to me then?"

He nodded. He finished cleaning up in silence and left, assuming he would never see her again.

51

GOING HOME

At his new hotel, still sore, Dragan lay on the bed, full of ibuprofen, ice packs on his ribs, drinking vodka. An old American western movie played on the television, dubbed in German. He phoned Paul Koslov.

"That's it, I'm done here," he told Paul. "Viggo had several of his biker thugs attack me by the canal, nearly killed me. This assignment isn't worth that. I'm going home."

Paul was silent at the other end. He was clearly surprised by the news. "They attacked you? Physically?"

"That's what attacked means, yes."

"Jesus. Are you okay?"

"Not really, but I'll get better. They did it to send a message, and I heard it. I got the message. I just want to tell you I'm leaving Denmark. I'm on the first plane to the United States tomorrow morning."

52

WAIL IN THE MIST

Paul Koslov stood in the middle of the living room in Lily Sandersen's apartment, glaring at her. She was in her underwear, without her usual makeup, looking drawn and tired, sprawled on her couch and staring up at the ceiling. Her hair was unbrushed, the soles of her bare feet dirty from the dusty floor. The apartment smelled of cannabis. Viggo was in the dining area, in front of the large painting of the policemen making an arrest, a tall glass of beer in front of him.

"What did you think you were doing?" Paul demanded. His eyes moved from Viggo, to Lily, and back.

"Taking care of it," said Viggo.

"By beating up Dragan Pavelovich Markov?" asked Paul. "Seriously? You think that's taking care of it?"

"Yes, we do," said Lily, in a sing-song lilt. Under the influence of the weed she appeared calm, to the point of boredom. "He left his hotel, we checked. He's frightened. He's on his way home."

"Jesus! Fuck me in the ear!" said Paul, pointing across the room at Viggo while still talking to Lily. "I told you to keep Viggo away from him!"

"We told you we would handle it," said Viggo. "And he ran away, like a baby, like we said he would."

"I'm not so sure," said Paul. "It was too easy."

Lily frowned. "You said he was hurt and afraid."

"According to him. I don't know how much of that was real. He's tougher than that."

"Hah," said Viggo. "He works for the same organization as you do. You're not tough."

"He's not like me. I was taught to handle money and audit books. They taught him to be a killer."

"What do you mean?" asked Lily. "A sport player is not like a tough guy!"

Viggo said, with a sneer, "Nina told me he was still like a boy who didn't know what he wanted to be when he grew up."

"I don't know how much I would believe of what Nina said," said Paul. He took a breath and started over. "Dragan and I worked together on that thing in Paris. Before he got here for it, I got a phone call from a friend of someone I know. It was just a heads up, telling me the reason Dragan wasn't an active agent any longer was that he killed someone back in America, some local guy who raped a girl. That's not the way Dragan tells the story, but it was a disaster, apparently. They barely got him out of there. The person who called me said the only reason they got away with it was they were able to bribe enough key people. I was supposed to be careful around him."

Lily pointed at Paul, twirling her finger in a tight circle. "That's why you always acted afraid of him."

"Well, yeah. And the way I heard it, he took down two of the gangsters that killed Benedikt and Nina Petroski. By himself. He's fucking dangerous, Viggo. You're playing with fire, is what I'm saying."

"But he's already on a plane back to America," Lily said with less confidence than before.

"He's been talking with Christina Koumba," said Paul. "I can check with her."

"Who is that?" asked Viggo.

"Pretty black woman with the nice clothes," said Lily. "Russian black woman."

"She's a colleague," Paul told Viggo.

"I don't like her," said Lily. "Full of herself. We need to go after her."

Horrified by her suggestion, Paul asked, "Why?"

"Dragan was with that bitch Nina," Lily explained, as if to a slow child. "I think he knows where our money is, because Nina told him. If he's with that Koumba woman he told her."

"Why would he do that?" asked Paul.

"There's no money anyway," said Viggo. "This is all ridiculous."

"Oh man." The exasperation in Paul's voice was like a wail in the mist. "Leave the Koumba woman alone. She's not 'with Dragan' whatever exactly you mean by that. Don't drag her into this. Forget I said anything."

"After I find out where my money is," said Lily, so quietly Paul barely heard her.

"No," said Paul. "I'm telling you, leave her alone."

She looked at the ceiling, thinking it through. "Now that Viggo scared Dragan away, she's the only connection left."

"I don't know if I can trust you," said Paul, which caused Viggo to raise his eyebrows and pay closer attention.

Lily propped herself up on her elbows to shout at Paul. "Trust me about what?"

Paul bit his lower lip and rocked from side to side. "I think you're a little out of control, that's all."

"Why is she out of control?" asked Viggo. The room became a little chillier.

"It doesn't matter," said Paul, with a small wave of his hand.

"It does matter," said Viggo.

Paul said, "Ask her." He pursed his lips and pointed them at Lily.

"I'm asking you." Viggo stared at Paul, challenging.

"She was the one blew up the newspaper office."

"You did?" asked Viggo, looking at Lily.

Lily fell back on the couch and folded her arms. "I did not blow up a newspaper office."

"You had it done," said Paul. "You told me you had it done."

"Bombs are what you do with the money I give you?" asked Viggo.

"The two of you are out of your minds," said Paul, but they weren't paying attention to him.

Viggo looked at Lily, shaking his head in disapproval. "Not a good idea."

"It was a horrific idea," said Paul.

"It had to be done," said Lily. "One small action after another."

"Oh my god," said Paul, putting his face in his hands. "Where is this going?"

"Stop complaining, I didn't bomb your apartment building," said Lily, "But if you keep harping on this I might have to."

Viggo shook his head in dismay. "Lily…"

"You need to control her," Paul said to Viggo. "I'm serious."

"Good job today everyone!" exclaimed Lily. "Thank you for stopping by Paul."

Paul realized he was being dismissed. He wasn't sure what to do. He looked from Lily to Viggo, and back again. He didn't want to leave.

"You should go home, rest, and think about how we're going to get information from that black Russian woman," she said. "These are your people, remember? Please, go home and start working on a plan."

Paul glanced fleetingly at Viggo and left.

When he heard the front door to the street close, Viggo turned to Lily and said, "He's going to turn on you one of these days."

"No he won't," she said. "He'll think about it. He'll think about a lot of things. But in the end he'll do nothing, which is the kind of person he is. People don't change who they are."

"He's right about leaving that woman alone. There's no money from that deal, and if there was, she wouldn't know about it. Nina and Ben emptied those accounts, I'm sure of it."

"Then what was Paul talking about that house in America for?"

"He probably thinks they have a lot of money and things hidden there."

"You mean my money? You just said…"

"A lot of other people's money, from other schemes. They were thieves." Viggo shrugged. "This bombing, are you hanging around with that Fedde again?"

"I have my own friends, my own hobbies."

Viggo snorted. "Hobbies? Is that what you're calling it? Fedde has to go. He's a bad influence. He's got you obsessing about politics all the time."

"Politics?" Her face became tight, like a fist. "I don't talk about politics. I talk about making things right. Fedde understands that. Leave him alone."

"Okay whatever," said Viggo. "Let's fuck."

"We should have taken more money back then," Lily said. "Then they couldn't have stolen it."

"But we all agreed not to, so we didn't attract attention. It seemed like the smart thing at the time."

"Not so smart, I'm thinking now," she said, her eyes tearing up in frustration.

"We thought Paul's friends couldn't be crooks because they were rich. Now we know that's probably how they got rich, by being crooks. We made the best choices we could at the time, babe."

"There might be more money in that house," she said, drifting back to that topic. "You said so yourself."

"Even if there is, there might not be any way for us to get to it now. We have to be realistic. You could chase this forever and get nothing out of it. The money I go after is real, and it's here."

"You do those things because you think it's fun to almost get caught. Because you're sick up here." She flipped her hand around at the side of her head, and grimaced.

He smiled but he didn't disagree with her. He said, "We need capital for what we want to do together. You know that."

She looked at him blankly.

He said, "So let's fuck."

"Okay," she said.

53

— · —

THREAT

Christina looked out of her office window and decided she needed fresh air, and while she was at it a coffee and a rhubarb horn. The sky was low and filled with grey clouds, and it felt like it wanted to snow, although it wasn't nearly cold enough and snow in Copenhagen early in the season was rare. She walked north alongside the university towards her favorite coffee shop a block and a half away. Leaving the shop she nearly collided with a woman who stepped out in front her.

Lily said, "You're Paul's Russian lady friend."

Christina eyed the woman's tights tucked into black boots, the brocaded sleeves on the wool coat, the dark bangs. She recognized her as Paul's ex-girlfriend Lily, but this Lily was different from the woman she met at the Christianborg Palace. The hair was pulled back in a ponytail rather than hanging to the shoulder, the nose and cheeks dotted with freckles. Without makeup the eyelashes were pale, and the eyes seemed smaller and full of sadness, set in a face both fuller and flatter than Christina remembered. It was the kind of face that could be twenty-two years old, or forty-two, and it gave the impression of a woman both fragile and fatigued.

"You're Lily," Christina said.

"Yeah, we know each other."

"No, I wouldn't say we know each other."

"Well, I know you," said Lily, taking a half-step forward. "I want my money."

"What are you talking about?" It took all her strength of will to hold her ground and not flee.

"That bitch Nina stole my money, and I think your boyfriend Dragan knows where it is. He tell you about it?"

"He's not my boyfriend. Why would he know where your money is?"

"He was fucking that bitch back in America. He knows." Lily was working hard to seem threatening, but Christina held her spot and gazed directly into Lily's eyes, attempting to understand what was in there.

"What does any of this have to do with me?" asked Christina.

"You can help me find out where the money is. It's mine, it was my idea, my plan, my money. I was going to get it out of Dragan sooner or later, but now he's left Denmark. So you're going to help us."

"He's gone?"

"He didn't tell you? Doesn't matter, you can still find out from him. He likes you. He'll tell you."

"You followed me from my office, didn't you?"

Lily nodded.

Christina realized the woman wasn't so much menacing as desperate. She thought, the best way to handle this bizarre situation is to pretend it's normal, to get the woman talking and she'll reveal a way to end this so she won't come around again. She said, "Walk with me part of the way back, we can talk."

Christina started back down the sidewalk. Lily followed and walked along.

"You were with Paul Koslov when we met," said Christina. "Why don't you ask him for help?"

"He's useless," said Lily. "He's afraid."

"Afraid of what?"

"Everything as far as I can tell. Now he's afraid of Dragan. I think he's afraid of you, too."

Christina took that in and tried to digest it. "Dragan tells me you have a brother here," she said. "Can't he help you?"

Lily looked up in surprise. "He told you that?"

"Yes."

Lily smiled slightly. "My brother" – she dragged the word out to twice its length – "is telling me to stop looking for the money. He says there is no money."

"Isn't your brother in a motorcycle club?"

"They won't help if he doesn't want them to. I'm by myself in this, so I need you."

She was no longer trying to intimidate Christina but pleading with her.

"I'll see what I can do," said Christina.

"Yes," said Lily. "To protect yourself."

That brought Christina up short. There was something in Lily's tone, something vaguely menacing. So much for being kind to her and hearing her out. "To protect myself? From you I suppose?"

Lily shrugged and looked down at the street.

"Is that what you're saying?" Christina was both appalled and angry. "I should do you favors, in order to protect myself from you? Are you threatening me?"

"Have it any way you want. But I want that information."

Christina had no intention of helping her, but asked, "How do I reach you?"

"Your boyfriend knows," Lily said over her shoulder as she crossed the street.

He's not my boyfriend, thought Christina. Far from it. She felt foolish, standing there on the corner, holding coffee and pastry. This craziness had to stop, at all costs. At all costs, of course, to anyone other than herself.

54

VODKA

Dragan had a late afternoon run that took him along the Solbjerg Park Cemetery and back past the brick homes on Kronprinsevsfej. It was a crisp, cool, sunny October day, and it felt good to be out in it. He was feeling much better, with most of the soreness gone and with only the last vestiges of the bruises on his body. When he left the hotel for any reason he wore a cap and sunglasses. Not that he thought the motorcycle gang would be actively looking for him – they would stick out in the upscale, leafy streets of Frederiksberg – but there was no reason to risk an unfortunate accident of being seen by the wrong person.

He also tried as best he could to disguise that he was Russian, claiming he was Czech if it came up in any way. This was not only to prevent some member of Viggo's gang hearing about a Russian man isolating himself in a hotel, it was also to sidestep uncomfortable conversations about the war. Early in the month Russian forces abandoned a number of Ukraine locations, allowing them to be retaken, and an entire Russian brigade had been decimated. People everywhere were becoming emboldened, feeling free to ridicule Russian military competence. Dragan had no interest in talking about any of it.

When he returned to the Grøn Engel hotel, feeling both energized and pleasantly tired, he was surprised to find Christina Koumba waiting for him in the lobby. Their greetings were awkward. She wanted to speak privately, so she would be neither seen nor overheard. In the elevator she asked how the hotel was; he told her it was better than he expected. In his room he offered vodka and apologized for being a sweaty mess. She told him not to bother showering, she wouldn't be there that long, but she did accept the vodka.

"Koslov's girlfriend Lily confronted me," she told him. "She said you had left Denmark, so I came over here to see for myself. What have you gotten me into?"

"Why would she talk to you at all? What did she want?"

"Something about money, that she claims the dead woman stole from her. She's convinced you know where it is, assumes you and I are lovers and that you've told me. She gives every sign of planning to harass me for as long as it takes for me to tell her what she wants to know. I don't think she's mentally stable, and she has me worried. You've now made such a catastrophe of things that you leaving the country won't help me out of this, since she already believes you've gone."

"I'm sorry this happened."

"That is so pointless to say now. I warned you. I begged you to leave me out of this. You didn't care, and now here we are."

"I don't see how this is my fault. How does she know about you in the first place, that we're talking?"

She ignored him. "Do you have this money?"

"No, of course not."

"I'm asking for the truth."

"I'm not entirely sure what money she's talking about, other than it has to do with the scheme they were running."

She tossed back the rest of the vodka in her glass and poured herself more. She asked, "Are you going to fix this?"

"I'm trying. New things that need to be fixed keep popping up."

"Prioritize my situation, please. What are going to do now?"

"I'm feeling much better, soreness mild, movement back mostly. So tomorrow I'll take a train to Roskilde and talk to Madsen, the history professor and semi-pro drug dealer. Let's see if I can scare up information about that money Lily is talking about."

55

TREASURE HUNT

Viggo, Anton and the Chen brothers lounged in a cheap motel off the Ring Nord north of Næstved, a town of less than forty-four thousand southwest of Copenhagen on the island of Zealand. They had been up all night, smoking meth and drinking whiskey and beer. They were planning their next big project, a sneak raid on the headquarters of a rival gang, the Ulvehoved Motorcycle Club. It was located further west, near a little village called Fodby. The Chen brothers, always less impressed by Viggo's schemes than he was, were raising objections to the project.

"We got away with less than we hoped on the last one," said Viggo.

"Is that so bad?" asked Alex, the Chen with the shaved head and goatee. "I thought it was still a good amount."

"Split four ways?" said Viggo. "After throwing a chunk into gang operations?"

"I'm confused," said Jin, the long-haired Chen. "What are you complaining to us about? You were the one who set up the last one."

"Hey," said Anton. "We're all in this together, right?"

"Sure," said Alex, trying to avoid an argument. "A little risky, though, going into their headquarters. A couple of lazy truck guards is one thing. These guys won't be lazy. What's the big attraction? What's the payoff for the risk?"

Viggo smiled a big smile. He asked, "You know what a bearer bond is?"

"Yeah, from the old days," said Anton. "Whoever had it could cash it, right? No history, no questions asked."

"Basically," said Viggo, enthusiastic. "It can't be traced back to the person who bought it. If it's in your hand you can redeem it."

"That nonsense is from movies," said Jin. "I don't think they make them anymore. It's like some kind of myth you're selling us here."

"They don't issue them," agreed his brother Alex. "I thought the EU was going to ban them. And the ones still around stopped earning interest a long time ago. You brought us down here for this ridiculous shit?"

"No, I'm telling you, this fucking gang has, in their back room, a box of European bearer bonds," said Viggo. "They were originally bought by London gangsters years ago looking to avoid paying taxes. I heard someone walked off with them last year, some woman who worked at the bank."

"Heard from who?" asked Alex.

"People. It doesn't matter who I heard it from. She disappeared for like seven months. Then they turned up in Amsterdam, a fence had them, but he was afraid to do anything with them because the gangsters were on to him, and he was being watched."

"Like I said, from a fucking movie," said Jin, laughing.

Viggo ignored him. "Then there was an incident, and the fence and three gangsters got shot up, and the bonds disappeared again until my guy said they turned up here. They're in a wooden box in the back of the headquarters along with a sack of cash in multiple currencies, all there for the taking."

"Your guy says?" asked Jin.

"Yeah."

"Oddly detailed," said Jin. He turned to his brother and said, "It's a movie. He saw this in a movie. This is a joke."

"Why hasn't the gang turned the bonds in?" asked Alex.

"Because they haven't done it yet," said Anton.

"That's helpful," said Jin. "Thank you."

"Fuck off," said Anton.

"Why hasn't your guy taken them for himself?" Alex asked Viggo.

"You think it's going to be easy?" asked Viggo. "It's going to take quality pros."

"Like us?" asked Alex, rolling his eyes.

"Yeah, like us," said Anton.

"This has me concerned," said Jin, looking directly at Anton, appealing to his common sense over his loyalty to Viggo. "High risk."

"And high reward," said Anton. "Right? Sky high reward."

Both Chens were unconvinced. Viggo believed they would come around eventually, so he waited.

His story about the bearer bonds was, in fact, utter nonsense. The Chens were correct, he had pulled it all from a couple of movies. He thought dangling something like that in front of the boys would lure them into doing the raid with him. It worked with Anton, of course, but he always forgot how smart the Chens were. They were pushovers, though, and always gave in if you waited long enough. He would never admit he had no idea what was actually in that gang headquarters, though he hoped it would be enough to make it worth the effort. He was only interested in robbing it because he was bored and he found the thrill of it ridiculously exciting and arrractive. To do it he needed all three of them, however.

Alex asked, "So how are we supposed to do this?"

And there it is, thought Viggo. This will be fun.

"It can't be complicated," said Anton.

"No, it isn't," said Viggo. "The Ulvehoved club is going on a big ride out to Aabenraa starting in a few hours. While they're gone there might be a couple of guys at the headquarters, or it will be empty. Jin and Alex wait in the van nearby like before. Anton and I will go up, knock on the door. If no one answers you bring the truck over, we break in, grab the goods, and leave. If they answer the door, we check out what's happening. One or two guys, we deal with it then same as before. If there's a big party going on we'll hear it before we knock and we leave. We'll know how to be."

"Because you're professionals?" asked Alex. Viggo grinned and nodded his head.

"Yeah, okay," said Jin. "As long as we leave if we see anything we don't like. We don't need an open conflict with another gang."

The meth was giving them all a sense of confidence. The booze took the edge off the meth and relaxed them. Time continued to drift by, until they were ready to make it happen. With the Chens driving the battered white van, and Anton and Viggo on their bikes, they headed into farmland.

On a back road near Fodby the quartet came to a large cluster of maples at the edge of an industrial farming operation. A dirt road, barely noticeable from the highway, skirted the trees and wrapped behind them. The road emptied at a large clearing, in which sat a low, ugly, brick building. They stopped at the edge of the clearing to take stock. The anxious downside of the meth high was starting to sneak up on them; combined with the booze they had been drinking they were now little more than agitated, wide-awake drunks.

No cars or motorcycles were visible from their spot, and they assumed – hoped – the place was empty. They drove up a little closer and followed their plan, with the Chens waiting off to the side as Viggo and Anton got off their bikes and walked up to the front door. Anton listened, then knocked and waited. No one answered. He knocked again and listened some more. Viggo waved the Chens to come closer with the van, then frowned as a thought occurred to him.

"We should have checked to see if there's any bikes parked in the back," said Viggo.

The door was opened by a yawning, middle-aged biker wearing no shirt and no shoes. He looked at Anton, and Anton looked at him, and before anyone could say anything Anton punched the man square in the face, sending him staggering back.

"Shit," Viggo said, and he and Anton stepped into the large hall with handguns pointed.

56

UNTOUCHABLES

Viggo and Anton swept eyes and gun barrels across the room. There was a bar to the right, tables and chairs in front of them, and a few ratty couches to the left. In the far corner was an area for weight training, and near the bar was a pool table covered with stacked boxes. On the couches four bikers were sleeping off the previous night.

"Everyone up and against the bar," Anton yelled in his awkward Danish. Jin and Alex looked into the room through the doorway, didn't like what they saw, and refused to enter, stepping off to the side where they could listen. The man who answered the door walked over to the bar first, holding his nose, blood trickling through his fingers. Two of the others, barely awake, followed. The fourth biker, however, did not. He was an angry-looking man with a deep scar on the side of his face. He slowly stood and puffed up his chest.

"Who the hell are you fools?" he asked.

"The guys with the guns," said Viggo.

"Jesus," said Jin to his brother, both of them still listening from outside. "From a fucking movie."

"The Untouchables Motorcycle Club sends their greetings," shouted Alex, thinking fast. His brother nodded in approval.

Scar-face spat on the floor, picked up a brown flat cap off the couch, and put it on his head. He said, "This is bullshit," pulled a gun out of the small of his back and fired, to the surprise of everyone in the room. The bullet whistled past Anton's ear, just nicking the edge, generating a thin but enthusiastic stream of blood. Both Anton and Viggo shot back, and scar-face dropped to the floor dead. The three bikers at the bar immediately took off for the other entrance across the hall, slamming against the door to push it open as Anton and Viggo turned their guns in that direction and sent bullets flying. All three of the men made it through the door but the third stumbled as he stepped outside.

"Dammit," said Viggo.

"I think I caught that last one in the leg," said Anton. But by the time they crossed the hall and opened the far door, all three of the Ulvehoved members were on their bikes and driving away.

"Scheisse," said Anton, looking over Viggo's shoulder.

Viggo shook his head in disgust. "We don't have much time now. Get the Chens in here to help." He entered the back rooms, joined a minute later by the others, and they tore the place apart as quickly as they could. They found several handguns, a rifle, three grenades, several kilos of weed, multiple plastic bags of unidentifiable pills, three padded envelopes full of euros in twenties, fifties, and hundreds, shelves of outdated canned goods, cases of beer and plenty of liquor. But, of course, no wooden box full of bearer bonds.

"We have to get out of here," said Alex. "If one of those guys had his phone with him there's already an army on its way."

With whatever loot they could carry in a single trip, they left the building. Everything was tossed into the back of the white van.

"We need to split up and lay low until we're sure none of this is going to blow back on us," said Viggo. "Jin and Alex, stash the take in one of your spots, then bury yourself with your people. Anton, the wharf house is good for you. I can't stay at Lily's more than a night or so, there's too many who know about it, I'll have to figure out where I can disappear. We'll stay in touch. It should only be a week or two."

All four nodded in agreement.

Viggo told Alex, "Smart move, that thing about the Untouchables club. If we're lucky they'll remember and if things get ugly around here it won't have anything to do with us. Later guys." Even as he said it he knew it wasn't true; soon enough the path was going to lead right to him and Anton.

They dispersed, three separate ways, making it safely out of the Næstved area as the first furious bikers arrived at the headquarters to take stock of the damage. Viggo pulled off the road outside of Ringsted, into the parking lot of an old, small brick church. He called Lily.

"I have to lay low," he said when she answered. "Things got a little fucked up."

"Oh that's a surprise," Lily said. "What did I tell you?"

"Shut up," he told her. "That's not helping."

"You're an idiot, Viggo."

"Shut up!"

"Where are you going?"

"I don't know. But we may have to leave for a while."

There was a pause. "What do you mean 'we'?" asked Lily.

"You and me. We have to be together in this."

"What do you mean 'leave'?"

"I don't know," Viggo said. "Out of the country. Things have turned bad."

"How bad?"

"Bad. We hit another gang's headquarters and one of their guys was killed. A few more got away."

"A few more got away... Tell me they saw your faces."

"Yeah they did."

"You fucking morons." Even through the phone Lily's simmering fury was palpable.

"This is not the time for an argument. That gang's going to start talking around."

"A guy with long gray hair, a big German, and two Chinese brothers," said Lily. "Jesus, Viggo, why not write your name and address on a note and post it on the door?"

"They didn't see the Chens. They stayed back."

"The brothers were always smarter than you."

"I have to pick up a few things then get lost."

"Fine but stop saying 'we' since I'm not sure I need more of this bullshit." She hung up on him. He growled as he took off again down the road.

57

— · —

Madsen

At Copenhagen Central Station, Dragan bought a round-trip ticket to Roskilde on Danish Rail. As he traveled through the suburbs he thought of the last time he was there. It was for the Roskilde Festival, over ninety thousand people converging for music and hanging out. A few days of a good time, long ago. The person he was back then would barely recognize what he had become.

He exited the train into a crowded station, commuters heading into the city. It was early morning and the town was still waking up, cafes and bakeries busy. The plan was to take Lucas Oliver Madsen by surprise, in his home. Dragan was hoping to bridge the gap between the money they made through drug financing, and the code hidden in the photo. Because somewhere in the dotted line between the two, the money disappeared, and this led to the murder of Nina and her husband. Dragan believed Paul Koslov was key, and his sometime partner Madsen might point the way forward.

Of course, afterwards Paul will hear about the conversation, know that Dragan did not leave the country and was still on the hunt, and tell Viggo and Lily. Which worked out fine: it maintained pressure on the three of them, while his exact whereabouts remained unknown.

As he walked through town Dragan considered why he was attacked that night by the canal. Clearly, Viggo sent those thugs. But there was nothing to suggest his involvement in the murders, and he had no known motivation. It's more likely Viggo saw Dragan as a pest, not a threat; yet for some reason enough of a pest to risk a public confrontation, which was not the smart move. Perhaps Viggo was trying to protect Lily, who had repeatedly claimed to be involved with the Petroskis, and that they owed her money. Though it seemed implausible she organized the hit in Philadelphia. Was Viggo protecting Paul? Not likely; Viggo didn't like Paul, and said Paul was the one who stole the money along with the Petroskis.

It felt like a circle rotating around an empty center.

He walked through a shopping area, down a few blocks of compact houses, and into a wooded area. A dirt path curled through trees, and he emerged at the edge of a small plot of cultivated land that looked like a collection of personal gardens. It was currently occupied by crows looking for seed. The ground gently sloped, with homes at the top. Dragan knew, from checking online, that Madsen lived in the two-story brick home with a hip roof of forest green tiles.

He cautiously moved along the edge of the field, hugging the tree line, keeping an eye on the house. A man, in his fifties, in pajamas and robe, came out the back door of Madsen's house to put a sack and some bottles in the bins, then returned inside. Mindful of sight lines, Dragan came to the same back door and to his surprise it was unlocked. He entered the house to find Madsen eating toast and melon in a small breakfast nook, reading the news on a digital tablet. Madsen jumped up in surprise and backed up to the wall.

"I didn't expect you so soon," said Madsen, in English, a little too loud.

Dragan recognized it as a warning, or a call for help, to someone else in the house. He took a butcher knife from the block on the counter and positioned himself near the kitchen entrance as someone very large hurried down from the second floor, heavy steps thudding. A thick young man entered the kitchen holding a wooden club in his hand. Dragan punched the man in the throat, and as he struggled to breath Dragan plunged the knife into and out of the arm holding the club. The weapon hit the floor. Dragan shoved the man to the back of the kitchen where he crumpled next to Madsen, coughing and holding his bleeding arm. Dragan took a folded cloth napkin from a stack sitting on the counter and tossed it to Madsen.

"Wrap his arm in this so he doesn't bleed all over the floor," said Dragan. "Then sit back down."

Dragan picked up the wooden club, which was short with a thick curved handle. "What is this?"

"It's a belaying pin," said Madsen, slipping into the breakfast nook. "I have a small collection." He spoke with an even, distant tone, a little too slowly, with a little too much emphasis on consonants.

Dragan returned the knife to the block but kept the pin in his hand. The man on the floor made no move to get up. He had no more fight in him, considering how little there was to begin with.

"You knew I was coming," said Dragan. "Paul Koslov told you, I assume?"

Madsen nodded.

"He's no bodyguard," said Dragan, gesturing to the miserable young man on the floor. "I hope I didn't cut an artery. He one of your students?"

"Yes. I was told I needed protection. He was open to earn a little money. I thought his size would be a deterrent."

"It just made him loud and slow. I was going to have a nice conversation with you, but now you've made me angry."

"I'm protected," said Madsen, defiance in his tone. He was matter of fact about it all, even though his bodyguard was bleeding on the floor and a stranger stood in his kitchen threatening him.

Dragan decided Madsen was either impressively confident or quite delusional. Either way things had to move along. He was running out of time. He said, "No, you aren't protected. You're a college professor who dabbles in drug dealing on the side. You come from money, which explains this house. The dealing is just a hobby and it's not the only side hustle you have going. You partner with Koslov in various money laundering schemes. So you see, I know who you are. I know you have some information that I need, and we'll sit here until you give it to me."

Madsen stared at him, then shook his head in refusal.

Dragan narrowed his eyes. "The university won't be happy to learn about what you've been up to. You'll lose your job."

"They won't believe you. You are some mobster, an outsider. Fuck off."

Dragan grabbed Madsen's wrist, pulled his arm across the table, and smashed his pinky with the belaying pin. Madsen screamed.

"We're going to start now, understand? I'm in a hurry."

Madsen, tears in his eyes, nodded.

58

PARKING MONEY

Dragan's voice was measured, but his hand stayed clasped around the belaying pin resting on the table. "Here's what I know, Mr. Madsen," he said. "A few years ago there was a turf war involving rival motorcycle gangs. It was ugly; people got shot, some died. The police were everywhere and up everyone's ass. It affected the drug trade. Sales dropped, product was hard to get, and the other gangs took business elsewhere to avoid all the police activity. But one gang, Tinhanhem Motorcycle Club, saw an opportunity. They had connections in Asia so they were able to get product, and they had the manpower to get it into the hands of the dealers on the street. Overnight they became market leaders in eastern Denmark."

"Who are you?"

"I'm running an investigation."

"Are you Interpol?"

"No."

"Paul said you were an American gangster and that I should defend myself. You dress American but to me you smell of the Balkans."

"Are we going to talk now?"

"Are you investigating me or Paul Koslov?"

"Koslov."

"Then I'll talk. He is not my favorite person right now."

Dragan looked at the man on the floor, to make sure he was staying put and not bleeding too much, then back to Madsen. He asked, "So where did they get the capital for that major play in the drug market?"

"Not from me," said Madsen. "And not from anyone I know."

"Why not? Why pass up a great business opportunity?"

"Tinhanhem was untested at that big an operation, and if they failed, it would backfire on the money people and taint their relationship with the other clubs." Madsen had tears in his eyes as he talked, cradling his damaged hand in his lap. "The established players think long-term like any good investors. They would rather wait it out, do a deal with whoever remains standing at the end. Less risky than making an early bet on who the winner would be."

"Where did the investment come from, then?"

"They needed fresh money. A small group came forward."

"Koslov put it together?"

"Yeah. Didn't involve me, I wasn't invited."

"Who were they?"

"I never met them. I heard some of them were supposed to be Americans, like you."

"What does that mean, 'supposed to be'?"

"The story I heard was the Americans spoke Russian to each other when they didn't want the bikers to know what they were talking about. Does that sound like Americans to you?"

"You didn't do any financial stuff with Koslov on that deal?"

"I got involved later. I just helped him clean and park money."

"The return on the investment?"

"Yeah. The investors put up the seed money, then as the deal started to generate revenue – which didn't take long, given the situation – the investors were paid back first, with interest, and they got a percentage of the earnings for a couple years after."

"That a typical thing?"

"Sometimes, in deals like this. It adds more long-term incentive for money people, and spreads out cash flow."

"What did you do with the cash?"

"Not much. Paul only trusted me with a few tasks, cleaning cash mostly. We converted to Euros, you have more options that way. Set up unsecured loans and mortgages on dummy businesses. On paper we made seed investments on projects that never happened. That sort of thing."

"The authorities didn't care?"

"If you're willing to take your time, you can hide money in plain sight even if you're not an expert. Things that attract notice when they happen quick, tend not to be noticed when they happen over a long time. You need to figure out where to park your money, and then pick your moments carefully about accessing it. Paul said they wanted to take their time."

"So where was the money parked?"

"I don't know. Paul handled the long-term stuff himself."

"How much?"

"I don't know the total. He was the one controlling the books, I didn't have access to the big picture. Also, he had other deals going on that didn't involve me."

"Substantial, though?"

"Oh yes, no doubt. You can do the math on the back of an envelope. The wholesale cost of opium in Thailand at that time was only about seven thousand krone per kilo, heroin about eighty thousand krone per kilo. You could get heroin for a lot less in Pakistan, along with morphine at about six thousand krone per kilo, if you had the contacts..."

Dragan held up a palm. "Jesus, I didn't ask for a maths lecture, you're just throwing out numbers."

Madsen sighed. "By the time the bikers hit the street with the product, it's being sold with a five- to six-thousand-percent markup. With the investment Tinhanhem got from that group, combined with their connections in Asia, they had direct control of the entire value chain after the product was manufactured. An investment of a few hundred thousand quickly becomes millions, with the right infrastructure."

"So we're talking about a lot of money."

"Keep in mind that's revenue, not profit. The trick is to keep the costs down to keep your margins up. You can imagine, there's a lot of people to pay: shipping, bribing the authorities, warehousing, preparation, packaging, security."

"I get it. It's a business."

"It's a business, where margins are more important than revenue."

"Considering the numbers, why didn't you do it?"

"Because Tinhanhem are a self-styled gang of immigrants. We don't need Denmark to be any more multi-cultural than it already is. A German gang, a Netherlands gang, I would do business. I would even do business with the Jews, they don't cause problems. But not with so many Asians and Muslims and people from I don't know where."

"Business isn't business?"

"They don't come alone. They never come alone. There's always a hole in the fence for their families and friends to wiggle through, with no desire to fit into Danish life. There's no future in my investing with them."

The would-be bodyguard recovering in the corner grunted and nodded in agreement. Dragan didn't expect to hear talk like this, he would have thought all money was good money to a drug dealer. It certainly verified what Bassel and Dewi told him that evening by the firepit.

"I had no interest in putting so much money into the pockets of people who would threaten our system, even if I benefitted in the process," continued Madsen. "It would be like wearing fancy new clothing while the house around me was torn down."

"If that's the way you feel, why are you irritated Koslov cut you out of this deal?"

"It would have been nice to be asked."

Dragan nodded at the twisted logic. "Did any of this involve the art world? Documenting purchases and sales of paintings and such?"

"No, of course not," said Madsen, astonished by the question. "None of us know anything about that. But I never heard the details, like I said. The only thing I heard was that Paul's American partners took all the money out of the places where it was parked, and cut him out of it. Cut everyone out. Paul and his people here were left with next to nothing."

"He was angry about that."

"When he told me the story, half drunk on the phone, he was furious."

"Angry enough to kill someone?"

"Is that what happened? Someone got killed over this? Yeah, he was probably angry enough. But I doubt he could do it. He's not the type of person to get revenge. He's the type to crawl off and feel sorry for himself."

Dragan stood up. It was time to go.

"He bought a fisherman's cottage out by the North Sea," Madsen said, "where I think he plans to kill himself, once he decides on the right moment."

"So I've heard."

"He's not a bad person, mostly just selfish. And a little lost." Madsen gestured toward Dragan with his uninjured hand. "Please remember I talked to you. That I helped. Leave me out of whatever you're doing, okay?"

Dragan put the belaying pin on the counter and walked out. He intended to get a train back to Copenhagen to confront Paul, and not be nice about it. He came up to a small house half the size of Madsen's, with a one-car garage attached. The garage door was raised, and a man walked out, in jeans and a dark hoodie, with long blonde hair under a watch cap. The man had a gun in his hand.

59

MIKKEL

The man who had been following Dragan around the city was not as young as he appeared from a distance, nor as slender. This was clearly no dilettante like Madsen, no overgrown child like the college student Madsen hoped would be his bodyguard. No bargain basement tough guy like the goons back in Philadelphia. This one had watchful, frigid eyes that said he would kill Dragan right there on the street if he needed to.

With a small movement of his head the man directed Dragan into the garage. Dragan smiled bitterly to himself. Just that morning, in a gesture of self-motivation, he told himself he didn't have much time left, not realizing he didn't have any time at all. So many things left undone. He wondered if anyone would miss him. The sky was a vibrant blue splashed with clouds, and he took one last look.

Dragan went to the rear of the garage, where lawn tools and a bicycle leaned against the wall. The man secured Dragan's wrists behind his back, and then tied him to built-in shelving and directed him to the floor. When the garage door came down the space was much darker, with only the light from two small windows draped with dust and cobwebs. The man pulled a folding chair off a hook on the wall, opened it, and sat down facing Dragan.

"No one in the house, I checked," the man said in awkward Russian.

"You've been shadowing me all over the city."

The man nodded vigorously. "I am so tired of it. I'm not being paid to follow you forever. This has now become ridiculous. I need to know what's happening. The client has gone quiet and I've been wasting my time. It ends here one way or another."

He took out his phone and dialed a number. He let it ring for a long time. When it was finally answered, Dragan heard a faint tinny voice coming from the other end.

"It's about time someone answered this line," said the blonde man. "I've been trying to reach Petroski for a week... Then where is he? I need to speak with him... Then who are you?... This is Mikkel, in Denmark. I have Dragan Markov with me, and I need to know what to do with him... Yes, Markov... If you don't know who that is let me speak with Petroski... No, I cannot wait, I need an answer now... Okay, call me back at this number within twenty minutes or I let him go and come looking for you to collect my payment." He ended the call, shook his head in disapproval.

"Is that your name, Mikkel?"

"Yes."

"Ben Petroski's father hired you to kill me?"

"Not exactly. He hired me to find you, then he would tell me what to do. Maybe kill you, maybe not. Maybe kidnap you. He would let me know. I found you, but he never told me what to do and I've been wandering around Copenhagen forever, waiting. So now we wait some more."

"Can we speak English? Your Russian is not very good."

"I would prefer English, actually."

"When I caught you following me I thought you were a little young to be doing this sort of work," said Dragan.

"I'm older than I look."

"I see that now."

"A lot of it is the clothing, my work outfit."

"I told someone you look like a skateboarder."

The blonde man laughed. "That is the idea, of course. I can walk anywhere in Europe and be ignored by everyone. You know Velizar Jelić? That was me."

Dragan was startled by this. Velizar Jelić was a Serb politician and a dodgy character with many enemies. He had been imprisoned briefly for suspicion of war crimes. He had public, often nasty disagreements with Kosovo Albanians, politicians, law enforcement agencies, and even angered regional crime organizations. There were many people who might want him gone. His car was firebombed once, but he wasn't in it, and many assumed he had done it himself in a bid to get sympathy. Then, as Dragan had heard it through trade gossip, the Russians decided they had enough of Jelić's incompetence and that it was time for him to step down. Which he refused to do. So one day, in broad daylight, in the middle of the city of Pristina, a man came out of the crowd on a scooter, shot Jelić, then disappeared just as quickly. Could this man really be responsible? And if he was, why on Earth was he sitting here bragging about it?

"How did you do it?"

"The Russians let it be known that a hit squad looking for Jelić had arrived in Kosovo on two planes. Descriptions were the usual cliché: hard men, black suits, dark glasses, duffel bags. Could be from anywhere. Everyone was looking for men just like that, before and after the shooting. No one was looking for a long-haired student doing a hiking tour between semesters."

Dragan wanted the conversation to continue. Perhaps he could talk his way out of the situation. He said, "That's brilliant."

"And of course, I train to develop my skills."

"It takes discipline."

"Of course. Michel Foucault writes of discipline as a type of power."

Dragan raised his eyebrows. "I don't hear Foucault referenced much, in my circle."

"Books are good." Mikkel smiled, and shrugged. "But I'm not special in my discipline. I'm sure it is the same for you, whatever you do for a living."

They could be chatting at a bar on a rainy night, Dragan and this strange young man named Mikkel who might, before the morning passed, kill dragan and leave him in the garage. They sat, waiting in the half-darkness. Mikkel didn't seem to mind it, he was calm and sat perfectly still on the chair.

"I hope I didn't offend you with the story about Jelić," said Mikkel. "Your name is Serbian, I think."

"On my mother's side. No worries. I don't really have a country any longer."

"Me neither. It is better that way, I think." Mikkel looked Dragan over. "Why can't my client make up his mind about you?"

"His son was murdered. He isn't sure whether to blame me or not. Some days he thinks I killed his son. Other days he thinks it was because of something he did or didn't do."

"Did you?"

"Did I what? Kill his son? No."

"Who did?"

"That's what I'm in Denmark trying to find out."

Mikkel's phone rang. He listened for some time. He said, "When did that happen?...Will I be paid for my time? I've had eyes on Markov for a while waiting to hear... No, of course you have no idea, you useless shit."

Mikkel ended the call and turned to Dragan.

"Well, it doesn't matter now," said Mikkel. "My client Petroski is dead. He fell out of his hotel room window in Miskolc. Seven stories. The woman said he was in Hungary talking with a psychic, trying to contact his dead son. Now I guess they can talk face to face. And I won't be paid for my time. This is very unethical."

"He was Ukrainian, and openly questioned the war," said Dragan. "I'm surprised he lasted this long."

Mikkel came over and cut the bindings. Dragan stood and brushed the dirt off his pants.

"Thank you for that night at the canal," said Dragan. "You may have saved my life. And you didn't kill me today, which I'm also very glad for."

"We're just being professional here."

Dragan considered the situation. Mikkel could be useful. He said, "How much does Petroski owe you?"

"Well, that would depend on what I was supposed to do with you. Murder you would be a different price than kidnap you."

"Understood. What if they didn't want you to do either of those, and just paid you for your time watching me?"

Mikkel thought a minute, did some quick calculations, and named an amount, in euros.

"That seems reasonable," said Dragan. "I'd like to compensate you for your time. Let me make up that difference."

60

ROSKILDE CATHEDRAL

Mikkel's eyes widened. "Why? You were the target, paying me is a little crazy."

"I owe you for the canal, and this way we can walk away feeling okay with how it ended."

"No, it doesn't seem honorable. I received half my fee up front, I'm okay with that."

"Let's split the difference, I'll pay half of what you're still owed, plus a bonus if you help me with something. I need a gun. I hope you can help me get one."

"It can be done. Why ask me?"

They left the garage and started toward downtown, like old colleagues heading out to have a drink together.

Dragan asked, "A woman told you I was coming here today, didn't she?"

Mikkel nodded. "She's been my local contact. I don't know who she is."

"That's okay, I do. It turns out everyone I know in this country is not to be trusted. That's why you. I'm looking for a compact nine-millimeter. Light, easy to conceal. I'm not trying to make a statement; I don't want people to know I have it until I need them to know."

"A twenty-two would be quieter."

"But not as effective. If I'm someplace where the noise is an issue I'll make sure to leave immediately."

"Gun laws here are strict. Hunting weapons only. Handguns are very hard to get, they think handguns are only for committing crimes. This isn't America, self-protection is not a good reason to own a gun here. It will be expensive."

"I understand."

Mikkel named a likely amount. "It will be clean. Untraceable. Likely virgin."

"Okay. And ammunition. I'll need some extra. How long will it take?"

"One day. I know a supplier who lives two towns over."

"Then I'll stay in town tonight. I'd rather not go back to the city until I'm armed."

Mikkel pointed to a small park adjacent to a pub a block away from them. "I will meet you there tomorrow, around two o'clock."

"Thank you." Dragan started to peel off, to take a different street, but he stopped and turned. He said, "A couple hours ago you were ready to shoot me."

"Probably not. I realized something was wrong when I couldn't talk to the client."

They both considered how close they had come to a different outcome of their meeting.

Mikkel asked, "You said you're involved somehow with my local contact, the woman?"

"Unfortunately."

"You should be very careful, then. More careful than you've been, I think. Those men by the canal, my client, this woman. You seem to have a lot of people who don't like you."

"It doesn't make any sense. I'm a lovely person, and normally everyone thinks I'm wonderful."

***

Dragan now had a lot to worry about. He had taken one step forward, with Mikkel no longer a threat and Benedikt's vengeful father out of the picture for good. But learning that Christina Koumba was an enemy – or at least a direct and serious danger – shoved him back two steps, or more. She had responded to Petroski's call for information about him, which set Mikkel on his trail. He was fairly sure when she would have done it, which was after she learned he was no longer an official part of foreign intelligence. It was almost certainly Paul Koslov who told her that, since the two of them, as Dragan now knew, had been in contact the entire time.

Madsen had known he was coming, because Paul told him, and Paul would have heard through Christina, since she was the only person who knew where Dragan was going and when. She probably wasn't telling Paul everything, but what little she shared was enough to compromise Dragan's actions. It was likely Paul passed it all along to Lily and Viggo.

Christina, who he thought might be an ally, had been betraying him nearly every step of the way. She warned him not to upset her compact, orderly life, and she delivered on the threat.

Dragan had to assume his continued presence in Denmark was common knowledge, as well as where he was staying. Paul would learn about the confrontation with Lucas Madsen soon enough, and he'd no doubt pass along that information as well. Dragan no longer had allies and was facing people who all had their own reasons for wanting him gone. Yet, incredibly, after all he had learned about the bad behavior of this crew, he still felt the core mystery remained out of reach.

Mikkel, Dragan acknowledged, had been correct: he needed to be a lot more careful. When he returned to the city he'd have to find a new hotel, prepare for the worst, and then act quickly. He would confront all four of them, see what came out. Dragan would save Paul for last, since he seemed to be at the center of the rat's nest. With luck the other three would given him enough information to finally break Paul.

That would be tomorrow. With time to kill, he had little to do other than play tourist. He strode over to Roskilde Cathedral, a dense and imposing example of brick gothic architecture. No soaring buttresses here, no ethereal vaulted ceilings held up by angels. This was a stolid building filled with dead Danish monarchs.

Dragan was amused by a little exhibition upstairs behind the altar, a series of scale models showing the development of the cathedral over the centuries, from the small initial structures lost to fires centuries ago, to the elaborate, barely contained beast it had become. What made the scale models so charming was they were crafted entirely in LEGOs. What could be more Danish than building architectural models in LEGOs? It reminded him of the LEGO model of Nina and Ben's beach house, sitting on the credenza in the dining room there. Dragan wondered if Ben and Nina had gotten the idea from a visit to this cathedral.

Then he had another idea, and stood thinking about it, staring at the models.

He booked a room in a modest hotel. After dinner he stepped into a bookstore and bought a collection of science fiction short stories in English by a writer he admired. Reading them he wondered if time does travel backwards as well as forwards and if so, did he already know how this adventure was going to end? When he fell asleep he dreamed of castles surrounded by moats where aliens quietly dozed, dreaming of him.

61

PURCHASE

D ragan was early to the park by the pub, watching off to the side in a doorway to ensure Mikkel arrived alone. He had no reason to think it would be a trap, but it didn't hurt to make sure. He saw Mikkel headed for a bench in an unhurried stride. He was concerned; Mikkel wasn't carrying anything. Perhaps there would be no weapons deal.

Dragan joined him on the bench. He said, "You're empty-handed."

Mikkel ignored that comment. "You ready?" he asked.

Dragan nodded, curious. He took a sealed envelope from an inside jacket pocket and handed it to Mikkel. "As agreed."

They walked to the shopping district on Algade, where automobiles were not permitted. They strolled along looking at the stores and came to a men's clothing store. There were racks of sale shirts and jackets on the street in front of the store and Mikkel began flipping through them.

"Looking for something?" asked Dragan.

"Enter the store," said Mikkel, "and purchase a couple of things. It doesn't matter what. Make sure you buy several items you would actually wear and spend enough to get one of their paper shopping bags with the strong handles; ask for one if you must. Buy items large enough to cover the bottom of the bag."

Dragan nodded and entered the store. In a few minutes he came back out, carrying a shopping bag.

"It took me a while to find two things I liked," said Dragan.

"It wasn't a fashion trip," said Mikkel.

They turned and walked back the way they came for half a block. They entered a liquor store nestled between a real estate office and a hair salon. It was cramped, with tall shelves all around. There was every manner of spirits and liqueurs, and wines, and beers imported from around the world.

Mikkel reached down casually and took the shopping bag out of Dragan's hand, then walked toward the cashier at the rear of the store. Pleasantries were exchanged. Dragan couldn't understand everything being said, but he picked up that Mikkel was looking for a particular type of lakka. The shop owner appeared, and indicated for Mikkel to come into the back. Dragan drifted through the store looking at wines until Mikkel reappeared and slipped the bag back into Dragan's hand. It was now much heavier. They left the store and walked toward the train station.

"I thought your source was two towns over," said Dragan.

"I don't know you, I couldn't trust you with the information that a good gun contact was the owner of the liquor store downtown. You could have trotted right there after we separated yesterday."

"Which would have gotten me nowhere with your contact, and only made you angry at me. You must think I'm a fool."

"More about me being cautious, than what I thought about you."

Dragan looked into the bag. At the top was the bottle of lakka Mikkel claimed to be looking for.

"So you were serious about this?" asked Dragan, taking the bottle out and looking at it.

"Well, it was the signal for the owner. But yes, I wanted to get a bottle of this, and have you pay for it."

"Expensive?"

"How to define cost versus value?"

"What's so great about it?"

"It's made with cloudberries, fruity and smooth. Good for the evening. Women like it." Mikkel grinned.

"Okay, then."

Dragan looked back into the bag. Laying in it was the charcoal grey wool scarf and the light cotton black crew-neck sweater from the men's store. He reached in and lifted the clothes. Under them was tissue paper, and under the tissue paper was a cardboard shipping box sealed and marked as if to be dropped off at the post office. He replaced the tissue paper, and the sweater, and the scarf.

"I was able to get you a compact nine-millimeter, as requested," said Mikkel. "It's small, about ten centimeters tall, barrel a little more than seven and a half centimeters. Just 454 grams with a full magazine. You won't be able to shoot a plane down from the sky, but if you're in a tight spot it will get you out of trouble."

"That's what I need."

"This one will be loud, compared to a twenty-two, as I warned."

"If I need to use it, I'm afraid a twenty-two won't have enough punch. As long as I'm not firing it in an apartment building in the middle of the night I'll probably be okay."

"Plan appropriately."

Dragan handed the bottle of lakka to Mikkel.

"I would be happy to work with you sometime," said Mikkel. "I am glad I didn't have to kill you. Your offer to compensate me for my time marks you as an ethical professional and I appreciate that. I think you might need some help while you are here." He handed Dragan a business card with only a phone number printed on it. "If you need to reach me, call this number and leave a message. I will get it."

"You never can tell," said Dragan. They shook hands. "Until next time."

He waited on the platform for the train to the city, planning a grand tour of his enemies. He was tired of this. He needed to end it, one way or another.

62

—·—

BETRAYAL

"I thought turnabout was only fair," said Dragan, sitting at the kitchen table across from Christina in her apartment in the city. "After you dropped in on me unannounced the last time."

He had banged on her door until she opened it, furious, refusing to let him in. He told her he would stay shouting and making noise until he changed her mind. She threatened to call the police if he did, and he pointed out how that would only draw more attention from her neighbors. Reluctantly she stepped out of the way and he slid in.

She put the water on for tea. Dragan noted she was tense and wary. She didn't expect him to return from Roskilde. Unless Mikkel was playing both sides of this game, however, she didn't yet realize he was aware of her betrayal. He was sad; he had liked her, despite her being a pain in the neck.

She asked, "Was your trip successful?"

"Partly. I understand the whole lot except the two most important things, which are who had Nina and Ben killed, and why. To find those out I'll have to get a lot more aggressive, I think."

"Oh good, and end up calling me when you're battered and bleeding again. Don't come crawling back here to be patched up, I told you no more."

"I understood. Anything new while I was gone?"

She frowned and looked at her watch. She wanted it to be clear this was an imposition. "Yes, actually. I've been talking with my Politiet friend. Do you remember the explosion at the offices of the newspaper, *Demokraten*? It turns out the newspaper is in the same part of town as Saint Paul's Church, and there's a street person who is something of a fixture in that neighborhood. I go to that church sometimes, and I've seen him. He calls himself Baldur. After the explosion he was telling people he had blown up the newspaper, that a woman gave him a lot of money to do it. He's not well mentally, he drinks, and he's prone to exaggeration. Typically no one pays attention."

"Did the police interview him?"

"Yes, of course, they were obligated by the way he was talking. They thought his story was outlandish. Something, though: he provided a detailed description of the woman as tall, dark hair with bangs, nice clothes, bold eye makeup. He claimed she had flowers on her coat, which sounds like brocade. That Lily woman was wearing a coat with brocaded flowers and plants on the sleeves when she confronted me."

"I've seen the coat."

"You told me she was a self-described revolutionary, correct? The owner is a news conglomerate based in Germany and the paper has become strongly right-wing. It wants to increase the size of the military, applauds the rise of nationalism in Western countries, and takes a hard line against immigrants in general, and Muslims in particular. Would that be enough for her?"

Dragan nodded. "Can your police friend arrange for us to talk to this Baldur?"

"That's not possible. Someone killed him with a petrol bomb. Threw it at him while he was sleeping in a cranny outside the church.

He was covered in blankets which all caught fire from the bomb. He burned to death. It even damaged the church."

"That's terrible."

"My friend said Baldur mentioned a small man with her, someone familiar. However, Baldur didn't want to talk about the man, he was fascinated by the woman, but he did mention the name Fedde. The police were aware of a playwright named Fedde, who hung around anarchists and such. When they stopped by for a talk, they found him dead in his apartment, bludgeoned and strangled."

"This is escalating. Someone is cleaning up."

"These are bad people. They're all so bad I couldn't guess who was behind those murders. If they're cleaning up what's to stop them from coming after you again, or after me? This is a filthy mess. You'll get no satisfaction from rummaging through it. Just let it go. I'm begging you, for the sake of all of us. Quit this, go home!"

He looked at her, nodded as if in solemn agreement, and sipped his tea. "I did figure a couple of things out while I was gone. You'll like this story, it's all about you. You said you checked with some contacts and learned I was no longer an active agent. But that first day you made it clear you had no contacts in America. You were isolated, you said. The only person you could have spoken to, who was aware of my status, was Paul Koslov. You were in contact with him even though you said you weren't. Ever since I arrived your information has pointed only at Lily and Viggo, and made Paul out to be little more than a drunk, a buffoon in over his head."

There were tears in her eyes. "That's really all he is."

"Now you're still happy to point to Lily and Viggo, with the bombings and the death of that man in his apartment, still pointing away from Paul and the money."

"I don't know where that money is. I told Lily that."

"But Paul knows, or at least he knew where it was, before the Petroskis stole it. Why are you protecting him?"

She looked at him in the silence of her kitchen. She wiped her eyes and found the energy to raise her chin in defiance. "He's the only family I have, as useless as he is. I need someone and he's it."

"Is that why you informed on me with the elder Petroski, knowing it might get me killed?"

She opened her mouth to protest, shaking her head in denial, but Dragan held up his hand to silence her.

"You were responsible for that man following me," he told her. "Viggo said it wasn't his guy, and I believed him. So it had to be connected to the reward Ben's father put out. I couldn't see Paul calling it in, he had no reason to want even more attention on him. The only other person who got that notice and knew my location was you. They sent a contract killer out after me, thank you very much. He first appeared the day we met at the café and talked about the drug trade. Who would have known I would be there, other than you?"

"You were stumbling around the city, kicking up dirt. You were going after Paul."

Dragan laughed at himself. "I didn't want to believe it. Like an idiot. But I had to accept it was you when the man showed up in Roskilde, since you were the only one I told."

"I thought your little quest would burn itself out, but you wouldn't give up. You were getting that biker and his wife agitated, sending Paul into a spin. Your messes would keep arriving on my doorstep even though I told you to keep them away from me. You insisted on making your problems my problems."

"That's not what…"

"You appear at the wrong time, where you're not wanted. You are intrusive, and annoying, and you threaten everything I've worked so hard to build here."

They stared at each other across the table. "Really, Christina, you went all in on Roskilde," he said. "You must have realized that if I saw the man there, I would know for sure you were betraying me. You were counting on him kidnapping me, or killing me."

She shook her head no. "I thought he just wanted to identify where you were. I had no reason to believe you were in danger."

"You couldn't possibly be that naïve. The only reason I'm still walking around is that the deal is called off, the older Petroski is dead. If you didn't already get whatever you were promised, you won't get it now. Though I don't think you did it for the reward."

"I don't care about the reward."

"No, I'm sure you don't. You did it just to be rid of me, which is worse. A weak moment of greed I can understand. Intentional, personal betrayal like this cuts a whole lot deeper."

He stood up. She took it as a threatening move and leaped out of her chair, knocking it backwards onto the floor, and stepped to the side. Her arm moved and a security baton telescoped with a crisp snap. Dragan was impressed; she had hidden it on her before she let him in, and he had no idea. He held up his hands.

"I was just taking my teacup to the counter and leaving."

"Don't come after me." It was a warning, and a plea.

"No, I won't. We're done, you and me. I'll be telling people what you did."

"I'm an agent in good standing. You're a disgraced failure who roamed off the farm. You're not official here. You'll come out worse in that fight."

"I'm already damaged material. If all I do is dirty your reputation and derail your perfect little life, that will be enough for me."

63

Spy Protocols

Dragan sat in an armchair in Lily's living room, holding a beer, while she sat across from him on the couch. On the table in front of her was a glass filled with vodka and the bottle it came from. As always, they were comfortable and relaxed together, even if one didn't trust the other.

"Is Viggo going to burst in on us?" asked Dragan. "I hope so. I need to talk to him."

"He did something stupid, as usual, now he's hiding out."

"Where is that?"

"I have no idea. He can't come here, that's the important thing. Whoever's looking for him would keep an eye on my place."

"He likes to take risks."

She snorted, and took a drink. "No secret you were still in the country."

"Paul told you." She nodded. "He tell you how he found out?" She shook her head. "That woman you confronted on the street, Christina Koumba? She told him. They've been in contact all along. You and I haven't had any secrets, it seems."

She scowled. In that light it seemed like a sharp amber light burned in her eyes. "He's always been a coward, and a lying piece of shit."

"Lily, listen to me. This has to stop now. If I find your money you can have it. But I can't find it unless I get some answers. You understand?"

She nodded.

"Why do you think I know where the money is?" he asked. "And why don't you already have it?"

"Your girlfriend and her husband stole it. She told you where it was."

"No, she didn't. It turns out there was a lot she didn't tell me."

She laughed, the nasty laugh of a drunk. "You aren't as smart as you think you are."

"Nobody is, especially me. One more lesson learned."

She laughed again. She said, "You're just a trusting soul."

"How did they steal the money from you? How could that happen?"

She took another solid gulp from her glass. "Paul said the five of us were like a corporation, and we would all have the same rights since we all brought something to the deal. After the Petroskis got their investment back we all got a bonus. Then we would get dividends, he said, over time. But later he changed that, said it would be in a few bigger payments."

"Why?"

"I don't know. To get more money sooner, I guess. It was a deal he worked out with the bikers. He told them if they agreed to this plan, the Petroskis will be open to investing with them in the future."

"Sounds like a way not just to get the funds sooner, but also to sever the relationship with the gang."

"Which is how it worked out."

"You were all fine with that?"

"All of us agreed except for Viggo."

"Wasn't he making the decisions for the bikers?"

"Viggo?" She snorted a laugh. "He's no leader. He has a crew of losers so he can swagger around, but the gang has a leader group. He's not in that. He just made the introductions to get the deal started, which earned him a little extra as a finder's fee."

"Then why wouldn't he agree to the terms?"

"He asked for a larger bonus, just that once, and to leave him out of the dividend scheme. He told me he thought the rest of his club wouldn't like it if he was still getting extra into his own pocket years after the deal."

"Which makes sense."

"The real reason, I think, is that he didn't trust the Petroskis, or Paul."

"Viggo's smarter than he looks."

"Told you. A smart guy who makes stupid decisions."

"More for the rest of you, then."

"That's how I saw it. The first payments from the club came in and we put the money in multiple banks, to keep it safe."

"It all happened that fast?"

"What fast?" Her words were becoming a little slurred.

"The Petroskis were only here for a couple of weeks."

"What? No! What planet are you on? They came back a bunch of times, keeping an eye on things. Fly in, stay for a few days, ask questions, act like they were the bosses, fly out. Rich people shit."

Dragan thought back to that period. It was humiliating, how little he was paying attention, and how much he missed.

Lily was thinking back, through the vodka haze, trying to get the sequence right. "After we got all the big interest payments Paul said we needed to lay low for a while, not get too much attention. He talked about fancy computer security things like we didn't understand what he was talking about, like we were all dumb. The account numbers and passwords were put on those USB-sticks, and they were encrypted. He tried to explain that to me, like I didn't know what encrypted meant."

"Why?"

"Because he's an asshole."

"No, why the flash drives?"

"Spy protocols."

Dragan wondered if she was serious or being sarcastic. She was drunk, and her eyes were red, sad, and angry. "What are spy protocols?"

"They were spies, right? Paul told me about them, and they laughed about it, said it was their hobby, which I thought was strange. They said for things like this it was good to use spy protocols. The password for the encryption, to get the account numbers and their passwords, was put on a photograph, on the license plates of trucks in the background. Paul said no one can remember a password of random letters and numbers, and you don't want to write them down somewhere where anyone could find it. But hidden in a photo like that is the best way, he said, and that it was a standard thing they did in his world. The photograph and the thumb drive were supposed to be kept in different locations."

"Paul told you all this?"

"There were written instructions. Spy protocols. How would you not know about these things? Paul said you were a spy too."

Dragan said nothing. He thought the story ridiculous – too ridiculous not to be true. The very idea of using those photographs was silly and anachronistic, like something from a novel. There were a dozen easier and more secure ways to accomplish what she described. Paul and the Petroskis played Lily and Viggo for fools. But to what end, exactly?

"There were two drives and two copies of the photo," continued Lily. "Paul and I had one, and your girlfriend and her husband had one. We all agreed to wait, then we would get together and divide the money. Paul said he would be the one responsible for checking the accounts, make sure none of us cheated." On that final word, she stabbed her index finger into the air.

"Wasn't that like asking the hawk to watch over the baby rabbits, considering his gambling debts?"

"That's what Viggo said! But the Americans thought it was okay, and I didn't think Paul would do anything wrong like that to me. So we agreed. After a while, he told me he checked the accounts and he couldn't get in."

"Nina and Ben changed the passwords on the accounts?"

"No, he said he couldn't even get that far. The code on the photograph didn't work on the thumb drive. The Americans locked us out. Paul said they were going to keep it all for themselves."

"That was bold."

"Yeah. Paul sat in the same chair you're in, holding his head in his hands, cursing them out."

"What did Viggo say?"

"That he warned us. He did, actually, to be fair. It didn't affect him, though, he was out of it. But me and Paul, we were planning on that money, which was a lot of money, and now it's gone."

"What did you all do about it?"

"I kept saying we should try to get into those accounts, get our money. Viggo thought there was no point. He said Nina and Ben would hide the money someplace else where we'll never find it."

"What about Paul?"

"He just got quiet. He never wants to talk about it."

Dragan could almost hear the pieces falling into place. There was only one question left. Which of these dreadful people were responsible for Nina? All of them?

"Is that why you had them killed?"

She looked at him with confusion. "Why would I do that if I needed them to give me my share? That's stupid. Them being dead cuts me off from it."

"But you're not above murder, are you? You did the bombing at the newspaper. You could have killed the security guard; it was a miracle he got away safe. But that street person you got to plant the bomb wasn't so lucky, was he? You killed him at the church, or had it done, because he started to talk about you. That was a horrible thing, Lily. All this talk about helping people who are struggling, but you don't think twice about sacrificing some poor street person, someone struggling the most."

"You have no proof of any of that." Her hand was shaking as she raised the vodka to her lips.

Dragan stood up to leave. "Your partner in that bombing was a little guy named Fedde, right?"

"How would you know about Fedde?"

"They found him dead in his apartment. Head bashed in and strangled. Did you do that, too? I hear he was a small guy, you'd be just strong enough, I'll bet."

The color drained from her face. "I don't believe you."

"Call him, see if I'm lying."

"Who would do that? He was harmless."

"If you didn't have it done, then you should ask your husband about it."

64

TRUSTWORTHY

Paul Koslov was back in the small second bedroom that he used as an office, where he had a desk and a small settee, with a stack of storage boxes in the corner. He was placing bets on La Liga games in Barcelona and Granada when someone knocked on his apartment door. He ignored it, but the knocking became more insistent. Paul opened the door to find Dragan standing there with a crooked grin.

"How did you get up…" was all Paul got out before Dragan shoved his foot into Paul's gut, sending him flying back into the apartment. Dragan closed the apartment door and stepped over to where Paul had stumbled and fallen. He pulled Paul to his feet. Dragan had at least six inches on Paul, and was in much better shape, so it was no trick to turn Paul around, yank his arm up behind his back, lift him off his feet and slam him into the birch top of the coffee table, knocking the wind out of him. A glass bowl that held a set of car keys and wristwatch flew into the air, fell on the edge of the table, and shattered, spreading shards of royal blue glass across the floor. Dragan used zip ties to secure Paul's hands behind his back, then rolled him off the table and propped him against the wall. Dragan crouched down and slapped Paul across the face, hard, to get his attention.

"You had Nina and Ben killed in Philadelphia," said Dragan, in an even, subdued voice that hid his fury. "I should cut your guts out and show them to you before you die."

Paul's eyes widened and he vehemently shook his head no. "I didn't do that. How could I do that?"

Dragan slapped him again. "You're the only one who would, and the only one with the means to make it happen."

"What about other people they pissed off? Stop hitting me!"

"They investigated all that and came up empty. It was you."

"Not me, not me, not me." Paul shook his head side to side, like a toddler.

Dragan sat on the ground so they would be at the same level. "It was the money that confused me, blurred my vision. I assumed there was a ton of it, a fortune. That might explain the murders, but people were acting too casual about a fortune being missing. Then I had a nice talk with your sometime partner Lucas Madsen out in Roskilde."

"He is not a trustworthy person!"

"He sorted out the financial part for me. The money from that drug deal wasn't enough to make anyone rich, was it? That little fact explains so much. It wasn't enough to make Viggo care, at least enough that he would risk everything to chase after it and get revenge when it was gone."

"He's a vicious bastard, he's totally capable of that."

"He no longer had a stake. He already got whatever he had coming. Lily confirmed that. He's the only one who came out of this in good shape, and he didn't give a crap any longer."

"He's dangerous, and unhinged."

"Now Lily, from her point of view the money was just enough to support her playtime terrorist thing, but no more. And no matter how badly she wanted it, it was still just something she would like to have. Plus, she would want them alive, so they could pay her."

"Yeah, but she gets really angry…"

"But you, my friend, you actually needed that money. You're in trouble from your gambling debts, and probably other things too – your kind is never stupid in only one place. Are you embezzling from work, too?"

"What? No! I'd never…"

"You needed that money from the drug deal to get out of the hole you put yourself in. You were in serious trouble, and furious about what Ben and Nina did. It was you, Paul."

"No! Absolutely not!"

Dragan nodded, then his fist shot out and hit Paul on the side of the head, snapping it back against the wall. Dragan said, "You lied to me about not being part of the drug deal. Madsen told me how you were the one who set up the banking scheme. You served as the gatekeeper on that deal. You negotiated terms with the bikers. You knew Nina and Ben ran away with the money and how they did it. I also think you were in on that scheme, at least in the beginning, until they screwed you over too. Which made you angry enough to have them killed. You're in the middle of this entire thing, and you're the one who would want revenge."

"That hurt… I'm dizzy…" Paul shook off the stars and tried to focus his eyes.

"What was the point of the ridiculous thing with the photograph? Why the flash drives, and the secret passcode in the photographs? The so-called spy protocols."

"You know about that?"

"Lily explained it all. What scam were you running on her?"

Paul, defeated and cornered, shrugged and smiled bitterly. "It was supposed to be ridiculous, it's why we did it."

"Who's we?"

"Ben and Nina and me. It was a joke, sort of. Viggo and Lily – Viggo especially – were condescending towards Benedikt and Nina, treating them like naïve rich people, like all they were good for was putting up the money. It annoyed Benedikt."

"Lily said the three of them were intimate."

"I'm not surprised she told you; she's a little obsessed about it. I think Ben and Nina did it to get some control over him, but it backfired, he just treated them with more contempt. Their money and connections meant nothing to Viggo and they weren't used to that. Ben's pride was hurting. One night Ben and Nina and me were sitting around drinking, talking about how we wanted to park the money in bank accounts for a while before we moved them, and she said we should dazzle Lily and Viggo with some supersecret spy stuff, have some fun with them. I didn't understand what she meant but Ben got it right away, and the two of them started working it out."

"It was a classic con. Make it complicated to distract them."

"Nina is the one who came up with it. They started throwing around phrases like cybersecurity and botnets and rootkits and digital warrant authorization protocols and it was all just gibberish. It was to confuse Lily and Viggo, give us something to laugh about behind their backs. It was supposed to be harmless. Nina sat down with Lily in a restaurant one night and explained how it would work."

"She believed it."

"She didn't object, neither of them did. Lily and Viggo act tough and street-smart, but I think a lot of the modern world, especially tech stuff, perplexes them. We all took a chunk of cash up front and hid the rest away, with an agreement on a certain date we would all reconvene and get the money."

"But you couldn't wait, could you? Lily said you checked the accounts early and couldn't get in. The password for the flash drive encryption didn't work. You contacted the Petroskis?"

"Of course. They said they couldn't trust us here. I asked to see the account financial statements. They refused. Then I demanded my share – just my share – right then and there, and they refused. I knew then they had moved the money."

"And you told Lily and Viggo?"

"Lily started asking for her share, too. In her mind the money was still in the accounts, they just weren't giving us access. She never accepted that the money was gone. Viggo recognized what happened right away."

"Wasn't he angry about it?"

"I assume he was a little, but only for Lily's sake, he wasn't really affected. Viggo always has this attitude that he can get more of whatever he wants."

"He was willing to just move on?"

"More or less. Me too, since I didn't have any choice. Lily was the one who couldn't let go."

Dragan slapped him again, twice, harder this time.

Paul bucked in protest. "What was that for?"

"For lying."

65

SHOE

"You and the Petroskis had a deal, didn't you?" said Dragan, more a statement than a question. "That thing with the photograph wasn't just a little charade. The three of you made that plan, to distract Lily with the stupid spy protocols stuff, and while she wasn't looking you were going to move all the money into your own accounts and leave Lily with nothing."

"No we..." Paul started to say, until Dragan hit him again. "Fuck! Stop it! Not nothing. She would have gotten some. I would have taken care of her."

"But you wanted your piece early, you had gambling debts to pay. That's when you found out Nina and Ben tricked you, too. Like I said, one of the oldest cons there is. That was the second part of it, when you realized Lily wasn't the mark, you were. They had you so focused on how you were going to rob someone else, you didn't feel their hands in your own pocket."

Paul nodded, humiliated, anger simmering underneath. "I talked to Nina multiple times. She told me to screw off. Said they're the ones who took the financial risk, I just did the introductions. Said what we already got was enough, that I didn't deserve a bigger share, any more than Lily did."

Dragan dragged the coffee table and placed it on top of Paul. "If you try to get up I'll hear it."

"I need to pee," complained Paul.

"Not till later. Wet yourself if you have to."

Dragan roamed the apartment, not sure what he was looking for. The bed was made. The closet held mostly business clothes, with stacks of shoe containers on the floor. He came across the pants of an ugly tracksuit in chocolate, sand, and olive, the match for the jacket in Christina's apartment. Dragan sighed in disappointment. He shouted to the other room, "Did you and Christina attempt to play a couple back in the day?"

"She doesn't like me."

"I don't blame her. But she still kept you informed about me."

"We're tied together at our waists. We're an official unit." He paused, and added, "You're unofficial and alone," echoing Christina. "You're in over your head."

The top of the dresser was neat and orderly. In the drawers were socks, underwear, sweaters, no surprises. In the office he found a couple of bills among a few pieces of mail on a side table, their envelopes slit open but the contents still inside, waiting for action. One was an invoice for electrical work, addressed to Paul's apartment, but specifying work done at an address in Siwardsted, a town Dragan had never heard of. He shoved the bill into his pocket. He searched the drawers of the desk in the office and found nothing important. He leaned over to look through Paul's laptop, but the security screen had come on, and required a fingerprint scan to unlock. He took the laptop into the front room and told Paul to unlock it.

"No, I'm not letting you into my personal machine, are you crazy?"

Dragan slapped him, again, this time harder.

"Jesus, stop that! You can't go into my files."

Dragan punched him, splitting his lip.

"Goddam it," said Paul, blood dripping onto his chin. He put his index finger on the reader.

The laptop unlocked, Dragan took it back into the office and sat at the desk in front of it. He randomly looked at documents, and scanned the browsing history. He quickly discovered all kinds of residue from Paul's gambling life, both in local casinos as well as online gaming. Paul had multiple e-sports betting accounts, wagering on handball and Superliga football on Danish sites, and English Premier League football on British sites, and EuroLeague basketball as well. From what Dragan could tell Paul wasn't good at it; all the accounts showed recent and consistent losses.

He opened Paul's personal email account. There was a lot of spam, and sports gambling content, and some conversations with what looked like relatives in Russia. In the search bar he entered the cryptic email address he had found on the back of the photograph from Nina's house. It was like opening a hatch in the ceiling of an old house and having a lifetime of hoarding rain down. It unfurled months of correspondence. The mystery account didn't belong to some black-market dealer, or a foreign espionage agent, or a gangster. It belonged to Nina. The most recent email was from a few weeks before Nina was murdered.

He scanned the threads, jumping through time, focusing on the most recent ones. Nina and Paul were pretty angry with each other, with Nina showing contempt for her Copenhagen partners. She referred to Lily as an unstable sociopath, Viggo as a common street thug, and Paul as an unstable junkie. Which was why, she claimed, she needed to be the adult.

Paul's emails to her were filled with threats over the betrayal, increasing in their fury. He warned her of injury and worse. In response

Nina said she would expose Paul's gambling, substance abuse, and intimate involvement with a criminal motorcycle gang to his keepers in the Russian foreign service. She said she and her husband could, and would, convincingly claim to be acting undercover to expose Paul's corruption and moral bankruptcy. With Ben's connections, she wrote, Paul wouldn't have a chance to win a finger-pointing contest. His service career would be over and he might be looking at prison, depending on what kind of example leadership wanted to set.

All of this made it clear Paul had plenty of motivation for killing Nina and Ben; not just in revenge for stealing the money, but also as a way of eliminating the danger they posed.

Dragan was so wrapped up in the email thread he didn't realize Paul had found one of the glass shards from the broken bowl on the floor and used it to saw through the zip tie. His hands free, stained by the blood from where he cut himself in his efforts, Paul quietly lifted the coffee table and got to his feet.

Dragan heard a noise behind him. He turned as Paul came tight, swinging his shoe like a war club. Dragan partly raised his arms, but the shoe caught the side of his head. He lurched forward onto the desktop, spilling papers and the computer mouse and a coffee cup full of pencils and pens. He tumbled onto the floor, dazed.

Paul grabbed keys and wallet, pulled a coat off the hook near the door, and ran out of the apartment. Through the spinning stars and roar in his head, Dragan heard Paul burst through the emergency exit and race down the stairs.

66

USELESS

A block away Paul had to stop running. He wasn't in any shape for this sort of thing. He was functioning on fear and adrenaline. He bent over, hands on his knees, and pulled out his phone.

"What do you want?" asked Lily on the other end.

"I need to talk to Viggo," said Paul, panting.

"He's not here. You sound like you're gasping for breath."

"I am gasping for breath."

"What's going on?"

"Where's Viggo?"

"I told you already, he's not here, what do you not understand about that? He fucked something up and now he's hiding out like a little baby coward."

"I need to call him. What's his number?"

"Viggo doesn't like me giving his number out."

"Even me?"

"Especially you. I'll call him and ask him to call you."

"Lily, this is an emergency. Dragan's in my apartment, going through my stuff."

"What kind of stuff?"

"Viggo! Please!"

"Alright," she screamed at the phone, and hung up.

Paul, stooped and anxious, was unsure of what to do. He decided he needed to leave the city. He had to get to the garage where he kept the car. He looked around – where was he? He recognized a couple of buildings, and realized he started in the wrong direction. Unsteady, afraid and with a foggy, uncertain mind, he headed off in search of his car. The phone in his hand buzzed.

"You wanted to talk?" asked Viggo on the other end of the line.

"Yeah," said Paul. "Dragan is in my apartment. He's rummaging through my things."

"He really should have gone back to America."

"Well, he didn't."

"What did you tell him?"

"Nothing! He already knows everything. He knows about the drug funding deal, about the banks, about the photographs. He's convinced I had Nina and Benedikt killed. I'm in serious trouble with my keepers."

"Yes, I see that. But I'm not in trouble with your people. He should be happy now, he has what he wants: he has you to blame. Why are we having this conversation?"

"You really think I wouldn't tell them all about you and Lily? That I wouldn't make it very clear you and Lily arranged for those murders?"

A woman cruised by on her bicycle, giving Paul a look of concern over his shouting and mention of murder.

"That's not true."

"Somebody did it, and it wasn't me," said Paul. "I moved some money around, but I'm not letting them blame me for the murder of two Russian agents. I'll make it obvious that it was you two."

"They'll still burn you for it."

"Then I'll take you down with me."

Viggo grunted. He said, "You won't last long enough to talk to them."

"You'll have to find me first. By then Dragan will be having Russian agents looking for all three of us. Your only chance to get out of this mess is to eliminate Dragan."

Viggo was quiet. Paul looked nervously at the shadows surrounding him. Why was the night so dark?

Paul asked, "What are you doing? I can hear you breathing."

"Where is he?"

"In my apartment. I hit him, I might have knocked him out."

"You should have killed him then."

"In my own apartment? Are you out of your mind?"

"God you're useless," said Viggo. "If I send anyone over there it will happen in your apartment anyway."

"But your guys can take care of it all, right? Get him out of there, do something with him, leave me out of it?"

"Sure, my friend, you'll be squeaky clean."

"That's what I want," said Paul. "I have to stay out of this stuff." He gave Viggo the code to his apartment.

"Wherever you go, inform us where you are," said Viggo. "We're all concerned about you."

"Sure, sure," said Paul before he hung up.

Paul stumbled half a block west, then walked south, and was thoroughly lost. Everything looked unfamiliar and shrouded in darkness. He felt ill. There were odd noises, and he was frightened. He managed to find his way to the garage. He got into the car and drove away, not expecting to return to his apartment, or to Copenhagen.

67

Loss of Control

Viggo had been nursing a beer in a small neighborhood bar when Lily called to say a panicked Paul Koslov needed to talk. His long gray hair was stuffed up into a knit cap, he had let his beard grow, and he wore the clothes of a factory worker. He had been hiding out in a friend's tiny apartment in the shadow of the Grundtvigs Kirke, the huge expressionist church dominating the Bispebjerg district in the northwest of the city, and he was feeling claustrophobic. He had to take some kind of action. The Ulvehoved Motorcycle Club would find him eventually.

He cursed and phoned Paul.

After they spoke he sat for a few moments and looked into his beer, seeking answers for how things had come to this. Lily was completely out of his control, and he feared what she might do next. Dragan was back, hellbent on causing trouble. Paul was falling apart, likely to drag them all down with him. It was bedlam.

Viggo liked the setup he had with his gang and his buddies, liked the freedom and excitement of his life, but it was probably over, or at least the version he had become used to. Some kind of change had to happen. He had been a fool to think he could keep things the same; nothing, and nobody, ever stayed the same for any length of time.

He had refused to accept that fundamental truth. He ignored it when he came out of prison to find Lily had taken up with Paul. He ignored it when Paul's American friends offered to invest in the drug deal. He ignored it when they stole the money and sent Lily over the edge, and when Dragan arrived in the city stirring things up. He thought if he just remained consistent, and put some pressure here, or took an action there, he could corral people and events to suit himself. But no, that wasn't how things worked.

He downed the remains of his beer.

Out in the parking lot, he made a call. When someone answered he asked for Anton, then someone else picked it up and he asked for Anton again.

"Anton, my brother," he said when his friend finally came on the line. "I need you to do something for me. Paul's American colleague Dragan Markov is still in Denmark. He has crossed the line and is now a serious problem."

"I told you."

"Well, no matter, the time has come. Grab a few guys and head over to Paul Koslov's apartment. Markov is there, gathering evidence to use against all of us. Take care of him and dispose of him completely, we don't need blowback from anything this guy is associated with." He gave Anton the address and the access code.

"What about Koslov? Aren't we tired of his shit?"

"We are extremely tired of his shit. He's now threatening me and has become a liability with no value to us. He has to go. But we have time to deal with him, first things first. Take the guys Markov messed up, if they're available, I'm sure they'll be happy to participate. Let them have a little fun."

"Yeah," said Anton, liking the suggestion. "Sounds like it will become messy."

"It isn't like Paul is ever going back there anyway. Call me when you're finished."

Viggo wandered over to one of the logs that defined the edge of the parking lot and sat down. He lit a thin joint. Decisions had to be made. He would need to leave the country. He had some money. His cousin Michael in the United States would put him up, get him situated. It was time to make a move.

The big problem was Lily. What to do about her? Eventually things will get attention from several quarters. If they looked hard at Paul, that would lead to Lily, and she would lead to Viggo. Paul and Dragan might be – with any luck would be – out of the picture, but she would be a loose thread. He couldn't do anything about her, however, it would cost too much of him. She was crazy, but he loved her... and despised her, and relied on her. Nonetheless, he couldn't leave her in Denmark, so he needed to bring her with him. He would have to lure her out of the country in pursuit of money that may or may not exist, and hope things took a turn for the better in America.

68

ANTON

Dragan sat up on the floor in Paul Koslov's apartment and tried to get himself together... How much time had passed?

Either Paul was running away blindly to hide, or he was getting help. It was prudent to assume the worst. If Paul was getting reinforcements Dragan had one chance and not much time. He couldn't have been dizzy very long, the laptop hadn't gone to the security screen. He made certain the door to the apartment was locked, then attacked the place. He gave the apartment a thorough search and found nothing of interest; Paul Koslov maintained an arid, empty life. Dragan sat on the bed, frustrated, painfully aware of time slipping away.

In a moment of inspiration he jumped off the bed, flipped up the mattress, and there it was, a cushioned envelope lying right in the middle. The envelope held a flash drive and a duplicate of the photo of Nina, Ben, and Paul in front of Paul's office. He hurried into the office, inserted the flash drive into the USB port. He entered the sequence of characters on the truck licenses from Paul's photo. Access was denied. He pulled out his phone and opened the copy of the photograph from Nina's townhouse. The characters on the license plates were different. Dragan entered the characters from Nina's image, and the flash drive opened for him.

"Son of a bitch," said Dragan to the empty apartment as he scanned the contents of the drive. It contained nothing but ebooks in the public domain, in English. Dozens of them. *The Adventures of Tom Sawyer, Pride and Prejudice, The Brothers Karamazov, Anna Karenina, Also Sprach Zarathustra, The Confessions of St. Augustine, The Decameron, The Wonderful Wizard of Oz, The Illiad*, and many more, all of them downloaded as raw text from some online source. For a moment he considered the contents formed some sort of secret code, but his heart wasn't in the theory. It was just a stick full of reading assignments.

Someone pushed the digits on the front door lock. Dragon turned and stood, expecting to see a defeated Paul returning to apologize. Instead, four men entered the apartment, looking mean and intimidating.

Dragan had miscalculated the time he had, and the reinforcements had arrived.

"I recognize you," Dragan said as Anton stepped into the office. "From Lily's apartment."

Right behind Anton came the wiry man with the long hair streaked with blue, held back in a ponytail. He had a bulge under his pant leg where the bandage was wrapped around the calf wound.

The other two men lingered in the living room, near the door. One was the shorter red-haired man with the tied-off beard who had followed Dragan from his hotel room the night he was attacked. The other was the big man in the ugly track suit, his nose still bandaged and surrounded by two fading black eyes.

"And I know the rest of you too," said Dragan, cheerily. He looked at the wiry man across the room and asked, "How's the leg?"

"Fuck you," he answered. He held a knife in his hand.

"You've stayed past your welcome," said Anton in heavily German-accented English. Anton held a short length of metal pipe.

"I'll try to do better next time."

"No next time," said Anton.

"You're right," said Dragan. He pulled out the nine-millimeter he bought in Roskilde and shot Anton in the neck. The big biker collapsed on the floor clutching his throat, blood already pumping through his fingers and down his arm. Dragan turned the gun towards the wiry biker with blue-streaked hair, who was stunned and frozen in place, his mouth gaping. Dragan shot him twice in the chest. He fell back against the wall and slowly slid down. The gunshots in the small room were like dynamite sticks exploding and Dragan's ears rang. This would bring the police for sure.

Dragan turned his attention to the front room. He saw the back of the red-haired man as he bolted out the door in panic. The big-nosed man, however, was not fleeing, but to Dragan's surprise was running toward him, howling, and he flung himself at Dragan before another shot could be fired.

The man collided with Dragan, sending him backwards into the office chair. Dragan slid off to the right as the biker kept moving forward to the left into the desk and the computer monitor, everything flying and crashing. Dragan brought the pistol hard on the biker's head. The biker was still able to whip his thick left hand to swipe Dragan's arm. Brass knuckles made it feel as if a tire iron had struck him, and Dragan dropped the gun.

The biker pulled up and turned around, ready to do damage. Dragan wasn't about to let him get anything behind a punch; he moved in close and hit the biker hard in the kidneys, twice, but it didn't seem to do serious damage. The biker shook it off and managed to get his arm cocked, and Dragan lurched forward with both arms between the biker's neck and fist to block the swing. Dragan snapped his inside elbow forward to the bandaged nose of the biker, who screamed and pulled back. Dragan then snapped his elbow forward again and struck the biker in the throat.

Dragan stepped backwards, towards the office doorway, just in time to miss a wild left jab the biker made toward Dragan's face. Still gagging and gasping from the blow to the throat, the biker had put his full weight behind the punch and had no balance. Dragan grabbed the man and shoved him forward, and the biker's head crunched against the far wall and he crumpled down onto Anton's body.

The biker, smeared in Anton's blood and still struggling for breath, looked down on the floor across the room, and Dragan followed his eyes to the gun on the floor. The biker reached for it.

Dragan pulled out his knife, opened it with a sharp click, took a step forward and dropped his knees onto the biker's back. He reached around with the knife in his right hand and stuck the blade into the side of the biker's neck and pulled back hard, cutting a deep and fatal gash in the biker's throat. Dragan got up on his feet again as the biker pitched forward, spasming and gurgling from his wound.

Dragan, delirious with adrenaline and the psychic rage of violence, lifted up his right leg and stomped on the back of the biker's head, shoving him face-down onto the floor.

Dragan retrieved the gun from the floor. He used the sweatshirt of the wiry man to clean off the gun and the knife. He used a towel from the kitchen to quickly wipe every hard surface he remembered touching, while listening for sirens.

He retrieved the photograph and the flash drive and put them back in the envelope and put the envelope into his coat. He grabbed Paul's personal laptop and shoved it into the computer bag with a second machine that sat off to the side, possibly Paul's work computer – he didn't want to leave either of them for the police or anyone else.

He left the building on the run. He was a block and a half away before he knelt near a bush and vomited from the violence, the blood, the sound and smell of the gun, the stress, the fear. He needed to sit for a few moments to retrieve his sense of self, to place himself back in reality. He wanted a drink and a shower and a good sleep but those had to wait.

The neighborhood was quiet, empty. He propped Paul's laptops against the curb and stomped on them to break them open. He removed the solid-state storage drives and put them in his pocket. Two blocks later he found a convenience store where he tossed the laptop shells and the bag into the large trash bin outside. He bought a dark grey knit beanie and a cheap pair of low-power reading glasses with the thickest black plastic frames he could find. He continued on until he came to an apartment building where he sat on the steps and called a taxi.

Keeping the glasses on, his hat down, and his coat collar up, he gave the driver cross streets near Lily's apartment. He chattered in poor French, mostly stock phrases about the weather, until the exasperated driver asked whether Dragan spoke Danish. Dragan said no but said he spoke a little English, and then started talking about how much he loved Danish dark bread in stilted English in a clumsy French accent. He said he had to stop by his friend's place to pick up a few things before going to the airport, that he was flying on Air France to Accra, Ghana, mostly for business, a little bit for pleasure; and several times he explicitly referred to himself as Sorrell and mentioned he sold computer parts. If the police investigating the murders managed to locate and interview this cabbie, he was going to have a lot of detailed misinformation to provide about the fare he picked up a kilometer from the crime scene.

After exiting the taxi a block from Lily's apartment, Dragan hung close to the shadows as he moved along the narrow, cobbled street. A light rain had given everything a slick sheen under the streetlights. Bicycles leaned against the wall on one side, while a parade of small cars were parked on the other. The neighborhood was quiet.

Dragan's plan was to go to the front door and ring the buzzer, to see what would happen. Beyond that he had nothing.

There was a decent chance Paul was hiding there, or Lily might be persuaded to divulge where he was. If he could get to Paul, Dragan might be able to secure him and relocate him to a safe location. He didn't want Paul roaming free. If the police got to him first it would create serious problems; it was likely they were already crawling over Paul's apartment and putting out bulletins in an attempt to locate him.

Dragan was half a block away from Lily's apartment when a motorcycle came from the opposite direction and pulled up in front of her building. He recognized the rider as Viggo, in boots and leather jacket, even though his distinctive long grey hair was hidden under a cap. Cursing the bad timing, Dragan stepped into the entryway of a building where he was hidden by shadow as he kept an eye on her apartment.

If Paul, Viggo and Lily were leaving together Dragan had no illusions he could stop them, not without someone else ending up dead. He hoped for good luck.

69

SPAT

I nside Lily's apartment things were tense.

"What are you talking about?" Lily screamed. "I'm not going anywhere."

"I'm telling you, everything is blown up," said Viggo as he gathered some boxes and a couple of suitcases in the living room. "We have to get out of Denmark."

"What's blown up? What else has happened?"

"Anton's dead."

"What the actual fuck?" Lily screamed. "Anton's dead?"

"Jesus keep your voice down," said Viggo. "Yes, he was killed in Paul's apartment with a couple of his boys."

She was astonished. "Paul did that?"

"Markov did it," said Viggo as he stuffed some clothes into a suitcase.

"That's not possible!"

"Paul asked for help so I sent Anton and a few guys to deal with the situation. I had no choice. Would you please help me get some things together? We don't have a lot of time. I have the Chens coming over."

"Do it yourself. How do you know they were killed?"

"One of them ran and called me. The police will be looking for Paul now, and they'll come here eventually."

"So we'll tell them about Dragan."

"Oh really?" Viggo stood and waved his arms in exasperation. "Some mysterious Russian from America walking around shooting people, for no reason? Is that the story you'll tell the police?"

"What about the guy who ran away? He was a witness!"

"Sure, he can explain why he and other members of a motorcycle club were in Paul's apartment, attacking some stranger. That would be a long and fun conversation. Every one of these scenarios will end up with me arrested, because Paul and Anton can be connected to us."

"Connected to you," she yelled, pointing a finger at him. "Paul and Anton can be connected to you! I'm just the girl. I'm just a waitress and an actress who lives in this crappy apartment."

"Plus the Ulvehoved club thing."

"That's your disaster. I told you not to do it."

"All of this is why we need to leave, now. You too. Let's get out of the country and start fresh in America, I've already set it up. Put these in your suitcase." Viggo handed her a pile of her clothes.

"The police won't look too long at me," she said, flinging the clothes across the room. "But you, they're going to like."

"They won't find me, unless they have help," he said. "Like before."

She looked at him sideways. "What does that mean?"

"You think I don't know you set me up last time?"

"You think that was me? You have rivals, remember?"

"It was you, lover, I just wonder why."

"The cops don't need my help," she said. "You're a street criminal, prison is where you're going to end up."

"Really? That's how you're going to play this? You're a terrorist! You don't think the police will trace that bombing to you?"

"Is that why you killed Fedde?"

Viggo snorted. "Oh, he's dead? That wasn't me. Fedde is the kind of guy who makes enemies everywhere he goes."

"No, he's not. He was a sad guy who sometimes annoyed people, that's all. You killed him."

"Somebody that annoying was on borrowed time."

"You shouldn't have killed him!"

"You shouldn't have been planting bombs!" He took a step forward to face her. He looked into her eyes and saw they were blazing; she was losing control. "And lower your voice."

"Bastard."

"Are you completely out of your mind? Bombing a newspaper? You think the law will just sit around while you do shit like that? You're the criminal here, you're a terrorist."

"I'm a revolutionary! And I walk the street proudly. You're the one who's been hiding like a frightened rabbit. You're a coward and a punk and a murderer and a loser and I'm sorry I married you."

He took two steps forward and smacked her across the face. She raced into the kitchen and grabbed a butcher knife from the drawer. She walked back into the living room with purpose, waving the knife in front of her, the side of her face red, her eyes pools of acid. She swung the knife hard and quick, but she wasn't trained and had no idea what she was doing. Viggo picked up a cushion from the couch and they battled for a bit, the knife flying across and down and jabbing toward Viggo's face, attacks deflected or absorbed by the cushion. She caught him a couple of times with the tip of the blade, bright lines of red appearing on his forearms, and one thrust just caught the side of his face, a thin line of blood appearing on his jaw line.

Viggo struck the inside of her arm, then managed to push Lily slightly off balance. As she tried to get her footing he grabbed her wrist and twisted, making her release the knife, sending it to the floor. He set his feet and shoved her back, staggering. As he reached down to pick up the knife Lily bounded over the couch to the dining area, picked up a chair, and clumsily flung it at Viggo. A chair leg caught him in the neck and nearly knocked him off his feet. He cursed and threw the knife at Lily, hard. It missed her face by a few inches and embedded itself deep into the sheetrock wall of the dining room, the impact sending the large painting crashing to the floor. Lily and Viggo stood their ground, glaring at each other across the apartment, as the downstairs neighbor banged on his ceiling and shouted his demand for a little quiet.

***

Outside Dragan lingered in the shadows, waiting for something to happen, to tell him what to do. A man in a raincoat and a trilby hat walked down the middle of the street, the leather soles of his oxfords slapping the wet cobblestones, his collar up against the steady drizzle. A young woman in a hooded down jacket rode her bicycle silently past, so close Dragan could have touched her.

A battered white Mercedes panel van entered the intersection and parked in front of Lily's apartment. Two men got out and Dragan recognized them as the brothers Alex and Jin Chen. He watched them remove several plastic storage containers from the back of the van and enter the building. This was turning into a party, far beyond Dragan's ability to confront or contain it. If they all came out, and Paul was among them, he would follow Paul who was his primary concern. If Paul wasn't with them, he would follow Lily, as she was the most likely one to lead him to Paul.

70

MOTIVATION

Jin and Alex Chen stood in the middle of Lily's apartment and took in the scene. A pile of suitcases and boxes sat near the door. Women's clothes were scattered across the furniture and the floor. Viggo had a nasty welt on his neck and his hair was in disarray. Both of his forearms and his jawline near his chin were bleeding. He held a glass with clear liquid, and a bottle of akvavit sat on the coffee table in front of him.

Cushions had been pulled from the couch and tossed around. A chair from the dining area was all the way on the other side of the room, on its side. The painting above the dining table had fallen onto the floor, with a large butcher knife embedded in the wall nearby. Two drawers in the kitchen were pulled completely out of the cabinet, their contents strewn about. A bottle lay in pieces in a pool of vodka where it had been thrown and broken. The brothers looked at each other, then at Viggo.

"I'll take the two small bags with me," said Viggo, pointing at the pile near the door, as if everything in the apartment was normal. "The rest of that bunch put in the basement of your family's old place."

"You coming back for it?" asked Alex Chen, stroking his beard.

"Of course I'm coming back for it," said Viggo. It was almost certainly a lie. "I have a thing to do."

"You going far?"

"Heading out of the country for a little bit."

The Chens both looked at the boxes.

"Lily going with you?" asked Jin.

"No," said Viggo, running his hand through his hair.

Jin looked at the knife sticking out of the wall. "She's not here?"

"She left. She's staying with a friend for a while, until things calm down."

Jin and Alex looked at each other again.

"You know who Paul Koslov is, right?" asked Viggo.

"He's that money guy. We've met him with you a few times," said Jin. "We don't like him."

"He's got to go. He's on the run now but he'll surface soon. He's probably at his cottage in a place called Siwardsted, out near Ribe." He handed them a piece of paper with an address. "I want you to find him before the police do and make him disappear completely. He'd give all of us up."

"He wouldn't give us up," said Alex, gesturing to himself and his brother. "He has no idea who we are. We aren't motivated to do that to him."

"Listen, you still have my take from the headquarters thing down near Fodby. Keep it. Keep it as payment for the inconvenience and for taking care of Paul."

"Okay," said Alex, after considering it for a minute. "Can't promise how soon..."

"One last thing," said Viggo. "I also want you to take care of Dragan Markov."

"No," said Jin Chen.

"What do you mean no?" asked Viggo. "What about the money I just gave you?"

"Not enough for that asshole," said Jin.

"We heard he took down Anton and his boys," said Alex. "He's not what he looks like."

"Paul Koslov we'll do, he's a pain and he knows too much," said Jin. "But this Markov guy is not happening. We got no beef with him, and it isn't worth the risk."

"Fuck you!" Viggo threw his drink down hard onto the coffee table, sending akvavit and shards of glass flying around the room. "He killed our brothers. You're not going to honor them?" He stood glaring at them.

Jin and Alex were unimpressed. Jin asked, "Do you want us to move your stuff out of here, or not?"

***

Dragan watched as the Chen brothers took several boxes out of the building and put them into the van. They closed the back door of the van as Viggo came out carrying two duffels. He said a few words in a tone that sounded harsh and impatient, secured the bags to the back of his bike, and roared off. The Chens entered the van and took off in a different direction.

As the sound of Viggo's motorcycle faded, the neighborhood became silent, and empty. Dragan waited for Lily to leave, but no one came out of, or entered, her building. Lights remained on in her apartment.

Dragan entered the building and quietly climbed to the second floor. He was surprised to find the door to Lily's apartment slightly ajar. Viggo hadn't even bothered to close it all the way, let alone lock it. This was not a good sign. Dragan cautiously entered, closing the door behind him. Lily could still be there, Koslov as well. Both of them would be unpredictable when cornered. He took a step into the living area and stopped short when he saw the mess. Taking care not to touch anything or make too much noise, he started wading through the chaos of the apartment.

He found her body stuffed in the bottom of the closet in her bedroom. He checked to make sure she was dead. There was bruising on her neck, as well as on her arms and face, and her open eyes were bloodshot. She appeared to have been strangled. There were signs of a beating on her face and her upper body. It was an echo of what happened to that man Fedde in his apartment.

Dragan cursed, and felt deeply sad and angry. Everything was going to hell, and it would get a lot worse before it got any better.

71

—·—

TRAPPED

A few blocks from Lily's apartment, Dragan found a small park where he could collect his thoughts. He sat on the bench of a picnic table, inside a small pavilion to protect him from the rain. Despite the late hour, teenagers talked under the roof on the upper part of the tiered seats by the asphalt-surfaced soccer field on the far side of the park.

Dragan phoned Julianna in Virginia.

"It's all gone to shit," he said when she answered, keeping his voice low. He told her about Paul attacking him in his apartment, about having to defend himself against the bikers, and about finding Lily's body.

"You've had a night," she said. "Are you at risk about what happened at the apartment?"

"Not immediately."

"Who killed the girl? Was it Koslov?"

"Possibly. I saw her husband, the biker, enter the apartment, then a little later connect with two of his buddies and leave. The husband could have done it, but I can't imagine what reason he would have. He might have discovered the body, like I did. If so, he's probably crazy angry right now."

"Was there enough time for Koslov to do it?"

"Just enough. He's become a desperate man. He and the girl had a tense relationship. I told him she gave me some key information, that could have made him angry, so this might have been my fault. But I still don't see Paul as the type."

"Anyone is capable of anything."

"Well, along that line of thought, it does appear almost certain that he had Ben and Nina killed, in a dispute over money. They were in a drug deal together, here in Denmark. The three of them double-crossed their local partners, then the Petroskis double-crossed Koslov. I found emails; Koslov was furious and threatened them. They threatened back. Everyone ends up looking badly."

"Oh no. If that gets into..."

"No worries. His machines are destroyed; I have the hard drives."

"That's my boy," she said, relieved. "Where's he going to run?"

"If it was me, I'd race overnight to another Schengen country before the Danish police find out I'm gone, and hide out there or get on a plane farther away. But Koslov isn't thinking straight. I believe he ran to a place out near the North Sea, to lay low."

"He has to realize he doesn't have much time."

Dragan could hear the calculation in Julianna's voice. He saw where this was headed, and he didn't like it. He said, "The police will learn about that cabin soon enough, so if that's where he's hiding he's trapped."

"If the biker finds him first that may solve our problem, but we can't count on that," she said. "If the police take Koslov it will be bad for us. If he's as dissolute and gutless as you say he is, he'll tell the police anything they want to hear, anything that might buy him favor. He'll turn on you in a hot second. Next thing he's talking about the

Pécy Bank operation and everything he can offer about our operation, trying to cut a deal."

"That's the kind of person he seems to be now."

"We can't afford that."

"Do you have people who can get to him inside the police here?"

"I'm sure we do, but it would be too late. A man like that will start talking before Danish police put him in the car. He's completely rogue and the window for pulling him in has closed. You need to find him and eliminate him."

"I can't do that."

"It has to be done."

"Not by me," said Dragan. "I'll find him and secure him, but you'll need to have someone come get him."

She grunted. "You said you think you know where he is."

"I have an idea."

"If you have an idea then, like you said, the police will have the same idea soon. They would be happy to arrest both of you. Not to mention there's a motorcycle gang that would love to find the American who killed their friends, so you're a target yourself. Are you seriously convinced you can track him down, capture him alone, and keep him stashed for a few days while you both remain safe? Because I don't think you can. You only have one option, and that's to eliminate him."

Dragan looked at the row of grey and cream nineteenth century apartments on the northside of the park opposite of him, and at the soulless modern apartment block faced in steel and fake brick next to him. He looked at the wooden structures in the park for children to climb on. He watched a car drive slowly past, looking for a space to park.

"Are you there?" asked Julianna.

"Yeah, I'm here. Look, there's a guy who might help me. It will cost you, though, he's a pro."

"Is he discreet?"

"Of course. If anything, he's overqualified."

"Okay, I trust your judgement," said Julianna. "Please keep me informed."

If it suits me, thought Dragan. Only then.

72

NORTH SEA

Dragan rented a Volkswagen four-door in the city, and very early the next morning he drove west. He pulled off the highway at an exit on the outskirts of the village of Baldersbrønde, where Mikkel waited for him carrying a small satchel. As agreed in their phone conversation the night before, Dragan had already transferred Mikkel's substantial fee to an account in Switzerland. The two of them continued on, driving southwest, crossing the Great Belt, through Nyborg, and south of Odense.

Mikkel looked over at Dragan. "You seem unhappy. You don't want to do this thing today?"

"No, I don't. And I don't want to talk about it."

Mikkel pursed his lips, nodded, and turned back to watching the farms and wetland grasses.

Near Kolding they turned southwest again and skirted Ribe. Towns receded and a small sign told them they were in Siwardsted, which was barely a hamlet. Dragan checked his hand-written directions and turned west on a narrow road, through farms and then reedy dunes. Beyond the dunes lay the North Sea, and fourteen hundred kilometers across the water sat northern England.

All together the trip west from Copenhagen to the edge of the world took a little over three hours.

About two hundred meters in front of them was a small, old cottage built for fishing or boating, or a maybe for the groundskeeper of some long-ago abandoned business. It looked much as it did in the photograph that hung on the wall in Paul Koslov's apartment, ochre walls and a dark red roof in a dune-covered landscape near the beach. A single-story retreat ideal for a poet, or suicidal drinker. Thoroughly isolated, with the nearest building half a kilometer south and the Mandø Island nature reserve about five kilometers offshore.

The reeds near the cottage were remarkably tall and sturdy. Dragan parked the car on the side of the road where it would be hidden from view of the cottage. Mikkel put on gloves and took a small pistol from the satchel and put it in the pocket of his coat, and they walked up the road. They swung a little wide so they approached the cottage at an angle, near the windowless corner by the carport. A single car sat there, a white Peugeot 208. Beyond the car was a rusting propane barbecue grill and a small wooden table with two chairs, under a corrugated plastic canopy. Leaning against the table was a bicycle. Dragan walked up to the front door as Mikkel stepped off to the side and around to the back.

Dragan knocked. He thought he heard noises of some kind from inside, then silence. He knocked again, louder. There was a creak of a wooden floorboard being walked on, and the door opened a crack. Half of Paul's face appeared. His eyes widened, he opened his mouth to say something then thought better of it. He froze.

"I thought we might have a talk," said Dragan.

Paul slammed the door shut and Dragan heard the deadbolt click.

"Son of a bitch," said Dragan out loud, as he kicked the door pointlessly. He ran around to the back to find the back door open. Mikkel stood in the kitchen.

"He ran out the back and saw me," said Mikkel. "He didn't expect that. He ran back in and I followed. But I don't think he's here."

They heard a muffled noise in the bedroom. When they investigated they saw on the rear wall a crude door. It opened into a shed of some type, and the exterior door of the shed was ajar.

"Pretty clever little emergency exit," said Dragan. "Some kind of storage space."

Mikkel stood on a tall dune to scan the water's edge.

"Did you see him?" asked Dragan, when he joined him.

"Yeah," said Mikkel. "He ran north along the shoreline. Should I go after him?"

"He won't get far," said Dragan. "I can't imagine he has any place to go, and he's in his shirtsleeves. We'll catch up to him." Dragan considered what to do next. "There's a bike on the side of the house. If it's usable, take it and follow that hiking trail. See if you can locate him. When you find him text me, I'll follow in the car. I have an idea."

Mikkel nodded and set out on the bicycle.

Dragan searched the cottage. There wasn't much to see. Wide-planked wood floors, whitewashed horizontal shiplap walls, four mismatched wood chairs around a small kitchen table. In the front sitting room, shelves held a small collection of books. On a small coffee table shaped like an avocado sat the Peugeot keys. He found an older cell phone in the drawer of the nightstand by the bed, which he put into his pocket. In its spot he placed two shells for the handgun he carried; it might support the fiction that the gun from Roskilde was Paul's all along, should there be an investigation.

Dragan's phone buzzed and he read the message from Mikkel. He took the keys from the coffee table, retrieved Mikkel's bag from the rental car, and drove Paul's Peugot north on the access road for close to a kilometer. He came across Mikkel waiting at the beginning of a dirt drive veering toward the sea, deep into the heart of the wetlands.

"Follow this, you can park at the end of it," said Mikkel.

The drive ended near the beach with a broad, irregularly-shaped area of turf and dirt probably used by fishermen and beach hikers. Mikkel had propped the bike against a post holding a sign with a list of activities that were forbidden on the beach.

"He's sitting on the sand looking at the sea, just over there," said Mikkel, pointing northwest.

Dragan nodded. He said, "Go a little further up, then circle back like you're taking a walk on the beach. Come over to say hello."

"Will he believe that?"

"He might. More likely he knows it's over and there's no more fight left in him. When the time comes, don't use yours, use this." He handed Mikkel the pistol he bought in Roskilde, the one he used against Anton and the bikers in Paul's apartment. "Hold it close, we'll want it to look like he did it himself. He's right handed." Mikkel nodded, took the gun and headed back down the gravel path.

Dragan walked to the top of the dune and surveyed the waterline. He saw Paul Koslov a little farther north, a small dark shape near the water. Dragan slid down and walked up to where Paul sat quietly, his arms on his knees.

Paul didn't look up. "I saw you coming, if you were trying to be sneaky."

"It's pretty out here," said Dragan. "The cottage is nice. Cozy."

Paul shrugged. After a little bit, he asked, "How did you find it?"

"You left documents at your place. Plus the photo on the wall."

Paul nodded. "I'm a terrible spy."

"You are. But that emergency exit out of the cabin was clever, I'll admit."

"My last good idea."

"I wasn't certain you would be here, but it was worth the trip to find out."

"Where else would I go?" Paul laughed and looked out at the surf. "The starlings flock here, doing that amazing thing they do, shapes in the sky. Twice a year. I didn't know that when I bought it, can you believe that? They come September to November, getting fat on insects before they cross the North Sea to winter in England." He pointed out across the sea. "Then in March and April they come back. Right here where we are. Hundreds of thousands of them, dancing up there together, swooping and whirling about, it looks like a monster made of dark quicksilver. They're so close together, there are so many of them, they turn the sky dark. Twice a year. I guess I'll miss the next one."

Yes, thought Dragan. Yes, you will.

73

BAD PEOPLE

Dragan and Paul sat together and looked out at the small waves breaking.

"I'm sorry I hit you," Paul said. "In the apartment."

"Do you think it's the worst thing between us at this point?"

"No." He dug into the sand in front of him, like an embarrassed child. "I fucked up. I got greedy, let Nina talk me into stealing the money. I was being set up."

"That's how a lot of people get conned. They're distracted, trying to con someone else."

"I'm no good at this, at any of this. I should have gotten out."

"Probably true."

Paul swept his hand in front of him, gesturing toward the water. "A thousand years ago merchant ships would leave from up near Ribe and do trading excursions over to York in England, or down to Hamburg, and places in Brussels. Up to Norway."

Dragan waited. For Mikkel, partly, and partly to see if Paul said something that would shed light on what happened.

"Do you know why I like gambling?" Paul asked, eventually.

"You like losing money?"

"I like gambling because when I win, I'm seen. Does that sound strange?" He turned and looked at Dragan. "I hate being anonymous. I hate having to play this part where I'm supposed to be invisible, to not even be myself. But when I win at a casino, everyone looks at me. I'm known. I'm the guy who won. And the next time I'm in there they remember, I'm the winner."

"When you lose, don't they remember that, too?"

"No. You're describing the way it works in the regular world. In an office, in a relationship, if you make a mistake or you fail at something, they remember forever. They forget the good things you've done. It becomes who you are, the person who made some big mistake all those years ago. But not at the casino. It's the opposite there. You have a good night, you win big, all the other nights no longer exist. They only remember the big win, because they want to be you."

Dragan could see Mikkel in the distance walking slowly along the waterline. He asked, "Why did you kill Benedikt and Nina?"

Paul shook his head sadly. "I didn't kill them. You think I did. You think Viggo had no motive and Lily didn't have the resources, that it had to be me because I had both. But I didn't do it. There was a list of people who hated those two enough to have them killed, given the opportunity. The Petroskis were a shit couple, Dragan, I'm sorry to tell you. She was worse than him. She said to me once, if you never screw people over then you won't survive. She was smiling as she said it, like it was a joke, but she lived it. She'd steal from her grandmother, and on the way out slap her in the head for complaining."

Paul noticed Mikkel walking by the surf. "We don't get a lot of beachcombers out here this late in the year," Paul said; then his eyes betrayed understanding of what was happening. A tiny light turned itself off inside, the eyes becoming a little duller, Paul's soul a little further away. He said, "I'm afraid Lily thinks, in some part of her, that I might have had the Petroskis killed. Would you convince her I didn't?"

He assumed she was alive, Dragan noted. That answered who strangled poor Lily in her apartment. But why would Viggo do such a thing?

"And I'm sorry about the Christina Koumba thing," added Paul, his eyes tearing up now. "But she warned you, just like she warned me. She'd do anything to protect the life she has. She's fierce."

That comment from Paul opened the door for Dragan, and the realization hit him. He felt light-headed. Yes, Christina would do anything to protect her ordered life. She had shown that. She didn't care about the money, only keeping control over what was hers.

The same could be said about Viggo.

Dragan had been so focused on Paul, so convinced that money was behind the murders in Philadelphia, that he was blind to other motivations. He didn't consider Viggo a likely candidate, despite his being a criminal, because the biker had no apparent stake in the missing money and thus, presumably, no thirst for revenge.

Dragan had looked at it all wrong. Protecting your corner of the world from change, holding on to what you have whether large or small, was one of the oldest drivers of violence.

Viggo had been the agent of chaos all along, Dragan realized. It was his hand behind the fate of the Petroskis, however he managed it. In a flash, Dragan understood how it could have played out. Viggo was okay at first with the drug funding scheme. It boosted his club and provided funds to him and Lily. When the Petroskis betrayed them, however, everything began to fall apart. Viggo lost whatever control he had, or imagined he had. Lily became increasingly unstable and obsessed. Paul spiraled into self-destruction and erratic behavior.

Dragan had witnessed how Viggo was a man who loved the risks in robbing a manufacturing plant, for example, or running drugs in Scandinavia, but only when it was on his terms. Viggo was a narcissist who felt certain he would win, and if anything went wrong he could improvise his way out of it. He was a bigger gambler than Paul. But he couldn't allow Lily and Paul to bring in new, unfamiliar risks and random pressures. It upset the balance Viggo maintained.

Viggo, sick of it all, must have thought it would be better if the Petroskis were dead. It would erase any possibility of getting that money, and then perhaps Lily would return to something closer to normal. Unfortunately, it just made things worse, while also bringing Dragan to pry and stir things up. Viggo could only stand off to the side and watch things fall completely apart.

He must have been desperate, killing Lily's friend Fedde and that street person, just to make the bombing trail go cold and protect her. Chasing after her and cleaning up must have been exhausting; how long and how often had he been doing that? All because protecting her also made his little world safe. Given how much he had invested in keeping the hounds away from Lily, it must have cost Viggo dearly to have ended her life.

Dragan's realization came far too late to benefit Paul, whose own actions had put him into a position where Russian intelligence needed him completely silenced. Nothing could stop that now. Mikkel walked up to the two of them and said some pleasantries, playing the beach-comber. The three of them talked about the weather, about the storm that sat far offshore.

Paul, though he fully understood why Mikkel was there, played along with the charade. It was, after all, what everyone said he wanted. It was why he bought the cottage, they said. The end was just made easier by the presence of a third party willing to help it along. Paul touched the sand and softly said he wished he could see the starlings one final time.

Dragan took a few steps back toward the dunes and looked away. The shot wasn't loud over the surf and the wind. Mikkel wiped the pistol to smear any of his or Dragan's prints. He reached across, took Paul's left hand, and forced a few partial prints on the sides and the barrel. Then he placed the pistol in Paul's right hand and shot another round into the sand to place gunshot residue. He picked up one of the ejected brass, dug the bullet out of the sand, and put them both in his pocket. Dragan slipped the Peugeot keys into Paul's coat. The two of them walked back in silence to the parking area where the bike was parked. Dragan grabbed Mikkels' satchel out of the Peugeot and handed it to him, along with a wad of additional cash.

"We need to separate," said Dragan. "Here's an extra two thousand euros, for your inconvenience. How's the bike?"

"It's quality, almost new. He must have bought it recently."

"Good. Take it to Ribe, it isn't that far, about five kilometers. There, leave the bike somewhere unlocked where it will be stolen, and catch a train. It will take a few hours but should be a pleasant trip. You'll be done with this."

"You're sad still," said Mikkel. "This was just a job. And you told me he murdered your friends."

"I did say that. But I was wrong."

Mikkel frowned. His face said what both he and Dragan knew, that mistakes like that were costly and dangerous, in their lines of work. He asked, "What will you do now, then?"

"I'm not sure."

"You hear of George Gurdjieff?"

"Yes, of course."

"He said awakening can only begin when a man realizes that he is going nowhere, and doesn't know where to go. You should meditate on that."

Dragan looked at this strange young assassin in front of him. "You read a lot, don't you?"

"I have a lot of time."

"Thank you for your help, it was good working with you."

Mikkel shook his hand with a broad smile, as if he hadn't just shot someone. He said, "We might have another journey, in the future."

Good lord, I hope not, thought Dragan. Mikkel was the kind of young man who only appeared when there was trouble, and Dragan had enough to last him.

74

CHEN BROTHERS

Dragan watched Mikkel pedal away. Then he headed on foot down the road, back to retrieve the Volkswagen. As he came up near the cabin he heard a car engine. He slipped into the reeds and crouched. A battered white panel van pulled up; Dragan recognized it as the one owned by the Chen brothers, and he saw them get out, both holding long rifles. In a replay of what he and Mikkel had done, Alex, with the shaved head and goatee, moved quickly to keep an eye on the back door, as his brother Jin, with the ponytail, walked up to the front door and knocked. When no one answered Jin tried the handle, and the door swung open. He entered, the rifle pointed forward. After a minute Alex walked away from the rear of the cabin toward the dunes, looking for Paul.

Dragan crept forward toward the rental car, hugging the edge of the reeds. He moved swiftly and was to the driver's door when Jin Chen came out and saw him. He immediately put the rifle to his shoulder and pointed it at Dragan, who stopped and raised his hands. They stood there for half a minute, neither one certain what to do next. Alex Chen came back around the cottage and took in the situation.

"Where is Koslov?" asked Alex.

"Dead. On the sand, about a kilometer north." Dragan gestured with his chin, not wanting to move his arms and spook the brothers. "He killed himself."

"I doubt it," said Alex, smiling slightly. "Maybe he had help."

"Maybe he did," said Dragan. "But he was in despair, things were closing in. That's the version that works for everyone."

Alex considered this. Dragan could hear the surf off behind the cottage, and the breeze came in off the water to caress them.

"We have no fight with you," said Alex.

"Nor I with you," said Dragan.

Jin finally lowered his rifle. Dragan brought down his hands to his sides.

Alex looked off in the direction Dragan had gestured. "If I walked there would I find him?" he asked.

"Yes. He's lying out in the open. Don't disturb the scene though, it tells the suicide story. You can claim credit with your people if it will benefit you."

Alex nodded in agreement.

Jin asked, "Did you kill Anton and his boys?"

"I didn't have any choice. I was defending myself."

"I believe it. They were reckless," said Alex. "We didn't like Anton and them, they were racist against Asians."

"They were thugs," said Jin. "Ignorant."

"You're more on the business side of things, then?" asked Dragan.

"Yeah," said Alex. "That sounds right."

"Then you're the top dealers now," said Dragan.

"We're commodity merchants, digga," said Alex.

"Fair enough," said Dragan. "Is it okay if I go?"

"Yes," said Jin. "We have not seen each other."

Dragan began walking half-backwards toward his car, so he could keep an eye on the brothers, but stopped when Alex called him.

"Viggo didn't tell us where he was going, but it was out of the country," Alex said, shouting to be heard over the wind. "You may find his trail, though. He usually leaves a mess."

"We worry about his woman," said Jin. "Keep a look out for her."

Dragan nodded to them, opened the car door, and started the engine. He did a three-point turn as quickly as he could, and drove away, just once checking the rear-view mirror to make sure a rifle wasn't trained on the back of his head.

As he came to the end of the access road, and turned onto the main route to head back to the highway and Copenhagen, he saw flashing lights ahead. A police car, siren off, passed him coming the other way. He slowed to watch it turn onto the access road. Apparently the police had also learned of Paul's cabin hideaway. Dragan didn't linger to see how the police and the Chen brothers dealt with each other.

As he drove he considered how Mikkel had been correct, he was going nowhere and had no idea where to go next. All he could do was hope that something emerged from the fog to point him in the right direction.

75

— · —

MICKEY

When Viggo landed at Philadelphia International Airport his cousin Mickey was waiting for him near the baggage carousel. The arriving families and business professionals were giving Mickey a wide berth, as he stood there in ill-fitting, stained jeans and black motorcycle jacket. On the back of the jacket was emblazoned his gang's name, in an arching embroidered fabric patch sewn into the leather: Archfiends.

"Hello cousin," said Viggo. He gave the aging biker with the thick drooping mustache and round glasses a once-over look, and abruptly hugged him.

"Where's your girl?" asked Mickey, with his squeaky voice and hint of a lisp.

"Not coming. Did you bring a car?"

"Of course. It's a Jeep."

"I want to go to the house in Philadelphia."

Mickey shook his head. "I told you on the phone, there's no point. There's nothing there."

"It's worth a look."

"You don't understand. There's literally nothing there. I looked through the windows. They cleaned the place out."

"The police?"

"No. Whoever those people worked for. Everything is gone, like no one has lived there for years. The three guys I hired? They found them by the railroad tracks in South Philly. These people are efficient."

"Fuck it then. How far to Arlington County near Washington?"

"D.C.? Like, two and a half to three hours."

"Seriously?" asked Viggo. "I thought Philadelphia and Washington were close."

"Closer than Philadelphia and Los Angeles, sure. But no, not so close. Plus the traffic."

"Okay," said Viggo. "Okay. I want to go there. I have an address for a house I want to check out. You have someone else up here can go with us, in case we need him?"

"Yeah, sure, there's a guy who'll come down for a few bucks, lives in Bentley, not so far. I got some buddies near D.C., too, if we need them."

They drove down to Bentley. Viggo looked at the desolate remains of the downtown shopping area.

"What happened here?" asked Viggo. "This is not what I imagined America would look like."

"Bentley is the oldest city in Pennsylvania," said Mickey, "and one of the most corrupt. My buddy D.G. lives near the university."

"Deegee?"

"Yeah. His initials are D and G."

They had to wait for a few minutes outside an old wood-frame two-story badly in need of paint while D.G. got his things together. He was a huge, bearded man in a leather vest over a sweatshirt with sleeves cut off at the elbow. He squeezed into the back seat and the car suddenly felt tiny.

By the time they reached Ivan Bortnik's house in Arlington, the street was quiet, everyone settled in for the evening. While Viggo assessed the neighborhood, Mickey and D.G. walked around toward the back, Mickey telling D.G. to check for an alarm system.

"Alarm's been disconnected," said D.G. when he joined Mickey at the back door.

"Sweet," said Mickey. He broke a window in the back door, reached in, and unlocked it from the inside. He and Mickey were like cartoon characters walking slowly through the first floor, D.G. a lumbering bear, the other like a shaggy ferret, crawling over and under things. Mickey opened the front door and beckoned Viggo to join them. They were surprised by the modern design and art objects inside the middle-class bungalow.

D.G. pointed to a small bronze and obsidian sculpture poised on a library table. "What the hell is this supposed to be?" he asked, but the other two weren't paying any attention to him.

"This Bertazzoni stove, I've read about them, they're expensive," said Mickey in the kitchen, admiring the high-end appliances.

Viggo explored upstairs. He surveyed the master bedroom and eyed the pull-down staircase to the attic, noting it as a place to thoroughly search. He returned to the ground floor.

"Okay," said Viggo, waving Mickey and D.G. over. "This was a confidential get-away house for rich people. If they had valuable secrets, and a stash of cash, they would be hidden here. We're looking for technology that could hold information, or that we could sell. Financial records, any documents about money – Mickey, you got people who work with documents like that, right?" Mickey half-nodded, not entirely sure. "And keep an eye out for money, they had a lot of it they needed to clean. Even if we don't find anything good, we still have a place to stay for a few days while we figure out our next move."

Mickey and D.G. glanced at each other, not sure what this man in the long grey hair meant by next move, but they let it go.

76

— ∙ —

ARCHFIENDS

When Dragan returned to Copenhagen after the incident on the beach with Paul Koslov, he still needed to lay low – Tinhanhem gang members were still on the lookout for him, and he wasn't sure if the police had his description. He chose a small hotel for its seclusion, and its distance from the other neighborhoods where he had been staying. Two days later, he was sitting in the bar of his new hotel when a call came in.

"I hope your holiday in a place you won't tell me is going well," said Leonid on the other end. "I have a present for you. That trap you set in Arlington has caught something." The cameras in Ivan's Arlington house had captured intruders.

"That was quick," said Dragan. "Describe them please."

"Three men. One tall with long grey or blond hair, who might be the one you told me about. He acts like the boss, though they all argue a lot. One is big, in all directions. The third one is older and smaller. You'll be interested in him. Remember, after the murders, you told me that one of the thugs was talking about getting messages from an archfiend? And we all thought he was high on something, just babbling?"

"Yeah."

"Well, the older man is wearing a leather motorcycle jacket. On the back is the name of his gang. The Archfiends."

"You're kidding."

"I looked them up. Small outfit in southeastern Pennsylvania, don't get in too much trouble, don't get in the news. No one made the connection."

"It wouldn't have made any sense back then if we did. We'd just wonder what a biker would have to do with the Petroskis."

"Does it make sense now?"

"The tall one with the gray hair ordered Ben and Nina killed, and the older one was the guy who actually hired the punks to do it. They're both hardcore bikers, so there's some connection between them and that's how it was arranged. How long have they been there?"

"Since last night."

"What are they doing?"

"The early part of the recording shows them roaming around the house, looking for things. Then they slept for a while, spent time drinking and watching television – we kept the utilities in place, like you asked. They looked through the house again. Eventually they found the camera and disconnected it."

"I want to be there when we take them down."

"I'm in," said Leonid.

"Okay. Have a team watch the house to make sure they don't disappear. I'll get the first flight I can and come into Dulles. I'll text you the info, you can pick me up. I'm also going to call Sacha, ask him to support."

"You two hate each other."

"It will thaw things a little. I'll ask him to coordinate with you."

"Okay. See you when you get here."

He phoned Sacha.

"We've cornered the people responsible for killing Nina and Benedikt in Ivan's house in Arlington County. A man who was in business with them in Denmark who ordered it, and some local men who actually had it done. I'm coming back to get them, and I thought you would want to be there."

Sacha was quiet. "Yes, I would," he said eventually.

"Leonid will pull in Lev. You should also bring someone. These are outlaw bikers, they'll be armed, most likely, and not held back by fear of consequences. I'll keep Leonid up to date and he'll pass things along to you. I'll tell more when I get there. I need to warn you, though, the story doesn't put Nina in a good light."

"I already understand much about her," said Sacha. "You should consider, I learned about her true nature earlier than you did. You cared about her more, so it took longer for you."

"You may be right."

"Thank you for this," said Sacha. "I'll do my best not to kill them on the spot. Please, you do the same."

77

Danish Friend

Dragan was able to catch a midday flight that brought him into Dulles before four, thanks to the time zone changes being in his favor. Leonid picked him up and they made their way to the meet at the Karpathos Deluxe diner in Arlington about a mile and a half from Ivan Bortnik's house.

"What is this you're driving?" asked Dragan as he looked around the interior of the car. "Big and heavy enough for you?"

Leonid grinned. "Two hundred sixty-eight horsepower three-point-five liter vee-six," he said. "I leave you in the dust but I don't even feel like I'm moving. And I look good doing it."

The outside of the Karpathos Deluxe was gleaming silver chrome bathed in scarlet, teal and gold neon. Inside, the walls were cream with wood trim, and chandeliers like fleshy mushrooms dangled from unexpectedly tall ceilings. A long counter featured side panels painted terra cotta, and a marble-looking top the color, Dragan assumed, of the beaches at Mykonos. Sacha, Lev, and Annika, the new woman on Sacha's team who Dragan had met at Ivan's house, were waiting in a large booth in the rear. Annika again wore tactical pants and a hooded sweatshirt. Sacha must be lusting after her, Dragan thought, to let the young woman get away with dressing like that when she was so new.

The group spoke only Russian to each other in subdued voices. They ate while Dragan told them the essential information they need- ed – as little as he felt he could get away with – about Viggo and what had happened. He was discreet about the fate of Paul Koslov, and didn't mention Christina Koumba or the assassin Mikkel at all. Everyone around the table understood he was withholding large parts of the story, but accepted it as normal practice. They took their time; they wanted to arrive in the target neighborhood under cover of night.

"Because they found the security camera, I haven't seen them for over a day," said Leonid. "I've had people watching the house. There's a Jeep in front with Pennsylvania plates we assume belongs to them, and it hasn't moved. One or two of them will leave to get food or alcohol. Once the agent watching didn't see them leave, but saw them return, so apparently they're also coming and going through the back and we're not catching it."

"Trying not to let the neighbors get a good look," said Lev.

"But the neighbors must have seen them," said Sacha. "Which makes it strange, the time they're spending in the house. It's risky."

"They think it's a secret hideaway for something. They're looking for what that something might be," said Dragan. "Also, Viggo doesn't have anywhere else to go."

"They can't stay forever," said Leonid. "They're probably making plans."

"Are they armed?" asked Lev.

"Almost certainly," said Dragan. "I don't think they'll hesitate to shoot their way out of a situation."

"But we want them alive," said Sacha. It was a statement not a question. Everyone nodded.

Dragan took a pen and drew a floor plan on a napkin. "It's a small house. Ivan opened up the first floor so it's one big space, but he left the mudroom behind the kitchen, where the back door is. Sacha and Lev, you go around the back and let yourself in, and wait in the mudroom for us to knock on the front door and approach them that way."

"How do we let ourselves in?" asked Lev.

Sacha held up a set of keys. "We still have a set. If we do this right the neighbors won't realize anything is going on. If it goes badly and there's gunfire, we won't have much time." He nodded at Annika.

"Arlington police have an average response time of seven to ten minutes from the first phone call for a non-urgent incident," she said in a crisp, professional tone. "A nosy neighbor calling 911 because she thinks she heard something would be considered non-urgent. It might take two callers saying they heard gunshots to get a real response. So in the case of shooting we'll only have as little as six or as much as twelve minutes to get out of there."

"If anything happens the priority is to get us all out safely," said Sacha. He looked at his watch, then up at Dragan. "Let's go visit your Danish friend."

78

CLEAN WATER

When they arrived at Ivan's street, Leonid parked half a block down, looking toward the house, Dragan in the front and Annika in the back next to a canvas satchel carrying weapons. Lev and Sacha were in an unmarked delivery van outfitted to carry prisoners; they drove around the block so they could park halfway to the corner, facing the other way. Dragan had a call open with Sacha, the phones on speaker so they could coordinate.

Leonid called the watcher on duty and spoke for a minute. "No one has left the house," he announced when he ended the call, as the agent drove his sedan slowly past them out of the neighborhood, "but my man can't guarantee they're all inside. He's concerned about them sometimes leaving through the back in the dark. I sent him away, we don't need someone not briefed getting in the way."

"We have to assume they're all in there, otherwise we could wait forever," said Dragan. "Are we about ready?"

"No, hold on please," said Annika from the back seat, to everyone's surprise. "I have an idea. There's a notebook and a pen in the pocket here."

"I like to make lists," Leonid said with a shrug.

She spoke both to Dragan, and to the phone, where Sacha listened on the other end. "With your permission, sir, I'd like to go to the front door, see who is in the house if I can. We don't have the camera on them any longer. It would help us be prepared."

Dragan nodded, and spoke into the phone. "Sacha?"

"Yes," came his voice out of the phone. "Be cautious."

Annika took the pen and pad, exited the car, and walked to Ivan's house. When she rang the bell the curtain covering the window moved and a bloodshot eye looked her over. It saw a young woman in a sweatshirt waiting nervously. The door opened and D.G., the big, bearded biker, towered above her.

"Hello," Annika said, with a big smile. She pretended to refer to the notebook. "Is Mr. Petroski here?"

"No, he's out." The biker struggled to focus on her.

"What does she want?" asked a voice from inside. Annika slid a few inches to her right to look into the room. The voice had come from the older biker with glasses and mustache, seated on the couch.

"Looking for a mister somebody," said D.G.

"Why?"

"Why?" D.G. asked Annika, as if she hadn't heard.

"I'm signing up donations for the Clean Water Foundation, and we were hoping Mr. Petroski would contribute. When will he be back?"

"She's looking for donations for clean water," D.G. told Mickey.

"Tell her to come inside, we'll give her donations."

"I don't know when he'll be back," D.G. said. "Soon. I like your accent. You want to come in and wait with us? We're having a little party." He tried for a smile but it came off as a leer.

"Sounds like fun, but I'll pass. I'll be back next week. Thank you!" She turned and walked off the porch, a woman on a mission to save Virginia's drinking water. She heard the door close behind her, and she stole a glance over her shoulder to make sure he wasn't following her.

"There are two in the living room," said Annika when she got back into the car as Dragan held up his phone so Sacha and Lev could hear. "A really big guy who answered the door, and an old guy on the couch. The guy on the couch looked like he was smoking something from a pipe, and the big one was drunk. I didn't see any weapons. The music is loud, so they won't hear anyone coming into that mudroom."

"You didn't see a tall guy with long grey hair?" asked Dragan.

"No. There were no lights on the second floor, so if he's up there he might be asleep."

"He doesn't seem like the napping type," said Dragan. He looked at Leonid and said to the phone, "I still think we should do it."

Leonid nodded. "If he's not there, we camp out inside and wait for him to return."

Sacha and Lev stated their agreement.

"Okay, let's go. Sacha and Lev, we'll give you a few minutes to slip into the mudroom in the back."

Dragan saw them get out of the van down the street and move quickly between the houses to the back. He and Leonid and Annika got out and walked quietly up to Ivan's porch. Dragan pressed his back against the brick on one side of the front door while Leonid did the same on the other side, as Annika stepped up, took a moment to put on a smile, and rang the bell. The huge biker answered, his face annoyed at being disturbed again, but softened when he saw who it was.

"Hi, darling," said D.G. "Changed your mind?"

She stuck a gun in his face. "Inside," she barked at him, and he stepped back into the room as Leonid came around the doorframe with his gun raised. Dragan followed and saw that Sacha and Lev had already moved into the living area.

Mickey jumped off the couch making a strange, guttural yelp and seemed to be reaching into his pockets for some kind of weapon. Sacha's arm, holding a baton, slashed down on the back of Mickey's head and the biker crumpled, his glasses skittering across the wood floor.

"Where is Viggo?" Dragan asked D.G., who stuttered until he could say, "Out."

Sacha lifted his eyes to the second floor and Lev cautiously moved upstairs to check, a gun in his hand. Annika bound D.G.'s hands behind his back. Leonid prompted him to get down on the floor. Annika tossed the duct tape to Sacha, who taped Mickey's wrists together and also his mouth.

"This one is wearing the jacket with 'Archfiends' on the back," said Sacha. "He's the one who hired the killers."

"He's yours now," said Dragan, with a nod.

Lev walked back down the stairs. "Empty. I even took a look in the attic."

Dragan grabbed D.G.'s hair and pulled his head up to face him. "Where did Viggo go?"

"We're out of booze," said D.G. "He's getting more."

"You smell like you drank it all." Dragan cursed and stood up, letting D.G.'s head drop to bounce off the floor. He said, "I'll set up across the street, cut off his escape if he runs."

He left the house. As he stepped off the porch and looked down the sidewalk he saw Viggo, carrying a bag, twenty feet away. Viggo stopped short, surprised to see Dragan. Time stopped. Frozen in place, they stared at each other.

79

———— ⋅ ————

Nowhere to Go

"What the fuck," said Viggo. He dropped the sack, liquor bottles crashing into each other and exploding as they hit the pavement. He bolted across the street, pulled himself up over the stone wall, and ran into the athletic fields of the private school. Dragan raced across the street in pursuit.

Sacha and Annika came out in response to the crash in time to see Dragan disappear as he dropped down on the other side of the wall.

"Stay with them," said Sacha. "Don't let Dragan kill him."

Annika leapt off the porch in a bound and was up and over the wall in a moment. When she hit the grass on the other side she could make out Dragan's shape ahead, walking slowly as he listened. She made her way to his side.

"He ran somewhere in that direction," he said, his arm in a short sweep to the left. "Stay close to the wall, look for him in case he tries to climb back over to the street."

She nodded and trotted off into the darkness. Dragan continued moving deeper into the athletic fields, listening, looking for movement at the edges of his vision. He heard Viggo break from whatever hiding place he was in and run through the different playing fields, first the soft thud of grass, then the high-pitched scuff as he trotted through the infield dirt of the baseball field. Dragan took off after him, following the sounds of his steps.

He heard Viggo scale a metal fence of some type, and when Dragan came up to it he saw the shadowy figure of Viggo come off the turf of the lacrosse field and leap over the fence on the other side. By the time Dragan had crossed the field he heard cursing in Danish, and a crash. He reached the source of the noise at the same time Annika did, to find Viggo tangled up in the netting of a portable hammer and discus cage. Viggo had collided into it hard, pulling one of the cage posts down on top of him. Annika pulled out her gun and trained it on Viggo, but it was unnecessary, he was too tangled up to find a way out.

Half an hour later Viggo was bound and gagged, sitting on the grass near the wall, watched over by Annika. Mickey and D.G. had been moved quietly into the delivery van, where Lev babysat them. The last task was to get an uncooperative Viggo over the wall and into the van, and Sacha and Leonid were discussing the best way to do it.

"I want to talk to him one last time," said Dragan. Sacha nodded. "Alone," Dragan added, "I'd like some privacy."

"No, it's not safe," said Sacha.

"What do you mean?" asked Dragan. "He's trussed up like an Easter lamb."

"Yes, you're safe. I meant not safe for him," said Sacha. "I don't trust you with him. I want to be there with you."

"If you're there he won't talk," said Dragan. "I need him to answer a couple of questions. I'll tell you what he says afterwards."

"Why would he talk to you?"

"He wants to," said Dragan. "He needs to tell someone his side of it. I'll take Annika, I think he'll talk in front of her."

"Because I'm just a girl?" asked Annika.

"Basically," said Dragan. Sacha hesitated, then nodded, and he and Lev stepped away. Dragan, followed by Annika, walked over to Viggo, who ignored him and stared into the space in front of him. Dragan crouched and took the duct tape off Viggo's mouth.

"You were surprised to see me," said Dragan.

"I expected you would show up eventually," Viggo said with a shrug. "Paul said that was the kind of person you were."

"What's your connection with the old biker?"

"Mickey? He's my cousin. The other one came for extra protection."

"Not the best choice, I think."

"Mickey does his best, but yeah, he's lost a step."

"When you had those men break into the townhouse, was it to kill the Petroskis, or to look for the money?"

"What does it matter now?"

"I'd like to understand you better, and her."

Annika gave a surprised side-eye toward Dragan, watching him. Viggo smiled slightly. "Why understand me?"

"You're a smart guy. You don't seem to hold grudges. But you did this thing. There was a reason."

"The money was gone. I told Lily that a hundred times. I could see it in Paul's face, he knew they had moved the money into their own accounts and there would be no way for us to find it, or to get it back. I was pretty sure that Paul was part of some scheme and they double-crossed him, too, because he's a fool. There was nothing to be done about it."

Dragan put as much empathy in his voice as he could. "But Lily wouldn't let it go."

"I thought if the two American pieces of shit were gone, she might give it up, move on."

"That just made it worse, I imagine. She became more desperate."

"She wasn't herself. The madness in her was always there, it was part of the appeal at first. Then it got worse, and she changed, and everything broke apart. It was very sad."

"Sad for her, or for you?"

"For everyone."

"So you killed her."

Viggo's nod was so slight as to be nearly unnoticeable. He said, "It's a tragedy, to stand in a room alone with someone you love, someone you've known for many years, and finally admit to yourself that they have lost their mind. They are unstable, and a danger to themselves, and to other people. You see this, and you are the only one in the world who does. The person goes to work, or gets coffee, where she chats with other people, and they don't know what's happening; they believe what she says, they have no reason to think she's lying or talking fantasy. They don't realize she is saying and doing crazy things. Some of them terrible things. And you are the only one who knows, because everyone else only sees a little part, and each little part seems fine, nothing too scary. It's only when you step back and look at it all that you realize the little parts don't come together into a whole person, the person you love. The parts no longer fit with each other. The person has become a jagged monster of mismatched bits, barely keeping its shape. Pieces fall off; she finds other pieces on the street and picks them up, sticks them somewhere."

Viggo no longer seemed aware Dragan and Annika were there; he was focused on a point in the darkness far in the distance.

He continued, "One night the person is in front of you with a knife promising they'll kill you while you sleep, and no matter what they said before, this time you believe them. This time they mean it. After everything you did to protect them, to protect both of you, to create some sort of future despite all the problems, after all that, they just want to blow the whole thing up because they can't help themselves, and you can't change it. It's a hell of a thing."

There was quiet. One man was tied up on the ground, about to disappear into the bowels of the Russian intelligence organization, never to emerge. The other crouched nearby, the winner of this battle, having fulfilled his mission but feeling a deep sense of loss and disappointment. Both men understood the common ground they shared. That was why Viggo had given that little speech, and why Dragan listened, and both accepted that. The biker wanted to be heard, and thought Dragan would understand. And Dragan did understand, to a point. But he was also keenly aware the self-pitying man in front of him was a sociopath who had murdered his business partners – one of them Dragan's lover – and when that didn't make him happy, murdered his wife.

"I was so tired of it all," said Viggo.

"Why did you come here?" Dragan gestured to the house across the street.

"I didn't know where else to go."

"You caused so much trouble."

Viggo smiled. "Yeah. That was the only fun part, knowing I kicked all the toys across the room and sent everyone running."

80

GIANT STEP

The days after the capture of Viggo were crowded with interviews, reports, and debriefs. Even the investigator Viktor, who Dragan had once called Nosferatu, showed up in an attempt to reach closure. Both Viggo and his cousin Mickey were made to confess to the Philadelphia murders fairly quickly. This, along with the evidence that had already been gathered regarding the dodgy side-gigs filling the pockets of Ben and Nina Petroski, and the abundance of information concerning money laundering on the hard drives Dragan took from Paul Koslov's laptops, exonerated Dragan fairly completely.

Any loose threads, Dragan heard, were tied up through two private conversations Russian agents had with Lucas Oliver Madsen in Roskilde. Julianna did her best to take credit for conceiving and directing the undercover operation, but privately everyone was at least mildly impressed with what Dragan had done entirely on his own, although few told him so to his face.

Dragan did not follow through on his threat to destroy Christina Koumba's career. He couldn't bring himself to do it, out of guilt for imposing on her life, and an acknowledgement that her suspicions of him as an unaffiliated, and therefore possibly rogue, operative were actually partially true. He also couldn't effectively damage her without bringing Mikkel into the conversation, and he thought the assassin was owed his anonymity. In the end she was officially commended for playing a key supporting role in the mission.

When things died down, and no one was watching him or asking where he was, Dragan packed a duffel with a laptop and other electronics, a few tools, and a notebook. He drove to Nina's place on the New Jersey shore. Once inside he took the model of the beach house in LEGOs from its spot on the credenza and placed it on the dining table. He carefully dismantled it, noting how it was constructed so he could put it back together when he was finished.

The epiphany had come that day in the Roskilde Cathedral, when he was amused by the LEGO models of the different versions of the cathedral over the centuries. It was easy to imagine Ben and Nina playing tourists, going to the Viking Museum at the south end of the fjord in Roskilde, then visiting the cathedral to look at the crypts of the monarchs. They would also have made it to the space behind the altar where the LEGO models were on display. It would have given them the idea, a private little joke.

After the top half of the LEGO beach house was removed, he focused on the dark blue rectangular shape representing the dining table – the same one he was working on. The block was hollow, and in the hollow was a flash drive. It was the twin of the flash drive he had found in Paul's apartment.

He fired up his laptop, stuck the drive in the port, and entered the passcode on the truck license plates in the photo he found in the keepsake box on the second floor of the beach house. The drive opened, revealing a handful of files documenting a set of bank accounts and the codes used to access them online, along with an email address and its password to use for second system security. There were also some documents related to tax codes in Denmark, Sweden, and Norway.

The first account he checked had only a small sum, enough to keep the account active; the same for the second; the same for the next. The same for the next six accounts. It was not a surprise. Nina and Ben had, indeed, emptied all the accounts.

One account at the bottom of the list was at a Swiss institution, not a Scandinavian bank like the others. And the notes showed an opening date well after the others. When he let himself in, and the account dashboard appeared on his screen, Dragan let out an involuntary grunt. Close to a million euros sat in that Swiss account. This was more than he expected to find from the drug deal, but he could have miscalculated. Or, possibly, this was an account where the Petroskis temporarily moved their illicit money, a waystation before they cleaned it. Then why were they still using the photo and flash drive gimmick? It was impossible to say. Dragan would never learn if there was anything serious behind it, or if it was just the joke Paul said it was.

He copied the files, uploaded another copy to his secure cloud account, closed the laptop and put it and the flash drive into his bag. He would need a plan for safely and discreetly transferring the money, but he would work that out later. As best he could, he reassembled the model of the house. It looked right when he was finished, at least no pieces were left over, and he returned it to the credenza.

Within a week the money was safely stowed in new, secure accounts known only to him, away from the prying eyes of his Russian keepers. It wasn't quite fuck-you money, but enough that he was taking a giant step away from the control Sergei and Julianna had over him.

81

TWO GLASSES

Dragan sat with Julianna in the room she called the library though it held no books. The shelves displayed her collection of small crystal and glass pieces; for some of the older ones, from the nineteenth and early twentieth century, Dragan had served as adviser. The weather had taken a sudden, unseasonable turn for the frosty, and the temperature had dropped over twenty degrees from the previous day, so a wood fire kept the cold at bay as it tried to seep through the tall windows. They sat on the couch, drinking coffee with a plate of cookies in front of them, looking out onto the lawn and the autumn leaves of the trees beyond.

"They are now officially stating the death of the Petroskis was an assassination by a cell of Ukraine terrorists operating in the United States," said Julianna. "It's a feeble attempt at propaganda, but it's all they can muster these days."

Other than that comment, and Julianna's observation that Sergei had been keeping a low profile, they avoided discussing the war with Ukraine. Things had not been going well for Russia. In October, Ukrainian forces had been steadily reclaiming territories: villages in the Svatove district in western Ukraine, as well as in Donetsk and Luhansk in the east. Large numbers of Russian military equipment had been captured, from artillery to vehicles to tanks. Yevgeny Prigozhin, head of his own mercenary group and a longtime Putin ally, had been publicly insulting and bickering with the commanders of the Russian army, and recently released a video of a man claimed to be a deserter having his head smashed in with a sledgehammer. All things considered, the war was a topic best not brought up. Especially since in a house that size you could never be sure who was listening, even among your own staff.

Julianna sighed. "We've arrived at the end of it."

"The end of it," Dragan said.

"Colleagues in the Copenhagen embassy tell me Danish authorities determined Paul Koslov committed suicide on the beach near his getaway cottage," said Julianna. "It's quite the story. It seems Koslov was heavily in debt to bookmakers in three countries, embezzling funds from his employer, and had a rather nasty opioid habit as well. He killed himself soon after a violent incident in his apartment. Several criminals who were known to the police were found dead there, all members of a motorcycle gang with ties to the drug trade. Two of the men were killed with the same gun he turned on himself. They think a drug deal may have gone sideways, as they say. He must have fled to his cottage on the coast immediately afterwards."

"Koslov knew the police would be at his doorstep soon enough. It makes sense to conclude he thought he had no other way out."

"He's also a suspect in the murder of a young woman, an ex-girlfriend. Her apartment showed signs of a struggle."

"That murder will never be solved. Might as well blame him for that as well."

"Sad ending for him, but a good one for us," she said. "Had the authorities arrested him alive, it would have been a significant security and operational risk."

"I want to put all of it behind me, if that's okay with you."

"I understand. Would you like to hear how the men captured at Ivan's house are doing?"

"No," he said. "I have no interest."

She raised her eyebrows and poured them both a little more coffee from the pot on the silver tray on the table in front of them. She said, "Thank you for being thorough."

"I really had no choice."

"I've heard that even Sacha is praising you to his colleagues, in subdued terms of course."

"We'll see how long it lasts."

"No sign yet of the money squirreled away in all those banks by the Petroskis. Such things have a way of falling into the status of legend fairly easily. It may be more entertaining if we never learn the answer."

Dragan nodded, and looked out at the gold and scarlet tree line.

***

An hour later, after coffee with Julianna, Dragan felt officially the matter was closed. Paul Koslov burdened the responsibility, Viggo and his American cousin disappeared into the Russian system, and any remaining details were swept under the furniture or simply ignored. No one was interested in him, which right at that moment suited him fine.

He took the scenic route, through Annapolis, over the bridge, across Kent Island and the flat farmland of Maryland's Eastern Shore, into Delaware where he caught the Lewes Ferry to Cape May. Forty minutes later he let himself into Nina's Stone Harbor beach house. The wind was biting by the ocean.

On the kitchen counter he placed a bottle of Stolichnaya Elit. He retrieved two tumblers from the cabinet and filled them with ice, then poured a double into each. He took the drinks to the table between two armchairs facing the rear picture windows and the ocean beyond. He watched the grey sky, listened to the groaning of the wind as it raced across the peninsula. He thought about Nina and the last time they were in this beach house together. He clicked his glass against the other on the table and had a sip. It would be his last visit there, and he wanted to savor the nostalgia, as painful as the memories might be.

Eventually his glass was empty. The one on the other side of the table, by the vacant chair, would not be consumed. That was Nina's. He had come to say an affectionate goodbye to his idealized memory of her, regret the person she turned out to actually be, and blame himself for not recognizing the gap. She had been a projection of his need, and a distraction from his own despair. In the end, he understood the problem was him, not her. She was who she was, and always had been, right in front of him the entire time.

He watched the waves aggressively caress the sand, and thought about what might come next. He needed to choose a direction and start heading there. Inertia was no longer an option. He cleaned the glasses and put them away, wiped down any surface he might have touched, packed up his things, and locked the door on his way out. He would dispose of the key somewhere along the drive home.

I hope you enjoyed this book. Please consider rating or reviewing it. This helps other readers discover it, and supports my work as an author. Thank you!

To receive updates on my books and other writings you can join my mailing list. Link below, or go to https://jrirwin.com/mailing-list/

Acknowledgements

Some deserve special thanks. Jill who has been exceptionally support-ive, gave clear and strongly worded feedback, and was a patient listener when I felt compelled to talk through things; she also originally had the idea of Russian agents anachronistically embedded in everyday American life. Nick and Jenna for their enthusiasm, creative feedback, and design and marketing ideas. Pam for being the most beta of all readers. Tony for the candid assessments and a key smack to the head reminding me of what I knew all along. Linda, who believed in me so many years ago and lobbied on my behalf; that faith in my work then has been today's foundation. And Dinty, Donna, Thomas, Tara, Emily, Jane, and Michael, who (often without realizing it) offered me a path back.

James Irwin was a college professor and held leadership roles in national and international marketing communication before turning full-time to writing. Prior to all that he was a widely exhibited, award-winning media artist whose work the *Los Angeles Times* called "witty and ingenious," and the *San Francisco Chronicle* described as "pithy – cerebral undercurrent sparked by sexual innuendo." He lives in northern New Jersey, and can be found at jrirwin.com   *(Photo by Jill Brillante Irwin)*

EXCERPT FROM BENT CITY

Bent City is book two of the Tajna Circle series. Look for it in 2026.

Chapter One: Stevedore

Half an hour after the meeting, Sara Jane Ott was still fuming that two members of the Police Athletic League board refused to accept the girls basketball program should be as robust as the boys. One of them, an old-school coach who always seemed in need of a shave and smelled faintly of bourbon, had the audacity to suggest too many girls quit athletics when they hit their teens so it wasn't worth investing the funds. She had to put them in their place, pointing out that if the girls program was better supported maybe more would stay, and they owed it to the ones who did stay to prepare them for the next level. The other board members looked at the table and waited for her tirade to finish. She prevailed at the end, of course, the board voting for gender equity, and she wanted to think she won them over with her passion and logic even though she realized the size of her annual donations was the most convincing argument. As everyone in that room understood, if she became disgusted enough with the men's club that still ran the organization she could take her money elsewhere.

She was so preoccupied with the events of the evening she failed to notice that the motion-activated floodlight was already shining on her driveway when she reached the house. She pulled the SUV to a stop a few feet from the low fence, and it finally registered that something had been walking around her property. She pursed her lips and looked around the side yard, and in the rearview mirror. The sensor was sensitive, she reminded herself, it could have been set off by a cat passing through. Deer followed the riverbank down to the parkland half a mile south, and often stopped to see if anything was tasty in the garden.

But something felt off.

Impulsively, to calm herself, she caressed the soft cordovan leather of the briefcase holding her notes and laptop. Small physical gestures grounded her and helped her focus. She was a woman in her late sixties, and while the neighborhood was full of families and reasonably safe, Peckham was still a city with its share of crime, even in the outskirts.

She exited the car into the cool early April evening. The clear sky was littered with stars, two airplane vapor trails like knife slashes alongside the moon. Music came from a backyard a few houses down and the odor of something burning was in the air, probably people sitting around a firepit. She walked along the path between the garden beds to the gate so see if everything was okay in the back.

Near the edge of her patio, before the ground tilted down toward the river, was a baby fox. It was curious, and brave too, taking a few tentative steps toward her. She knew the cub was from the brood that had taken up residence in the neighborhood. She had been watching them for a week as they scrambled in and out of groundhog tunnels, tussling and exploring while mom hunted. This little one, fuzzy and brown, stopped ten feet away and was giving Sara Jane a thorough inspection until its mother, somewhere in the darkness of the bushes, emitted a sharp, raspy bark and the cub, duly warned, turned and ran back down the hill.

Sara Jane smiled and waved goodbye.

Everything appeared secure in the back. She lived in a three-story small factory space she and her late husband had purchased and converted decades before, and they kept the rear metal door with its bar lock. Burglars would have an easier time dynamiting a hole in the wall than they would getting through that door.

She looked across the Bearfort River to the lights in the windows of the new condominiums in Cutterton on the other side, sighed, and told herself to let goof her frustrations from the meeting. People are people, she reminded herself, and generally speaking they eventually do the right thing. It just takes them too long, in her opinion.

As she walked around to the front someone emerged from the darkness of the trees lining the pavement. The soft orange glow of the streetlight illuminated a thick man, built like a stevedore, wearing a dark trench coat over a dark suit, the two top buttons of the white dress shirt undone. He was middle aged, and wore a hat that gave him the air of a film noir character. He didn't match what Sara Jane imagined a common mugger would look like, and he wasn't a street person, but he carried with him an aura of menace. His face was emotionless, and he did not look like he belonged in the neighborhood. She cradled the can of pepper spray in her coat pocket.

Ashe came closer she could see his clothes were high quality, and tailored to fit his thick frame. Gray chest hair and a thick gold chain peaked out from the open vee at his neck. She had seen men like him many times in northern New Jersey, drinking and laughing at fundraising events, or dining with younger women at white table-cloth Italian restaurants. In her mind they all resembled mobsters, even though they might actually have been lawyers, shop foremen, or dentists.

"Evening, Ms. Ott," he said, smiling. She flinched in surprise to hear her name. "A woman as elderly and vulnerable as yourself shouldn't be walking around here this late." His voice was deep, and smooth, and had the casual assertiveness of someone accustomed to being listened to and obeyed. His eyes were dark pools and they never left her face.

"I live here." She'd kick him in the groin if he called her elderly again.

"I know," he said. "It's just that you make a target of yourself. You're a woman, and a temptation. Or at least that expensive briefcase is, anyway."

He wasn't moving toward her, at least, but he stood between her and her front door. She held the pepper spray more tightly. She said, "I just left a meeting, and if I don't text them that I'm safe at home they'll send someone looking." As soon as it came out of her mouth she knew it was a silly thing to say.

The man chuckled. "Oh please," he said. "I know about you, about your money and the good works you do everywhere. You're a fucking humanitarian. You have committees and board meetings all the time. You aren't sending texts after each one."

He stepped forward. She stepped back, readying the spray. He glanced down at her right arm, her hand hidden in the pocket.

"Don't spray me lady," he said. "I'm just here to give you a message. Leave the Blake Dorcey nomination alone. Don't tell your bullshit stories, don't give any depositions." He spoke calmly, and took another small step toward her.

She stared back at him, both furious and terrified. Why was there no one else about, she wondered, there were always a few people on the street in this neighborhood. If she screamed would the people around that firepit hear?

"The stories are true," she said. "They're relevant, if they're really thinking of approving that man."

He shrugged. "After all this time who knows what's true and what's not? You could be mistaken. You could be delusional. You could just be old, and not as sharp as you once were, making you untrustworthy. Maybe you have a political axe to grind."

"None of those are true."

"There are so many ways you could be painted as a liar or a crank," he said. "And you will be. You'll be humiliated in front of everyone. You won't be able to buy groceries without people whispering behind your back."

"I'll tell my story," she said, her voice cracking. "Let people decide."

The man sighed and shook his head. He moved close to her, and took hold of her arm, keeping it in her pocket. He filled her field of vision, blotting out the street with his bulk, his breath warm and she could see the small scar at the top of his cheek, and the gray hairs in his eyebrows. "No, you won't," he said, with more urgency, more threat, like a man forcing himself to swallow his urge to violence. "You'll keep things to yourself. Don't make me come back here."

The man turned and walked back the way he came, the darkness folding around him. The stars above seemed to darken and spin. Sara Jane needed to sit down. She hurried to her door, closed and locked it behind her. As her breathing calmed, she laughed at herself, astonished at her own naivete.

How could she have thought there wouldn't be consequences for attempting to derail a nomination to the U.S. Supreme Court?